DEAD MAN'S CHEST

Concept and Design: Lance Hawvermale

Writing Team: Lance Hawvermale, Rob Mason, Robert Hunter, Patrick Goulah, Greg Ragland, Matt McGee, Chris Bernhardt, Casey W. Christofferson, Chad Coulter, Skeeter Green, and Travis Hawvermale

Additional Contributers: Erica Balsley, Lindsey Barrentine, Jay Decker, Rachel Mason, and Nadine Oatmeyer

5E Conversion: Edwin Nagy

Developers: Erical Balsley, Bill Webb, and Skeeter Green

Producer: Bill Webb

Editors: Pat Lawinger, John, Ling, Edwin Nagy, and Karen McDonald

Art Direction: Casey Christofferson

Cover Art: Adrian Landeros

Interior Art: Julio De Cravahlo, Brian LeBlance, and Eric Lofgren

Layout and Graphic Design: Charles A. Wright

Fantasy Grounds Conversion: Michael W. Potter

ADVENTURES WORTH WINNING

FROG GOD GAMES

ISBN: 978-1-62283-798-4

FROG GOD GAMES IS:

Bill Webb, Matthew J. Finch, Zach Glazar, Charles A. Wright, Edwin Nagy, Mike Badalato

TABLE OF CONTENTS

Dead Man's Chest
Introduction

No place offers more adventure than the ocean. No dungeon is as deep, no jungle as full of exotic and dangerous life. Most folk spend their lives on dry ground, unaware that entire civilizations thrive beneath the waves, sometimes far more ancient and steeped in mystery than any of the world's surface. Though characters have long grown familiar with the air-breathing world above, seldom do they venture into the depths, and when they do, they discover wonders they never dreamed existed. The ocean environment is radically different from the surface world, in at least three very important ways: an insufficiency or complete absence of sunlight, the ever-increasing ambient pressure, and the fact that water rather than air is the omnipresent medium for respiration, movement, and all other activities. Because of these and other factors, the ocean offers a venue for adventure that is at once alien and appealing. Strange things exist down there, as perilous as they are compelling.

But the water's surface is also a world unto itself. Great ships vie for control of the trading lanes. Dangerous reefs protect lost islands full of treasures yet unearthed. *Dead Man's Chest* lays bare the ocean. Within these pages you'll find rules variants to add to your game, many new spells, and wondrous items, but also information on the science of oceanography.

Chapter 1: An Oceanography Primer

The ocean contains a variety of natural occurrences that can enliven any campaign. You shouldn't be dependent solely on monstrous encounters to make your player's character's life eventful on the high seas. This chapter reveals a short summary on many oceanic features, enabling you to present the characters with a more realistic description of the world that they will find themselves in.

Each entry also explains how best to use that particular feature in your own campaign.

Mid-Ocean Ridge

The mid-ocean ridge is the region along the ocean floor where new seafloor is created. This typically takes place near the center of an ocean basin, though it exists in any location where two ocean plates spread apart from one another. Mid-ocean ridges are featured throughout the world, stretching over 40,000 miles in length. Their pattern winds across the globe in a fashion that is often likened to the seams of a baseball. They appear as mountainous formations or merely as mild swells upon the seafloor up to 2400 miles wide. Their crest is marked with a V-shaped depression running throughout its range, up to a mile deep and 10 to 20 miles wide. This rift valley is actually a volcanic fissure from which the new seafloor extends from below gradually over time.

The origin of the seafloor naturally begins beneath the surface. Within the rift where the two tectonic plates diverge, the reduction of pressure affecting the mantle allows the rock of the asthenosphere (the upper layer of the mantle) to rise and melt. The upwelling leads to the formation of magma chambers just beneath the mid-ocean ridge, acting as focal reservoirs of the material needed to produce new ocean crust. Molten rock from the depths of the magma chamber gradually hardens, producing several miles of coarse rock. Vertical sheets of magma from within the chamber rise up through fissures in the overlying crust, creating dikes. Portions of this uprising magma will break through to the surface, oozing along the seafloor exterior. The outer layer of the surface lava solidifies immediately in the near-freezing seawater, forming a pillowed layer of volcanic basalt — the surface of the new seafloor.

The mid-ocean ridge axis is marked with deep, jagged indentations known as fracture zones. These appear in frequent intervals across the ridge, offsetting its crest up to hundreds of miles in either direction. The fracture zones appearing between two offset segments of the ridge are recognized as transform faults, and the fracture zones outside of these segments are simply remnants of the plate's movement over millions of years. The segmented ridge is generally widest and highest in the middle of the offset, and slimmest and shortest near the ends, and is believed to occur due to an interaction between fracturing of the seafloor and magma accumulation.

Another feature of interest to be found on the mid-ocean ridge is hot springs, or hydrothermal vents. Hydrothermal vent fields are areas of underwater geysers that form in places along the mid-ocean ridge axis. When seawater creeps into deep cracks and fissures found in the flanks of the ridge, it reacts with the hot volcanic rock, chemically altering and heating it up to temperatures reaching 700° Fahrenheit. This superheated fluid rises, dissolving metals found within the rocks on its way back up to the surface. Continuous streams of thick black or white immensely hot fluid projects straight up through vents in the surface, showering the surroundings with precipitated minerals.

The fluids in vents known as black smokers precipitate so quickly as they cool in the seawater that the metal sulfides form solid, smokestack structures, typically a couple of stories high (the largest ever discovered is 160 feet tall). In regions where the altered seawater is substantially cooled before reaching the surface, the ejected fluid is usually spread out among numerous vents in the area and takes on a diffused, clear glow. These diffuse vents are often found among larger more focused black smokers.

Life on the ocean floor is known for its scarcity, but hydrothermal vent fields are packed with an abundance and variety of life in one of the most volatile and unlikely of places. Organisms such as tubeworms, mussels, clams, and crustaceans gather or attach themselves near vents in incredibly dense clumps. However, it is the sulfur-eating bacteria found around and inside those creatures that grants them nourishment. The sulfide-oxidizing bacteria convert the vent chemicals into energy for the organisms through a process called chemosynthesis. This localized ecosystem is one of few known to exist independent of sunlight and photosynthesis.

Using Mid-Ocean Ridges in the Campaign

In campaign worlds, mid-ocean ridges should be an important feature of the ocean. They mark the birthplace of the seafloor, directly influencing the geography of the planet, and provide an unlikely though successful site for life. The ridge shapes and sizes vary slightly from ocean to ocean, as does their productivity. In certain areas of the mid-ocean ridge, profuse magma accumulation beneath the ridge may produce large volcanic islands bisected by the active spreading ridge, such as Iceland in the North Atlantic.

Given the importance and regional nature of the mid-ocean ridge, implementing them into your game should prove simple and rewarding. Moderately intelligent ocean life dwelling on or near the ocean floor would certainly hold some opinion of it. Whether or not they fully understand its significance and true nature, some races may believe it to be sacred territory, or even a place where the deities exercise their direct will through volatile bursts of eruption. Denizens of the deep might even go to war over the rights to claim such land for spiritual and ancestral beliefs and practice. Races like sahuagin place great value on these areas. Furthermore, in specific places along the mid-ocean ridge, valuable minerals and metals could be discharged into the ocean in addition to seafloor, ripe for harvesting, and for conflict.

Ocean Floor

From the time of its birth within the mid-ocean ridge, the young ocean floor is in constant motion. From the flanks of the ridge axis, gravity causes the new crust to fall away, accentuating the peaks of the ridge formation. Continuing, it becomes colder and contracts with time, growing denser and settling further. Sediment accumulation obscures its rock and hill-laden topography gradually, resulting in vast flatlands. Eventually, its existence will conclude in the inevitable return to the planet's mantle in deep trenches, some thousand miles away and millions of years later.

The ocean floor is a place of mystery. By its very nature it is not prone to exploration. At the average depth of the ocean floor at 13,000 feet, near-freezing seafloor water, crushing water pressure, and complete lack of sunlight make for a very uninviting environment. For these reasons, ocean floor exploration has been a slow and educating process. The topography of the ocean floor is every bit as varied as the land we're more familiar with. Stretching flatlands, peaking mountains, rolling hills, and plummeting canyons are all common ocean floor features. But as is often the case, the features that characterize the ocean have the tendency to be larger in scale, more severe, and more frequent than on land. In addition to the mid-ocean ridge and ocean trenches (both explained in detail elsewhere within the chapter), the following ocean floor features are of special significance:

Abyssal Hills. The abyssal hills emerge in the wake of seafloor spreading at the mid-ocean ridge. They are composed most generally in linear rows stretching parallel to the spreading ridge axis, appearing as fractured, elongated peaks up to over 3000 feet high and about 6 to 12 miles across. These hills are the most prominent geologic feature of the planet's surface. It is generally agreed that they are caused by an interaction of the faulting and eruptions taking place within the mid-ocean ridge axis. However, little of their formation and development is well understood.

Abyssal Plains. The abyssal plains are the flat regions of the ocean floor, constituting roughly half of the planet's topography. In fact, there is no flatter location on the plant, with a gradient no greater than .05 degrees. They are produced when the rocky terrain of the abyssal hills is obscured by sediment accumulation over the course of millions of years. The most significant contributor to the abyssal plains' flatness is the submarine flow of density-heavy currents called turbidity currents. These currents are basically underwater sediment avalanches, generated by earthquakes or simply acting as continuations of enduring river outlets. They transport mostly terrigenous (land originating) sediment from its settled location along the continental shelf to the continental slope and into the deep sea.

Sediment composition is varied throughout the ocean, based largely on a particular basin's history and location. The most abundant sediment composition is comprised of assorted clays, silts, and sands originating from land, metal-rich sediments, pebbles, and stone from the spreading ridges, and oozes consisting of calcareous and siliceous skeletal remains. On average, the thickness of sediment cover on the ocean floor is over half a mile. Typically, it is thickest near continental masses and thinnest near the center of an ocean basin, but other circumstances impact its accumulation. For instance, the Pacific Ocean's immense size places the inner regions of its basin out of reach from turbidity currents and most wind-carried sediments. In addition, its basin is nearly surrounded by hundreds of deep ocean trenches that funnel and trap a great deal of the sediments within their depths. As such, the abyssal hills comprise approximately three-quarters of the Pacific. The floor of the Atlantic Ocean, much smaller and with few trenches of significant size for sediments to escape, is nearly half-featured with abyssal hills.

Seamounts. Punctuating the ocean floor are seamounts, isolated seafloor volcanoes of heights greater than 600 miles (dwarfing Mount Everest's almost 6-mile height). They are most often conical, and have a recessed caldera within their summit. Seamounts that have flattened tops due to excessive erosion caused by water currents are called guyots. There are thousands of seamounts on the ocean floor, and many serve as great habitats of life. Creatures classified as suspension feeders adorn the steep slopes of seamounts near the top to intercept organic matter passing by in the water currents. Various coral polyps, sponges, and xenophyophores (single celled creatures similar to fungi that can grow up to 8 inches across) cling to seamounts to feed in this manner. Their presence also attracts other ocean wildlife. Seamounts are also larvae catchers; the very currents that provide food for seamount communities also provide for its continued population.

A small percentage of seamounts appear to have been created at the mid-ocean ridge. However, most are formed above regions known as hot spots, exceedingly hot locations within the mantle where plumes of magma have risen and melted through the oceanic lithosphere. The majority of these seamounts are no longer volcanically active, having been carried away from the magma source by the movement of the ocean plate. The seamounts created by exceptionally prolific hotspots break the surface of the ocean, often producing a chain of volcanic islands. As the oceanic crust glides over the excessive hot spot, one by one and oldest to youngest, an arcing trail of volcanic islands forms. A notable real-life example of this is the Hawaiian Islands. Chains of these seamount islands can extend many thousands of miles.

Life on the ocean floor — its presence, diversity, and development — is constantly being redefined. As we further explore the great depths of the ocean, the perceptions of a stale and stagnant seafloor largely devoid of life are being shattered. Despite the relative scarcity of life to be found there, it is startlingly diverse. The possible number of species is projected to soar well beyond one million, and possibly possessing more biodiversity than the rain forest. Among the countless species of life inhabiting the deep seas are grenadier fish, slime-secreting eel-like hagfish, echinoderms such as sea cucumbers and brittle stars, and various species of crustaceans and invertebrates.

The primary source of food for many of these bottom-dwellers is organic debris that falls from the surface waters. This organic detritus, or marine snow, consists of microscopic, one-celled plant (phytoplankton) and animal (zooplankton) remains, along with various dissolved particulates that have clumped together into tiny flakes. Throughout the oceans, marine snow falls, raining down in sporadic pulses. In the summer, the spring-born plankton die in great numbers and immerse the ocean in a blizzard of organic matter, blanketing some spots on the ocean floor in a thick green blanket of dead matter. This, in addition to the rare arrival of whole animal carcasses, is what feeds the majority of the ocean floor life.

Using the Ocean Floor in the Game

Adventure in the deep ocean should be highlighted with a constant hint of danger and suspense to keep the characters on edge. Those brave enough to defy the pulverizing pressure, near-freezing water, and utter blackness of the sea at those depths should be rewarded with an eventful experience. Whether it's subterranean monsters burrowing within the mud-packed sediment floor of the abyssal plains; ancient civilizations living in the abyssal hills, forced to migrate towards the mid-ocean ridge as their habitat is slowly consumed with sediments; or perhaps even elemental-driven turbidity currents sweeping throughout the sea like colossal sand storms, the ocean floor should provide plenty of excitement, and endless possibilities in your campaign.

Reefs

An important part of oceanic life, reefs are defined as elevated ridges along shallow places on the seafloor. Reefs are formed from creatures known as coral polyps, hence the popular name coral reef. Upon death, these tiny coral polyps leave behind hardened exoskeletons made of a calcerous (calcium-containing), stony material. These small bits of limestone, when combined with similar deposits from countless polyps, form the beautiful and labyrinthine structures that are coral reefs.

Depending on the number of polyps that die in the area, coral reefs grow at rates between 1 to 40 inches each year. Coral reefs are found exclusively in tropical regions of the ocean, never beyond 30 degrees north or south of the planet's equator and never in waters cooler than 61° Fahrenheit. Two primary types of coral exist — hard and soft. Categories of hard coral include brain coral and elkhorn coral, both of which have hard limestone frames. Soft corals such as sea fingers and sea whips do not form reefs.

Most campaign worlds boast at least three different kinds of coral reefs, though there is no limit on the variety of reef that can appear in a fantasy setting. One such example is listed below, along with the three typical types of reefs.

Barrier Reefs. These reefs always run parallel to the shoreline, but several yards out and separated by a lagoon. Because these reefs form a kind of protective palisade around the beach, they are known as barrier reefs.

Coral Atolls. These are rings of coral atop old, sunken volcanoes. Coral atolls begin as fringe reefs surrounding volcanic islands, but when the island sinks, the reef keeps growing and is classified as a coral atoll. Horseshoe-shaped collections of coral, atolls form rings around small lagoons that fill the caldera of inactive volcanoes.

Fringing Reefs. Running directly along the coastline, the fringing reefs are found built close to the continental shelf in the shallow waters near shore.

Spherical Reef. One example of the kind of reef found in a fantasy world is the spherical reef. Also known as reef globes, these huge structures of coral are formed into great spheres by some unknown natural process. The walls of the reef globe are hard enough that the spheres can act as a temporary shelter for marine travelers.

Regardless of the exact nature of the reef, all such coral mazes are robust ecosystems supporting a variety of marine life. The reef's far layer consists of the living polyps, while below them are the calcerous reef framework, containing filamentous green algae. These algae provide nourishment for many of the animals that make their home in or near the reef. Fish and other creatures abound. A brief list of a reef's inhabitants includes the following: sponges, nudibranchs, reef sharks, groupers, clown fish, eels, snappers, jellyfish, anemones, sea stars, crabs, shrimps, lobsters, sea snakes, snails, octopi, nautilus, and clams.

USING REEFS IN THE GAME

Coral reefs make excellent sites for exotic adventure. Imagine a villain's underwater lair constructed from confusing coral passages. Spherical reefs can serve as hideouts for all manners of creatures, or hauled onto shore to use as part of an NPC's elaborate home. The stereotypical dungeon maze can take on a new form when made of coral; the winding coral corridors can present characters with a challenging labyrinth to solve. Reefs are notorious haunts for many dangerous beasts, such as eels, sharks, and octopi. Societies of sea elves can use coral to make armor, weapons, and other trade goods. Reefs are also known to conceal sunken ships beneath their protective arms of coral.

TECTONIC PLATES

The surface of the planet is essentially a rigid shell, a layer of thick rock comprised of continental or oceanic crust along with the uppermost portion of the mantle. This layer of the planet is known as the lithosphere. The oceanic lithosphere is on average 6 miles thick, while the continental lithosphere can be up to 60 miles thick. It is broken up into a dozen or more slabs or plates, known commonly as tectonic plates, which move and interact in relation to one another as they glide upon the asthenosphere, the partially molten rock region of the planet's mantle. The size and position of these tectonic plates are constantly changing, though only at rates of inches per year.

Tectonic plates interact with one another in several different ways, and the results of these interactions have a severe impact upon the topography and geology of the planet. In divergent boundaries, plates pull away from each other, creating new crust in the process. Since the size of the planet does not change, older crust must be destroyed simultaneously as new crust is formed. This occurs in the areas known as convergent boundaries, where two tectonic plates commit a slow collision. Transform boundaries, or transform-fault boundaries, are where two lithospheric plates simply glide or shift past the other.

Tectonic activity is never more evident, nor more crucial, than in the ocean. Geology occurs foremost at plate boundaries, and the plate boundaries of the ocean floor are of particular consequence to the rest of the planet as seismic and volcanic events occurring anywhere on the globe can be traced to activity at an ocean plate boundary. Furthermore, the phenomenon of seafloor spreading in divergent boundaries and the imminent result of ocean floor subduction in convergent boundaries points directly towards the composition and layout of the rest of the planet's surface.

USING TECTONIC ACTIVITY IN THE GAME

Tectonic plates are the origin of many large-scale events on any planet. Continental shelves are constantly moving — and sometimes this movement results in the release of a monster that had been contained for millennia deep in the crust of the earth. An NPC sorcerer who wants to wreak havoc on the world above could cause a great explosion at the juncture of two lithospheric plates, resulting in massive land shifts. The movement of the plates can result in tidal waves and earthquakes. Seeing this, it's no surprise that powerful NPCs might contrive to take control of certain points on the ocean floor, places where they can use their magic to command tectonic activity.

TIDES AND WAVES

So much depends upon the tides. As one of the most fundamental aspects of oceanography, the importance of tides and tidal activity cannot be overstated. Without the constant movement of the tides, life below the surface would be greatly different, as would the lives of those dependent upon the incoming and outgoing waters along the coast. Any capable sailor is well-versed in tidal lore. The study of the nature of tides involves unraveling some of the core tenets of the universe, namely mass and gravity. Quite simply, tides are the occasional rise and fall of a planet's waters, including oceans, seas, and bays. This constant up-and-down motion is due directly to the gravitational forces exerted upon the planet by the sun and moon.

Lunar pull accounts for most of the tidal activity on the planet. In a game world that has no moon, or on a planet with multiple moons, the tides will behave differently depending on the amount of gravitational pull being exerted at any one time. On an earth-like planet, two "high water" and two "low water" occur every lunar day. This rising and falling of water results in lateral water movements called tidal currents (not to be confused with ocean currents). Tidal currents flow in a shoreward or upstream direction during high water then reverses flow during low water.

Waves are the result of the wind. Generally speaking, the greater the wind speed, the higher the waves. Note that waves do not move horizontally, but only up and down. Another type of wave, the tsunami, can cause vast and terrible damage to structures when it crashes upon the shore. Tsunamis are not caused by tides, but rather by tectonic activity such as earthquakes and undersea volcanoes.

WAVE HEIGHT TABLE (DAY)

	Height in feet			
1d00	Summer	Winter	Autumn	Spring
01–10	5	15	20	15
11–20	25	18	20	15
21–30	42	20	15	35
31–40	20	35	15	25
41–50	18	10	5	22
51–60	35	18	20	15
61–70	15	30	10	22
71–80	17	25	20	10
81–90	45	20	30	15
91–00	10	10	25	20

	Height in feet			
1d100	Summer	Winter	Autumn	Spring
01–10	25	18	25	15
11–20	42	20	20	35
21–30	20	35	15	25
31–40	18	10	5	22
41–50	35	18	20	15
51–60	15	30	10	22
61–70	17	25	20	10
71–80	45	20	30	15
81–90	10	10	25	20
91–00	5	15	20	15

Using Tides and Waves in the Game

Tides can be used to reveal or conceal sunken ships, the entrances to hidden lairs, or other things. Waves can make life miserable for anyone trying to travel across the open sea. Refer to the Wave Height table for a quick way to determine wave height. Roll 1d00 and consult either the day or night portion of the chart.

Big waves can cause trouble for those aboard ships. The Wave Effects table shows what happens when waves of a certain size wash over the sides, or gunwales, of ships.

The following are guidelines for using the table.

Wave Size. Compare the wave height from the Wave Height table to the height of the ship's gunwale to determine "wave size." This is the amount by which the wave is taller than the ship's side.

Dexterity Check Modifier. Anyone forced to make a Dexterity check for any reason does so at a penalty when large waves wash over the ship.

Creature Size. This is the size of creature that a particular wave can effect.

Wave Effects. Any of these effects can be resisted with a Strength saving throw, the DC is indicated in the final column.

Knocked Prone. Creatures who fail their save are knocked prone by the force of the wave and swept in a random direction 1d6 feet.

Checked. Creatures who fail their save are unable to move against the force of the wave, and can take no action that round but that of stabilizing themselves.

Swept Overboard. Creatures who fail their save are knocked prone and carried 1d4 x 10 feet, taking 1d4 points bludgeoning damage per 10 feet traveled. If the distance traveled extends beyond the sides of the deck, the creature is tossed overboard.

Trenches

Ocean trenches are deep and narrow subterranean depressions within the ocean floor. They mark the deepest areas on the planet. It is in these trenches that the seafloor, now denser and well over 200 million years older, returns to the mantle where it is effectively recycled. Most often appearing adjacent to continental masses, their length can stretch up to thousands of miles. The depth of these trenches varies anywhere from the 20,000 feet necessary to generally be considered a trench, to over 35,000 feet.

Trenches form in the convergent plate boundaries known as subduction zones. General theory suggests that in these zones, an oceanic plate meets either another oceanic plate or continental plate and slides beneath it. The denser lithospheric ocean plate commits a slow plummet towards the mantle below, dragging the edge of the non-subducting plate down with it, producing the linear V-shaped trench. The dense lithosphere of older, thicker oceanic plates subducts quickly and steeply into the mantle, whereas the buoyant young lithosphere that is thinner and warmer bends slowly, creating a gentle trench slope.

The process of subduction has many consequences that impact the surrounding area, most notably the sweeping arcs of volcanoes. Over millions of years the convergence of the two plates leads to volcanic arc formations appearing on the overriding plate parallel to the subduction zone. As the descending oceanic plate lunges deeper

Wave Effects Table

Wave Force	Wave Size	Dexterity Check Modifier	Creature Size	Wave Effect on Creatures	Strength Saving Throw DC
Light	0–2 feet	—	Any	None	—
Moderate	3–5 feet	—	Any	None	—
Strong	6–10 feet	−2	Tiny	Knocked prone	10
		—	Small or larger	None	—
Severe	11–30 feet	−4	Tiny	Swept overboard	15
		−2	Small	Knocked Prone	15
		—	Medium	Checked	15
		—	Large or larger	None	—
Windstorm	31–50 feet	−4	Small or smaller	Swept overboard	18
		−2	Medium	Knocked Prone	18
		—	Large or Huge	Checked	18
		—	Gargantuan	None	—
Hurricane	51–100 feet	Impossible	Medium or smaller	Swept overboard	20
		−4	Large	Knocked Prone	20
		—	Huge	Checked	20
		—	Gargantuan	None	—
Tornado	101+ feet	Impossible	Large or smaller	Swept overboard	30
		−4	Huge	Knocked Prone	30
		—	Gargantuan	Checked	30

towards the mantle below, it is subjected to greater pressure and rising temperatures. Eventually the surface water of the crust and hydrated minerals from within the basaltic portions of the subducting plate are discharged into the mantle portion of the overlying lithospheric plate. As the water interacts with the mantle, it decreases the mantle's melting temperature, allowing it to melt. A supply of the magma created rises through the crust of the overriding plate and forms the volcanic arc. When subduction zones involve two oceanic plates, the chains of volcanoes that break the ocean surface are called volcanic island arcs.

Other side effects characterize subduction zones. Interactions between the two converging plates generate some of the most seismically powerful earthquakes in the world. The plot of the subducting plate's ascension can be outlined by the seismic activity occurring deeper and deeper within the planet's mantle, several hundred thousand kilometers beneath the surface. The earthquakes focused along subduction zones tend to be cyclic and reactionary. Subduction zone earthquakes can also wreak havoc upon the coastal areas by causing the incredibly destructive waves called tsunamis. Tsunamis caused by the subduction zone earthquakes or earthquake-triggered submarine landslides can be catastrophic events, wiping out miles of coastlands.

Despite frequent sediment-dense avalanches along the slopes, ocean trenches provide fairly hospitable homes for creatures that are capable of withstanding the crushing water pressure. The water temperature and seawater salinity found in trenches is identical to the other areas of the deep sea, and sources of food tend to be slightly less scarce. The trench profile traps generous amounts of organic matter within, distributing it down to even the deepest dwellers. Their proximity to the coasts also grants access to especially plankton-rich surface waters raining in nourishment from above. Additionally, cold methane seeps exist along the slopes of some trenches, packed with methane-eating bacteria that nourish the creatures nearby through chemosynthesis. Anemones, crustaceans, bristle worms, and most prominently, holothurians (sea cucumbers), make homes in ocean trenches.

USING TRENCHES IN THE GAME

In campaign worlds, trenches serve as perhaps the most remote locations of the planet — much like in reality. Very few would likely know of their existence, and fewer still would be willing to explore them. However, those that take the proper precautions and brave the seemingly bottomless depths of these trenches should have plenty of sights to see. Long-abandoned ruins of ancient civilizations found along the trench walls or partially submerged treasures of immeasurable worth within the sediment-filled valley are but a couple enticements. A strong downward suction could exist within the trench formation, or the subduction zone might cease and become dormant. This is to say nothing of the possibilities as to what terrors might exist within these fearsome depths.

CHAPTER 2: UNDERWATER ADVENTURING

The oceans hide a world that most adventures and adventurers never explore. It is a world fraught with danger and discovery, mystery and the unknown.

VARIANTS

Many factors come into play when the characters venture beneath the water's surface. The following are all self-contained variant rules that can be added to your campaign to add a sense of verisimilitude. This is not to say that it will add realism, but in a seafaring campaign, these rules attempt to address issue that might draw your players out of the story you are attempting to tell.

You should feel free to modify them as you feel is appropriate for your campaign.

ENCUMBRANCE

While not necessarily required, this rules variant slightly modifies how much a character can carry without being affected. The effects of these rules affect all the following rules, but are not necessary to use them.

A creature's Strength score determines the amount of weight it can bear. The following terms define what the creature can lift or carry. Ignore the any Strength requirements for armor.

Carrying Capacity. Carrying capacity has three levels: Encumbered, Heavily Encumbered, and Maximum Capacity.

Encumbered. If a creature carries weight in excess of 5 times its Strength score, the creature is encumbered. An encumbered creature's speed drops by 10 feet.

Heavily Encumbered. If a creature carries weight in excess of 10 times its Strength score, up to its maximum carrying capacity, the creature is instead heavily encumbered. A heavily encumbered creature's speed drops by 20 feet and it has disadvantage on ability checks, attack rolls, and saving throws that use Strength or Dexterity.

Maximum Carrying Capacity. A creature's maximum carrying capacity is its Strength score times 15. If a creature reaches its maximum carrying capacity, its speed drops to 5 feet.

Push, Drag, or Lift. A creature can push, drag, or lift a weight in pounds up to twice its maximum carrying capacity (or 30 times its Strength score), and while pushing or dragging weight in excess of its maximum carrying capacity, its speed drops to 5 feet.

Size and Strength. Larger creatures can bear more weight, whereas Tiny creatures can carry less. For each size category above Medium, double the creature's carrying capacity at all levels, and the amount it can push, drag, or lift. For a Tiny creatures, halve these weights.

SWIMMING

A creature with a swimming speed does not need to worry overmuch about rough surf or strong currents, save for supernatural ones. A creature that lacks a swimming speed — such as the majority of the characters' racial options — is at a distinct disadvantage while in water. These disadvantages are heightened by what type of armor that creature is wearing, and what types of actions they are attempting to take while swimming.

The easiest way for a creature to gain a swimming speed is to utilize one of the benefits of the *alter self* spell: Aquatic Adaptation. The following rules detail the disadvantages that a creature suffers when it does not have such a boon.

Actions. Normally, it does not require an action to swim, unless another effect requires that a creature use their action to swim.

Speed. A creature without a swim speed can swim at half their normal walking speed in normal surf. They may need to make a DC 15 Strength (Athletics) check in rough water, or have disadvantage on the check if the waters are frothy from storm. Supernatural effects, such as the *control water* spell, dictate what ability checks may be necessary to survive within the magic's area.

When other effects modify a creature's speed, such as the *haste* spell or the amount of weight a creature carries, don't apply the effects of swimming until all other factors have been imposed.

Dashing. A character without a swim speed can still dash to swim further as their action (or bonus action as appropriate). However, swimming is taxing when done for long periods of time. If a creature uses the Dash action to swim farther more times than their Constitution modifier, they must make a DC 10 Constitution saving throw for each successive Dash action or gain one level of exhaustion.

Armor. Swimming in armor is a dangerous affair to be involved in. Even light armor can be cumbersome to the uninitiated. While wearing **light armor** that a creature is proficient in, they have no difficulties swimming unless another effect would impose it, such as the *control water* spell. A creature that lacks proficiency in light armor but tries to swim in it has disadvantage on any ability check made to do so.

Swimming in **medium armor** is somewhat difficult. The weight of the armor makes a creature negatively buoyant, causing them to sink if a character cannot continue swimming. A paralyzed or restrained creature that's wearing medium armor in water sinks at a rate of 10 feet at the end of each of its turns. A creature wearing medium armor moves at half their normal movement rate; a creature with a swimming speed is unaffected. Because a creature already moves at half their normal movement rate while swimming, this effectively forces the character to swim at one quarter their swimming speed.

Swimming in **heavy armor** is dangerous. A creature must use their action to swim or stay afloat by making a DC 10 Strength (Athletics) check. On a failed check, a creature sinks 15 feet at the end of each of their turns.

VISION

Seeing underwater is a difficult question to address, and will need to be taken in two steps: available light and turbidity, or clarity of the water.

SUNLIGHT

For the purposes of sunlight into the open ocean, the depths of the ocean are divided into three separate sections: the sunlight, twilight, and midnight zones. In the absence of sunlight — such as on a moonlit night — the ocean is complete darkness beneath 15 feet of water, and dim light to the surface.

The Sunlight (Euphotic) Zone. The sunlight zone occupies a depth down to 650 feet. Within this zone, sunlight allows vision to work normally absent any other conditions.

The Twilight (Dysphotic) Zone. The twilight zone occupies the deep from 650 feet down to 3000 feet. In this zone, sunlight rapidly decreases and it is considered dim light absent any other conditions.

The Midnight (Aphotic) Zone. The midnight zone begins at 3000 feet and continues to the bottom. In this zone, it is complete darkness.

VISIBILITY

Water's visibility is based on its turbidity, or the measure of the relative clarity of the liquid medium. Unlike the diffusion of sunlight by the passage of water, this is when material affects how clear a body of water is by turning the water cloudy or opaque. A body of water's turbidity is always a function of external circumstance, such as the body of water's location or excessive churning of the water from storms.

An area of water's turbidity breaks down into four categories: low, medium, high, and occluded.

LOW TURBIDITY

Areas of low turbidity have a visibility distance of 180 (4d8 x 10) feet. Creatures or objects beyond this distance are heavily obscured, and creatures beyond half that distance are lightly obscured. Areas of low turbidity are most commonly found in deep water and occasionally in tropical coastal areas.

MEDIUM TURBIDITY

Areas of medium turbidity include sounds, bays, and coastal waters, caused by their relatively shallow depth and the sea currents which flow through them. An area of medium turbidity has a visibility distance of 90 (2d8 x 10) feet, beyond which creatures and objects are heavily obscured. Creature and objects are lightly obscured beyond half that distance.

HIGH TURBIDITY

Rivers and harbors always have high turbidity. The areas have sediment and silt from river mouths, which cause creatures to be heavily obscured beyond 30 (1d6 x 10) feet, and lightly obscured beyond half that distance.

OCCLUDED

Reserved for the most turbulent waters, occluded waters have a visibility distance of 10 (1d4 x 5) feet, beyond which creatures are heavily obscured. Creatures and objects are lightly obscured within half that distance. Areas of occluded visibility occur in the strongest currents, such as those churned by storms or underwater events like eruptions and earthquakes, like the turbidity currents that cross the abyssal plains.

BREATHING

The most obvious way to handle breathing under water is the *water breathing* spell. Its utility and breadth makes it a necessity in seafaring adventures. However, if a creature does not possess it or another feature that allows them to breath under water, you can utilize the following rules.

A creature can hold its breath for a number of minutes equal to 1 + its Constitution modifier (minimum of 30 seconds) if a creature does nothing but use their turn to swim in normal surf.

A creature that is holding their breath when they take damage from any source must make a Constitution saving throw. The DC equals 10 or half the damage taken from the effect, whichever is higher. On a failure, they exhale and run out of breath.

If a creature runs out of breath, it can then survive a number of rounds equal to their Constitution modifier (minimum 1 round). At the start of its next turn, it drops to 0 hit points and is dying, and it can't regain hit points or be stabilized until it can breathe again.

PRESSURE

Pressure is a function of a creature's depth, caused by the weight of the water above them. For creatures of the land, this is an unknown and dangerous world. A creature that strays too deep risks having their blood pushed from their veins and into their lungs, where they drown on it.

Depth Rating. A depth rating is a number of increments of 30 feet, and it is these ratings that determine how deep a creature can go before suffering from the effects of pressure. A creature's maximum depth rating is equal to their Constitution ability score x 30. For example, a creature with a Constitution of 10 can survive the pressure up to 300 feet without ill effects — assuming they have a source of magic or another feature that allows them to avoid drowning.

Once a creature reaches this depth, the effects of pressure become noticeable.

Water Breathing. A creature that can breathe water, either through magical or natural means, doubles their maximum depth rating. This is cumulative if a creature is an aquatic creature.

Creatures. A creature that is native to aquatic environments, such as one that has a swim speed like the killer whale, also doubles their maximum depth rating. This is cumulative with the ability to breathe water natively.

Damage. A creature takes a cumulative 1d6 bludgeoning damage at the end of each of their turns for every 30 feet past their maximum depth rating. This has an effect on a creature's ability to hold their breath, as detailed above.

PRESSURE SUMMARY

Creature Type	Depth Rating
Non-aquatic creature that can't breathe water	Constitution score x 30 ft.
Can breathe water *or* aquatic creature	Constitution score x 60 ft.
Can breathe water *and* aquatic creature	Constitution score x 120 ft.

THE REAL WORLD

This is not that far off from real world norms — at least for creatures.

If one considers a killer whale, its Constitution score is 13, meaning that it can survive without ill effects dives of up to 780 feet according to the above rules. An average minimum for killer whale depth in the real world is at least 328 feet, while the deepest dive, performed under experimental conditions, was 850 feet. Some species of whales have been recorded as deep as 866 feet in the North Pacific.

To continue the example, a hunter shark — a creature that can only breath water and is an aquatic creature — has a Constitution score of 15. This hunter shark would be able to swim without suffering the effects of pressure up to 1800 feet. To equate that to a real world equivalent, studies have shown that the average tiger shark would be recorded at 1100 feet, and possibly even deeper.

UNDERWATER COMBAT

The rules for underwater combat are fairly straightforward, but the following can add a bit of fun during combat.

Melee Weapon Attacks. While underwater, when a creature makes a melee weapon attack a creature that doesn't have a swimming speed (either naturally or granted by spells like *alter self*) has disadvantage on the attack roll unless the weapon is a dagger, javelin, shortsword, spear, or trident.

Ranged Weapon Attacks. A creature automatically misses a ranged weapon attack if the target is beyond the weapon's normal range, and has disadvantage on the attack roll if the target is within normal range unless the weapon is a crossbow, net, or a weapon that is thrown like a javelin (including a spear, trident, or dart).

From Land to Sea. Attacks that originate from above the surface to below the surface have special rules.

If a creature is floating on the surface of the water, they can be targeted by attacks from creature above the surface normally. However, if a creature is fully submerged but still within range of a surface creature's melee attack, a creature has half cover from creatures on or above the surface, to account for water's bending of light which obscures their vision.

If a creature makes a ranged weapon attack from on or above the surface at a target that is 5 feet or shallower beneath the surface, the attack is resolved normally. However, a creature that is deeper than 5 feet below the surface has three-quarters cover from attacks made from on or above the surface.

CASTING SPELLS

A creature that is incapable of breathing underwater is unable to cast spells with verbal components. In addition, in salt water, spells that deal lightning damage are more effective: creatures have disadvantage on saving throws to resist its effects and a creature has advantage on attack rolls with spells that deal lightning damage.

The bulk of this chapter contains daily weather entries, small capsules that describe the weather for a particular day, including high and low temperatures, wind speed, and other events. Preceding this information, however, is a look at certain weather-related factors that impact the data in the daily weather entries.

CHAPTER 3: WEATHER

TEMPERATURE

Temperature in the daily weather entries is listed in Fahrenheit and Celsius, with both highs and lows. For example, you might find this entry: Temp H 92/34 L 71/22. This means that the high temperature for that day will be 92° F or 34° C, with lows of 71° and 22° respectively.

HUMIDITY AND WIND CHILL

Two factors that combine with temperature to cause misery to travelers are humidity and wind chill. Though it might actually be 85°, a high humidity can make it feel like an unbearable 105°, while a strong wind can drop that and make it feel like a comfortable 72°. High humidity prohibits the body from being able to cool itself properly. Thus the body perceives the temperature as being higher than it actually is. This perceived temperature is called the heat index. The daily weather entries show you the base high and low temperatures, but you may optionally alter these temperatures by adding the effects of humidity and wind chill. On warm days, roll on the Random Humidity Table to find the percentage of humidity. When humidity is 50% or higher, refer to the daily weather entry to find the day's high temperature, then use the Heat Index Table to see how hot a character feels in such conditions. On days where the cold can be a problem, read the wind speed in the daily weather entry, then refer to the Wind Chill Table.

TEMPERATURE EFFECTS

Extremely high and low temperatures have serious effects on characters who are unprotected from the elements. Some of these effects are detailed in the daily weather entries. Other effects include the following:

Temperature Below 40° F. An unprotected character must succeed on a DC 10 Constitution (Survival) check each hour or take 3 (1d6) cold damage and gain one level of exhaustion. For each check of this type a character fails, the DC of subsequent checks increases by 1. The DC resets to 10 once the character regains at least one lost level of cold-based exhaustion. Characters wearing winter clothing need not make these checks.

Temperature Below 0° F. In conditions of severe cold or exposure, an unprotected character must succeed on a DC 12 Constitution (Survival) check once every 10 minutes or take 3 (1d6) cold damage and gain one level of exhaustion. For each check of this type a character fails, the DC of subsequent checks increases by 1. The DC resets to 10 once the character regains at least one lost level of cold-based exhaustion. Characters wearing winter clothing only need to make this check once per hour.

Temperature Below –20° F. Extreme cold forces unprotected characters to succeed on a DC 14 Constitution (Survival) check every minute or take 3 (1d6) cold damage and gain one level of exhaustion. For each check of this type a character fails, the DC of subsequent checks increases by 1. The DC resets to 10 once the character regains at least one lost level of cold-based exhaustion. Characters wearing winter clothing only need to make this check every 30 minutes. Those failing their check and wearing metal armor take an additional 3 (1d6) cold damage and have disadvantage on attack rolls and ability checks until they doff the armor.

Temperature Above 90° F. A character in very hot conditions must succeed on a DC 10 Constitution (Survival) check every hour or take 2 (1d4) fire damage and gain one level of exhaustion. For each check of this type a character fails, the DC of subsequent checks increases by 1. The DC resets to 10 once the character regains at least one lost level of heat-based exhaustion. Characters wearing heavy clothing or any sort of armor have disadvantage on these checks.

Temperature Above 110° F. In severe heat, a character must succeed on a DC 12 Constitution (Survival) check once every 10 minutes or take 2 (1d4) fire damage and gain one level of exhaustion. For each check of this type a character fails, the DC of subsequent checks increases by 1. The DC resets to 10 once the character regains at least one lost level of heat-based exhaustion. Characters wearing heavy clothing or any sort of armor have disadvantage on these checks.

Temperature Above 140° F. Exposure to these temperatures requires that characters succeed on a DC 14 Constitution (Survival) check every minute or take 3 (1d6) fire damage. For each check of this type a character fails, the DC of subsequent checks increases by 1. The DC resets to 10 once the character regains at least one lost level of heat-based exhaustion. Those wearing heavy clothing or any sort of armor have disadvantage on these checks. Those failing their check and wearing metal armor take an additional 3 (1d6) fire damage and have disadvantage on attack rolls and ability checks until they doff the armor.

RANDOM HUMIDITY

1d20	Arctic	Tropical	Temperate	Equatorial
1–2	10%	50%	10%	60%
3–6	10%	60%	20%	70%
7–10	20%	70%	30%	80%
11–14	30%	80%	40%	80%
15–18	40%	80%	50%	90%
19	50%	90%	60%	90%
20	50%	90%	70%	90%

HEAT INDEX TABLE

Temp.	50%	60%	70%	80%	90%
80	80	81	82	84	85
85	86	90	92	96	101
90	94	99	105	113	121
100	118	129	142	161	178

WIND

A typical entry for wind might look like this: Wind — 10–15 mph. This means that the wind is moving between 10 and 15 miles per hour. Note that this is the base wind speed. You may, at your discretion, roll 4d6 and add the result to the base wind speed.

Wind Direction. To determine the direction of the wind, consult the Wind Direction table.

RANDOM WIND DIRECTION

Roll 1d4, then 1d8

	1–2		3–4
1d8	Wind Direction	1d8	Wind Direction
1	NNE	1	SSW
2	NE	2	SW
3	ENE	3	WSW
4	E	4	W
5	ESE	5	WNW
6	SE	6	NW
7	SSE	7	NNW
8	S	8	N

Temp. (F)	Wind Speed (mph)											
	5	10	15	20	25	30	35	40	45	50	55	60
40	36	34	32	30	29	28	28	27	26	26	25	25
35	31	27	25	24	23	22	21	20	19	19	18	17
30	25	21	19	17	16	15	14	13	12	12	11	10
25	19	15	13	11	9	8	7	6	5	4	4	3
20	13	9	6	4	3	1	0	−1	−2	−3	−3	−4
15	7	3	0	−2	−4	−5	−7	−8	−9	−10	−11	−11
10	1	−4	−7	−9	−11	−12	−14	−15	−16	−17	−18	−19
5	−5	−10	−13	−15	−17	−19	−21	−22	−23	−24	−25	−26
0	−11	−16	−19	−22	−24	−26	−27	−29	−30	−31	−32	−33
−5	−16	−22	−26	−29	−31	−33	−34	−36	−37	−38	−39	−40
−10	−22	−28	−32	−35	−37	−39	−41	−43	−44	−45	−46	−48
−15	−28	−35	−39	−42	−44	−46	−48	−50	−51	−52	−54	−55
−20	−34	−41	−45	−48	−51	−53	−55	−57	−58	−60	−61	−62
−25	−40	−47	−51	−55	−58	−60	−62	−64	−65	−67	−68	−69
−30	−46	−53	−58	−61	−64	−67	−69	−71	−72	−74	−75	−76
−35	−52	−59	−61	−68	−71	−73	−76	−78	−79	−81	−82	−84
−40	−57	−66	−71	−74	−78	−80	−82	−84	−86	−88	−89	−91
−45	−63	−72	−77	−81	−84	−87	−89	−91	−93	−95	−97	−98

DAILY WEATHER

The remainder of this chapter comprises daily weather entries. The information is broken into several parts. To determine daily weather, find the current season (Spring, Summer, Autumn, Winter). Then find the appropriate terrain type (Tropical, Equatorial, Temperate, or Arctic). At this point you can select from one of the following 4 options: Rain/Day, Rain/Night, Dry/Day, Dry/Night. It's up to you to decide whether it's day or night, but for purposes of rain, roll 1d20 and use the Precipitation at Sea table. Note that this table in no way represents realistic precipitation chances, but simply provides a ready means to determine random weather. Finally, roll 1d100 to find the exact weather entry for that day.

PRECIPITATION AT SEA

	Dry	Rain/Snow
Arctic Sea	1–6	7–20
Desert Coast	1–18	19–20
Jungle Coast	1–4	5–20
Swamp Coast	1–9	10–20
Temperate Sea	1–12	13–20
Tropical Sea	1–7	8–20

Summer

Tropical

Heat stroke is a risk for any who travel the warm regions of the world. Those exerting themselves must succeed on a DC 10 Constitution saving throw for each hour of strenuous work or gain a level of exhaustion. For each cumulative hour of strenuous work, the DC of subsequent saves increases by 1. Resting in shaded areas for 10 minutes per hour negates the +1 to the DC for that hour. Spell components run a 10% chance of spoiling in humidity, if you determine they are subject to such damage.

Rain/Day

01–20	A gentle breeze blows, adding a pleasant cooling to the warm rain falling. Large drops patter along the deck, occasional sunshine warms the deck, quickly evaporating the rain and adding to the humidity. A sticky aspect of the air grows throughout the day as the humidity rises. Sunlight glints off the water like numerous smaller suns, blinding those not ready for the effect. Waves are large in width but not in height, rocking the ship with their passage. (Temp H 92/34 L 71/22, Wind — 10–15 mph. Characters on deck have disadvantage on concentration checks.)
21–40	Steady rain pummels the ship and those on board, quickly soaking all equipment and people. The waves are sedated, rarely topping 5 feet, seemingly held down with the rain. The sun tries to pierce the cloud cover with its intense glare, only succeeding in raising the temperature. Wind is non-existent, hammered to submission by the heavy rain (Temp H 91/33 L 80/27, Wind — 0–5 mph.)
41–60	Seemingly in rhythm with the lapping waves, periodic rain drops in vast amounts, quickly soaking all surfaces and washing away loose items. Between rainfalls, the sun attempts to burn away the moisture with blistering heat. Waves roll languidly, topping 6 feet in height but not steep enough to make more than an exaggerated rocking motion. The wind blows merrily, billowing out the sails of the ship and propelling the vessel over the large waves. (Temp H 89/32 L 71/22, Wind – 10–15 mph. Characters moving on deck during a deluge must succeed on a DC 6 Dexterity (Acrobatics) check or be knocked prone and pushed 10 feet in a random direction, and all exposed areas of the ship count as difficult terrain.)
61–80	A drizzle of rain, sometimes hard and sometimes light, falls continuously throughout the day. All surfaces are thoroughly soaked and heavy with water. The warmth of the occasional sun is diminished slightly by the cool rain, keeping it tolerable for all involved. Waves are present but pose no real threat to the direction of the ship or her course. The wind blows constantly, keeping the sails full but not pushing the limit of its capabilities. (Temp H 87/31 L 78/26, Wind — 15–20 mph.)
81–00	Heavy rain from unseen clouds pummels the ship and those on deck. Waves like great gray-green boulders smashing against the ship every minute. The overhead clouds have descended to a point where it seems the ship is in a large chamber. Wind hurtles against the vessel and its sail, trying to rip it from the mast and rigging. All loose items on deck vie for attention from the crashing waves or the blustery wind. (Temp H 91/33 L 80/27, Wind – 50–55 mph. Characters moving on deck must succeed on a DC 10 Dexterity (Acrobatics) check each round or be knocked prone and pushed 10 feet in a random direction. All exposed areas of the ship are lightly obscured and count as difficult terrain. Characters on deck also have disadvantage on Strength (Athletics) checks involving climbing and Constitution saving throws made to maintain concentration on a spell.)

Rain/Night

01–20	The cool of the night is accompanied by the patter of rain upon the deck. The humidity keeps the coolness of the night from being comfortable. The moon makes itself known through the clouds, illuminating a portion of the night sky to milky white. The waves crash against the hull as if trying to keep the ship from reaching its goal. The bounce of the ship as it passes over the waves keeps all but the soundest sleepers awake. (Temp H 33/90 L 22/71, Wind — 0–5 mph.)
21–40	Heavy rain from unseen clouds pummel the ship and those on deck. Waves can be seen in the dark like great gray-green boulders smashing against the ship every minute. The clouds press on the ship, cloaking all details over 10 feet away. Wind crashes against the vessel and its sail, trying to tear it from its supports. All loose items on deck vie for attention from the crashing waves or the blustery wind. (Temp H 33/91 L 27/80, Wind — 60–65 mph. Characters moving on deck must succeed on a DC 8 Dexterity (Acrobatics) check each round or be knocked prone and pushed 10 feet in a random direction. All exposed areas of the ship are lightly obscured and count as difficult terrain. Characters on deck also have disadvantage on Strength (Athletics) checks involving climbing and Constitution saving throws made to maintain concentration on a spell.)
41–60	Seemingly in rhythm with the lapping waves, periodic rain drops in vast amounts, quickly soaking all surfaces and washing away loose items. Waves roll languidly, topping 6 feet in height but not steep enough to make more than an exaggerated rocking motion. A light wind blows, carrying mist from the still warm water, visible in the occasional moonlight. (Temp H 76/25 L 71/22, Wind — 5–10 mph. Vision is reduced to 1/2 from the mist and the darkness. Darkvision is unaffected. Characters moving on deck must succeed on a DC 6 Dexterity (Acrobatics) check or be knocked prone. All exposed areas of the ship are lightly obscured and count as difficult terrain.)
61–80	A drizzle of rain, varying in strength continuously throughout the nighttime hours. All surfaces are thoroughly soaked and heavy with water. The warmth of the day rapidly disappears, replaced with the humidity of the still evaporating water around the ship. Waves are present but pose no real threat to the direction of the ship. The wind blows constantly, keeping the sails full but not pushing the limit of its capabilities. (Temp H 80/27 L 78/26, Wind — 12–18 mph.)
81–00	A constant rain falls from gray clouds overhead, keeping all within it thoroughly soaked. The wind propels the ship slowly, seemingly held back by the rain, over the large hillock-shaped waves. Occasional lightning flashes illuminate the depth of the rain, looking like iron bars for as far as the eye can see, peppering the water. (Temp H 79/27 L 71/22, Wind — 5–10 mph. All exposed areas of the ship are lightly obscured and count as difficult terrain.)

Dry/Day

01–20	The large sun dominates the sky but a swift breeze keeps the temperature to a more moderate level. Spray pulled up from the many waves, capped in white froth. The horizon is marked with a large bank of gray clouds, promising rain in the next day or two. (Temp H 90/33 L 75/24, Wind — 10–15 mph.)
21–40	Clouds run amok along the sky, occasionally blocking the sun and its warmth. The wind seemingly growls as it tears across the water at the ship. The sail quivers, trying to keep the wind from escaping. Waves rise up and crash against the hull of the ship, each impact like a bludgeon from nature itself. (Temp H 89/32 L 77/26, Wind — 45–50 mph. Characters moving on deck must succeed on a DC 8 Dexterity (Acrobatics) check each round or be knocked prone. All exposed areas of the ship count as difficult terrain, and characters on deck have disadvantage on Strength (Athletics) checks involving climbing and Wisdom (Perception) checks that rely on hearing.)

41–60	A crystal clear sky magnifies the sun, directing its heat against the ship and her crew. The wind puffs slowly, not enough to extinguish a candle, let alone cool the flesh of those in the open. Waves move across the water like a herd, trying to carry the ship along in their wake, fighting the vessel should it try to turn away. The spray carries over the rail into the faces of those on deck, quickly drying to leave powdered salt. (Temp H 92/34 L 87/31, Wind — 0–5 mph.)
61–80	The thick clouds overhead threaten to release their burden but maintain their hold for now. The moderate wind moves both the ship and the clouds, lifting the waves to heights of 10 feet, launching the spray into the air. The ship rolls with the impacts as it tips down one wave and up another, the prow having difficulty cutting through the water. (Temp H 89/32 L 82/29, Wind — 10–12 mph.)
81–00	The sky is clear, dotted with numerous small unimposing puffs of cloud. A steady wind blows, determined to cart items away in its embrace. The sun, high overhead, seems a greater distance than usual given the lack of heat generated. Abundant waves run to the horizon, making up for size with numbers. Churned to a gray-green only a few feet under the surface can be seen with any clarity; another indicator of the weak sun. (Temp H 79/27 L 77/26, Wind — 18–20 mph.)

Dry/Night

01–20	Clear sky provides a view of the numerous constellations and guiding stars. Wind gusts from the North East create a flapping staccato to match the waves breaking on the hull of the ship. White-capped waves, visible in the moonlight, reach for the sailors on board, topping 7-8 feet. A slight mist can be felt in the wind; consequently, all surfaces are slick and shiny with moisture. (Temp H 80/27 L 79/27, Wind — 15–25 mph. Characters moving on deck must succeed on a DC 8 Dexterity (Acrobatics) check each round or be knocked prone. All exposed areas of the ship count as difficult terrain, and characters take a –1 penalty to Strength (Athletics) checks involving climbing and Wisdom (Perception) checks that rely on hearing.)
21–40	Clouds of stone gray run from horizon to horizon, extinguishing the stars and moon from view. The absence of wind allows the sails and rigging to hang listless, like cloth in a shop window. The water is unmarked, calm for many miles around the ship, waves visible in the far distance. Pressure seems to build, raising the temperature over several hours to just above a comfortable level. (Temp H 78/26 L 75/24, Wind — 0–5 mph. Experienced sailors know a storm is coming. Reroll on Tropical rain/day chart in 1d4 hours for result.)
41–60	The cool of the night is identified by the daytime heat escaping the decking, misting the moisture collected through the daylight hours. Raising the humidity to an uncomfortable level, it deadens the night sounds of the creaking riggings and lapping waves. Lone trenches of waves roll the ship as it moves through them like long strides of a great beast. Occasional clouds plunge the ship into darkness, allowing the moon and stars to peer through again in a few moments. (Temp H 90/33 L 78/26, Wind — 10–20 mph.)
61–80	Moon and gray clouds do battle overhead for dominance, sometimes plunging the world into darkness or a dim twilight. Numerous waves about the size of a man run the length of the water as far as the eye can see, all topped with a cone of greenish white froth. The rigging and sails have rivulets of collected water, which pools on the deck. Lines are heavy with water and deck boards are slick and shiny, sometimes reflecting the occasional starlight. (Temp H 78/26 L 75/24, Wind — 20–25 mph. Characters moving on deck must succeed on a DC 8 Dexterity (Acrobatics) check each round or be knocked prone. All exposed areas of the ship are lightly obscured and count as difficult terrain.)

81–00	Clear ebony night overhead provides astronomers and navigators a fine view of the stars and planets. A gentle wind blows from the West, flapping the sail and nettings. Small waves lap against the side of the boat like a heartbeat, reflections of the moon on the waves stand out against the black background of the water and night sky. (Temp H 79/27 L 75/24, Wind — 5–10 mph.)

TEMPERATE

Rain/Day

01–20	A gentle breeze blows, adding a slight chill to the damp air. Large drops patter along the deck, occasionally warmed by the sun and quickly evaporating. Gray white clouds fill the sky from horizon to horizon, predicting a constant rainfall. Waves are large in width but not in height, rocking the ship with the passage. (Temp H 70/22 L 54/13, Wind — 5–10 mph.)
21–40	Intense rain from ebony clouds pummel the ship and those unfortunate enough to be on deck. Waves like great gray-green boulders smashing against the ship every minute. The overhead clouds have descended to a point where it seems the ship is in a large subterranean chamber. The sail struggles to remain attached to the mast as the wind tries to rip it from the rigging. All loose items on deck vie for attention from the crashing waves or the blustery wind. (Temp H 64/18 L 62/17, Wind — 70–75 mph. Characters moving on deck must succeed on a DC 12 Dexterity (Acrobatics) check each round or be knocked prone and pushed 10 feet in a random direction. All exposed areas of the ship are lightly obscured and count as difficult terrain. Characters on deck have disadvantage on Strength (Athletics) checks involving climbing and Constitution saving throws made to maintain concentration on a spell.)
41–60	The sky carries a darker shade than normal, clouds so thick they block out all trace of light. Rain is propelled horizontally with the wind, hitting like daggers and needles, reducing vision to mere feet around each person. Winds blow loose objects and people unprepared for its force off course. Waves 15-30 feet high assault the ship, blowing over the rail and soaking sailors with its frigid embrace. (Temp H 79/27 L 75/24, Wind — 27–35 mph. Characters moving on deck must succeed on a DC 12 Dexterity (Acrobatics) check each round or be knocked prone and pushed 10 feet in a random direction. All exposed areas of the ship are heavily obscured and count as difficult terrain. Characters on deck also have disadvantage on Dexterity checks involving fine motor skills and Constitution saving throws made to maintain concentration on a spell.)
61–80	A constant rain falls from gray clouds overhead, keeping all within it thoroughly soaked. The wind propels the ship slowly, seemingly held back by the rain, over the large hillock-shaped waves. Occasional lightning flashes illuminate the depth of the rain, looking like iron bars for as far as the eye can see, peppering the water. (Temp H 61/17 L 53/12, Wind — 5–10 mph. All exposed areas of the ship are lightly obscured and count as difficult terrain. Characters on deck also have disadvantage on Strength (Athletics) checks involving climbing.)
81–00	A simple rain falls, creating a constant drone of rain on the wooden deck. The wind is not strong enough to alter the vertical direction of the rain, letting the sail hang like a soaked rag from the mast. The subtle waves rock the ship almost undetectably as they move on under currents. Clouds looking like an inverted mountain range press down upon the ship and crew. (Temp H 48/9 L 44/2, Wind — 5–20 mph.)

01–20	Lightning-rippled clouds streak by overhead, waves lift like cliffs (6-15 feet) around the vessel. Rain alternates from side to side and straight down with the force of a hammer blow. Rivers of water course around the deck from the rain and waves, creating treacherous footing for all on board. The sails snap and crack as it fills with the wind, dropping deluges of collected rain to the deck below. Periodically, the sky lights up with a lightning blast nearby, painting everything in shades of white and gray; all other times, the charcoal sky and water bestow a sense of isolation. (Temp H 37/3 L 36/2, Wind — 55–60 mph. Characters moving on deck must succeed on a DC 14 Dexterity (Acrobatics) check each round or be knocked prone and pushed 15 feet in a random direction. All exposed areas of the ship are lightly obscured and count as difficult terrain. Characters on deck have disadvantage on Dexterity checks involving fine motor skills, Strength (Athletics) checks involving climbing, and Constitution saving throws made to maintain concentration on a spell.)
21–40	A constant rain falls from gray clouds overhead, keeping all within it thoroughly soaked. The wind propels the ship slowly, seemingly held back by the rain, over the large hillock-shaped waves. Occasional lightning flashes illuminate the depth of the rain, looking like iron bars for as far as the eye can see, peppering the water. (Temp H 42/6 L 39/5, Wind — 5–10 mph NE-E. All exposed areas of the ship are lightly obscured and count as difficult terrain. Characters on deck take a –1 penalty to Strength (Athletics) checks involving climbing.)
41–60	Thick rolling clouds erupt constantly with thunder and rain beating upon the wooden planks. The percussion of the rain is accented with the occasional spray of mountainous waves carried on the wind. Gusts of wind blow across the ship, attempting to pull everything along in its wake. Sight is reduced to feet, distance eliminated with the thick sheets of rain. (Temp H 59/16 L 48/10, Wind — 15–20 mph. Characters moving on deck must succeed on a DC 12 Dexterity (Acrobatics) check each round or be knocked prone. All exposed areas of the ship are heavily obscured and count as difficult terrain. Characters on deck have disadvantage on Dexterity checks involving fine motor skills, Strength (Athletics) checks involving climbing, and Constitution saving throws made to maintain concentration on a spell.)
61–80	Hurricane force rain and wind, the ship is tossed like a child's doll. Huge waves like mountains threaten to topple the vessel and launch the sailors into the unforgiving sea. Wind blows fiercely lifting all heavy objects not lashed down and propelling them around and off the ship. The sky and water are distinguishable, erasing the horizon as both are steel gray. (Temp H 62/17 L 54/13, Wind — 60–80 mph. Characters on deck must succeed on a DC 14 Dexterity (Acrobatics) check each round or be knocked prone and pushed 20 feet in a random direction. All exposed areas of the ship are heavily obscured and count as difficult terrain. Characters on deck have disadvantage on Dexterity checks and saving throws, Strength (Athletics) checks involving climbing, and Constitution saving throws made to maintain concentration on a spell.)
81–00	A simple rain falls, creating a constant drone of rain on the wooden deck. The wind is not strong enough to alter the vertical direction of the rain, letting the sail hang like a soaked rag from the mast. The subtle waves rock the ship almost undetectably as they move on under currents. Clouds looking like an inverted mountain range press down upon the ship and crew. Navigation can only be done through compass or landmarks. (Temp H 59/16 L 58/15, Wind — 5–10 mph.)

01–20	The large sun dominates the sky, but a swift breeze keeps the temperature to a cooler level. Spray pulled up from the many waves, capped in white froth and thrown across the deck. The horizon is marked with a large bank of gray clouds, promising rain in the next day or two. (Temp H 48/10 L 35/2, Wind — 10–15 mph.)
21–40	The sky is clear, dotted with numerous small unimposing puffs of cloud. A steady wind blows determined to cart items away in its embrace. The sun, high overhead seems a greater distance than usual given the lack of heat generated. Abundant waves run to the horizon, making up for size with numbers. Churned to a gray-green only a few feet under the surface can be seen with any clarity; another indicator of the weak sun. (Temp H 70/22 L 54/13, Wind — 18–20 mph.)
41–60	A crystal clear sky magnifies the sun directing its heat against the ship and her crew. The wind puffs slowly, not enough to extinguish a candle let alone cool the flesh of those warmer than usual day. Waves move across the water like a herd, trying to carry the ship along in their wake, fighting the vessel should it try to turn away. The spray carries over the rail into the faces of those on deck, quickly drying to leave traces of powdered salt. (Temp H 82/29 L 68/21, Wind — 5–10 mph. Sun stroke in 3d8 rounds unless properly attired for the sun. Characters on deck take a –1 penalty to Wisdom (Perception) checks that rely on sight and have disadvantage on Constitution saving throws made to maintain concentration on a spell.)
61–80	Sun and gray clouds do battle overhead for dominance, sometimes plunging the water into a dark twilight or bright daylight. Numerous waves, about the size of a man run the length of the water as far as the eye can see, all topped with a cone of white froth. The wind picks this froth from each and carries it along and coats all surfaces. This cooling spray makes the trip enjoyable for most on board, even in the shade. The rigging and sails flap in the breeze, occasionally dropping additional sprays to the deck, glinting like jewels in the periodic sun. (Temp H 75/25 L 61/17, Wind — 18–20 mph.)
81–00	Gray the colour of stone has been painted from horizon to horizon, plunging the day into twilight. The absence of wind allows the sails and rigging to hang listless, like cloth in a shop window. The water is unmarked, calm for many miles around the ship, waves visible in the far distance. Pressure seems to build, raising the temperature over several hours to a more comfortable level. (Temp H 64/18 L 51/11, Wind — 5–10 mph. Reroll in 4 game hours on the wet-day chart for the approaching storm.)

01–20	Clear sky provides a view of the numerous constellations and guiding stars. Wind gusts from the North East creating a flapping staccato to match the waves breaking on the hull of the ship. White capped waves, visible in the moonlight reach for the sailors on board, topping 7-8 feet. A slight mist can be felt in the wind; consequently, all surfaces are slick and shiny with moisture (Temp G 39/5 L 37/3, Wind — 15–25 mph. Characters moving on deck must succeed on a DC 6 Dexterity (Acrobatics) check each round or be knocked prone. Characters on deck take a –1 penalty to Wisdom (Perception) checks that rely on hearing and Strength (Athletics) checks involving climbing.)
21–40	Clear ebony night overhead provides astronomers and navigators a fine view of the stars and planets. A gentle wind blows from the South flapping the sail and nettings. Small waves lap against the side of the boat like a heartbeat; small white caps stand out stark against the black background of the water and night sky. (Temp H 64/18 L 62/17, Wind — 15–25 mph.)

41–60	An overcast sky blocks the view of all but the brightest stars and planets. Some navigation can still be done by experienced sailors. A breeze comes and goes, proving to be a fickle asset for the sails on the ship, waves playing tag rock the ship gently back and forth. (Temp H 79/27 L 75/24, Wind — 5–10 mph.)
61–80	Numerous stars turn the night sky into a twilight gray, offsetting the jet black of the calm water. A steady soft wind blows propelling the ship along on its way. The sound of the surf being cut by the hull is seemingly alone, periodically joined by the creak of the rigging and the soft voice of a sailor. (Temp H 61/17 L 53/12, Wind — 10–15 mph.)
81–00	A severe wind blows threatening to rip the sail form the mast, propelling the vessel over the waves like a toy. Thick ribbons of cloud race overhead like gray gashes in the constellations. Many large waves run the length of vision, occasionally growing to such a large size (45 feet) they threaten to topple the ship like flotsam. (Temp H 48/9 L 44/2, Wind — 60–65 mph. Characters on deck take a –1 penalty to Strength (Athletics) checks involving climbing and Constitution saving throws made to maintain concentration on a spell.)

ARCTIC

Wind chill is a real concern when the temperature drops below 32° F. Exposure to the wind risks frostbite for flesh. The effective temperature, for purposes of calculating potential harm caused by extreme cold, can be found in the Wind Chill Table.

RAIN/DAY

01–20	White gray clouds span from horizon to horizon, periodic deluges of snow drop upon the water and ship. The deck is quickly covered in a white blanket of snow, making progress slow around the ship. Finding equipment is difficult for the inexperienced sailor, boxes and barrels becoming nondescript objects in the snow. The wind moves the snow in various directions as it descends, moving the sails to half full with their strongest force. (Temp H –10/–23 L –15/–26, Wind — 10–15 mph. All exposed areas of the ship count as difficult terrain. See rules above for the consequences of exposure to extreme temperatures.)
21–40	Sleet drops like sheets of needles upon sailors in the open. The wind drives the sleet almost horizontally across the waves. Large mountains of water move across the area threatening to bash the vessel into submission. The steel gray sky rolls like the underside of a surf promising many hours of attack. The rigging creaks and sails moan ominously in the barrage of the storm. Movement along the deck is perilous at best; those in the upper reaches of the vessel cling for their lives. (Temp H –15/–27 L –25/–31, Wind — 20–25 mph. See rules above for the consequences of exposure to extreme temperatures. Characters moving on deck must succeed a DC 10 Dexterity (Acrobatics) check each round or be knocked prone and be pushed 10 feet in a random direction. All exposed areas of the ship are lightly obscured and count as difficult terrain. Characters on deck have disadvantage on Dexterity checks involving fine motor skills, Strength (Athletics) checks involving climbing, and Constitution saving throws made to maintain concentration on a spell.)
41–60	Freezing mist falls like a cloud landing on water. Wind is present but too weak to fill sails. Ice flows move on the sunken currents, dancing around the ship at great distances. Waves are subdued, seemingly moving in numerous directions, no pattern discernable. Ice forms on most surfaces with extended exposure, sails and rigging becoming rigid and hazardous with each passing hour. (Temp H –15/–26 L –20/–29, Wind — 0–5 mph. See rules above for the consequences of exposure to extreme temperatures. Characters moving on deck must succeed on a DC 10 Dexterity (Acrobatics) check each round or be knocked prone. All exposed areas of the ship are lightly obscured and count as difficult terrain.)

61–80	Lightning-rippled clouds streak by overhead, waves lift like cliffs (6–15 feet) around the vessel. Rain and sleet alternate from side to side and straight down with the force of a hammer blow. Ice coats all exposed surfaces in minutes, creating treacherous areas on the ship and rigging. The sails snap and crack as it fills with the wind, snow, and ice, chunks of collected ice dropping ice dropping to the deck below. Periodically, the sky lights up with a lightning blast nearby painting everything with in shades of white and gray, all other times the charcoal sky and water bestow a sense of isolation. (Temp H –20/–29 L –31/–35, Wind — 25–35 mph N. All exposed areas of the ship are lightly obscured and count as difficult terrain. 10% chance of course change required for ice formation in path of ship. See rules above for the consequences of exposure to extreme temperatures.)
81–00	The sky carries a darker shade than normal, clouds so thick they block out all trace of light. Rain is propelled horizontally with the wind, hitting like daggers and needles reducing vision to mere feet around each person. Ice forms on all surfaces, making passage difficult on deck. Winds blow loose objects and people unprepared for its force off course. Waves 5–30 feet high assault the ship, blowing over the rail and soaking sailors with its frigid embrace. (Temp H –20/–29 L –29/–34 mph. See rules above for the consequences of exposure to extreme temperatures. Characters moving on deck must succeed on a DC 14 Dexterity (Acrobatics) check each round or be knocked prone and pushed 10 feet in a random direction. All exposed areas of the ship are heavily obscured and count as difficult terrain. Characters on deck have disadvantage on Dexterity checks involving fine motor skills, Strength (Athletics) checks involving climbing, Wisdom (Perception) checks that rely on hearing.)

RAIN/NIGHT

01–20	Lightning-rippled clouds streak by overhead, waves lift like cliffs (6–15 feet) around the vessel. Hail alternates from side-to-side and straight down with the force of a hammer blow. Ice coats all exposed surfaces in minutes, creating treacherous areas on the ship and rigging. The sails snap and crack as it fills with the wind, snow, and ice, dropping chunks of ice to the deck below. Periodically, the sky lights up with a lightning blast nearby painting everything within shades of white and gray; all other times, the charcoal sky and water bestow a sense of isolation. (Temp H –20/–29 L –31/–35, Wind - 45–50 mph. Characters moving on deck must succeed on a DC 12 Dexterity (Acrobatics) check each round or be knocked prone and pushed 10 feet in a random direction. All exposed areas of the ship are heavily obscured and count as difficult terrain. Characters on deck have disadvantage on Strength (Acrobatics) checks involving climbing and Wisdom (Perception) checks that rely on hearing. See rules above for the consequences of exposure to extreme temperatures.)
21–40	Freezing mist falls like a cloud landing on the water. Wind is present but too weak to fill sails. Ice flows move on the sunken currents, dancing around the ship at great distances. Waves are subdued, seemingly moving in numerous directions, no pattern discernable. Ice forms on most surfaces with extended exposure, sails and rigging becoming rigid and hazardous with each passing hour. (Temp H –15/–23 L –20/–29, Wind - 0–5 mph. Characters moving on deck must succeed on a DC 10 Dexterity (Acrobatics) check each round or be knocked prone. All exposed areas of the ship are lightly obscured and count as difficult terrain. Characters on deck have disadvantage on Strength (Athletics) checks involving climbing and Wisdom (Perception) checks that rely on hearing. See rules above for the consequences of exposure to extreme temperatures.)

41–60 The night sky carries a darker shade than normal, clouds so thick they block out all trace of light. Rain is propelled horizontally with the wind, hitting like daggers and needles reducing vision to mere feet around each person. Ice forms on all surfaces making passage difficult on deck. Winds blow loose objects and people unprepared for its force off course. Waves 15–30 feet high assault the ship, blowing over the rail and soaking sailors with its frigid embrace. (Temp H –20/–29 L –29/–34, Wind - 27–35 mph. Characters moving on deck must succeed on a DC 14 Dexterity (Acrobatics) check each round or be knocked prone and pushed 10 feet in a random direction. All exposed areas of the ship are lightly obscured and count as difficult terrain. Characters on deck have disadvantage on Dexterity checks involving fine motor skills, Strength (Athletics) checks involving climbing, and Wisdom (Perception) checks that rely on hearing. See rules above for the consequences of exposure to extreme temperatures.)

61–80 Constant icy drizzle settles on all surfaces, turning the dark night into a dark gray, reducing vision to nearly non-existent. Frigid temperatures freeze the moisture within minutes on every surface. Travel across deck is difficult but manageable to those familiar with surroundings. Sound is subdued with the ice pellets, adding a muffling effect to conversations. Waves are unseen but can be felt hitting the deck every few seconds, occasionally bathing the deck with its spray, a testament to their height of several feet. (Temp H –10/–23 L –15/–26, Wind — 5–10 mph. Characters moving on deck must succeed on a DC 8 Dexterity (Acrobatics) check each round or be knocked prone. All exposed areas of the ship are lightly obscured and count as difficult terrain. Characters on deck take a –1 penalty to Wisdom (Perception) checks that rely on hearing.)

81–00 Large thick flakes drop around the ship, landing softly on the water before melting. Equipment and decking are quickly covered in a thick blanket of white snow. Waves roll languidly topping 6 feet in height but not steep enough to make more than an exaggerated rocking motion. A light wind blows carrying the flakes on the air currents, visible in the occasional moonlight. (Temp H 19/–7 L –2/–19, Wind — 5–10 mph. Characters moving on deck must succeed on a DC 6 Dexterity (Acrobatics) check each round or be knocked prone. All exposed areas of the ship are lightly obscured and count as difficult terrain.)

Dry/Day

01–20 Clear blue sky overhead provides ample room for the bright sun to shine. Wind gusts from the North East, flapping the sail and nettings. White-capped waves, topping 7–8 feet high seem to pushing large chunks of ice along in their grasp. (Temp H –21/–29 L –28/–33, Wind — 10–15 mph. Those working while facing the sun must succeed on a DC 10 Constitution saving throw or be blinded for 1d4 hours. Characters with a natural sensitivity to light have disadvantage on this saving throw. 10% chance of course changed required for ice flow in path of ship.)

21–40 Sun and gray clouds do battle overhead for dominance, sometimes plunging the water into a dark twilight or bright daylight. Numerous waves, about the size of a man run the length of the water as far as the eye can see, all topped with a cone of white froth. The wind picks this froth from each and carries it along, freezing it to any surface it covers. The rigging and sails labour under the extra weight of the ice, glinting like jewels in the periodic sun. (Temp H –25/–32 L –32/–36, Wind — 20–25 mph. Characters moving on deck must succeed on a DC 10 Dexterity (Acrobatics) check each round or be knocked prone. All exposed areas of the ship count as difficult terrain. Characters on deck also take a –1 penalty to Strength (Athletics) checks involving climbing. 12% chance of course change required for ice flow in path of ship.)

41–60 Gray, the color of stone, has been painted from horizon to horizon, plunging the day into twilight. The absence of wind allows the sails and rigging to hang listless, like cloth in a shop window. The water is unmarked, calm for many miles around the ship, waves visible in the far distance. Pressure seems to build, raising the temperature over several hours to a more comfortable level. Icebergs in the distance hold steady like islands. (Temp H –17/–27 L –20/–29, Wind — 0–5 mph. Experienced sailors know a storm is coming. Reroll on Arctic day-rain chart in 1d4 hours for result. 2% chance of course change for icebergs in path of ship.)

61–80 Streamers of billowy clouds race overhead in the wind. Large waves buffet the ship attempting to carry it along with them. Wind assaults the vessel hard form the west, never wavering or letting up. Tacking into the wind seems impossible from its vicious force while tacking with the wind runs a risk of never getting control of the ship back. (Temp H –20/–29 L –27/–33, Wind — 35–40 mph. Characters moving on deck must succeed on a DC 6 Dexterity (Acrobatics) check each round or be knocked prone and pushed 5 feet in a random direction.)

81–00 The air burns with the wind chill, crusting ice all over the ship, the sun adding no aid to the frigid temperature. Clouds are non-existent in the sky, collecting only on the horizons. While filling the sails, the wind steals the breath from those on deck freezing exposed flesh in minutes. (Temp H –18/–28 L –35/–37, Wind — 45–50 mph. Characters moving on deck must succeed on a DC 8 Dexterity (Acrobatics) check each round or be knocked prone and pushed 10 feet in a random direction. All exposed areas of the ship count as difficult terrain. Characters on deck take a –1 penalty on Strength (Athletics) checks involving climbing.)

Dry/Night

01–20 Clear ebony night overhead provides astronomers and navigators a fine view of the stars and planets. A gentle wind blows from the South, flapping the sail and nettings. Small waves lap against the side of the boat like a heartbeat, icebergs stand out stark white against the black background of the water and night sky. (Temp H –20/–29 L –25/–32, Wind — 5–10 mph. 10% chance of course changes required for ice flow in path of ship.)

21–40 Large clouds move overhead, blocking the stars and moon with their bulk. The ship rolls gently on the waves as it rides through the water. Occasionally, larger waves provide a small drop for the vessel as it is carried over the lip of the wave. The strong wind takes the ship along with it, filling the sails and pulling at cloaks of those on board. (Temp H –22/–30 L –26/–32, Wind — 10–15 mph. Characters on deck take a –1 penalty to Wisdom (Perception) checks that rely on hearing.)

41–60 Clouds block all stars and only hint at the location of the moon, adding a claustrophobic feel to the trip. The absence of wind allows the sails and rigging to hang listless, like cloth in a shop window. The ebony water ripples in the soft breeze, white caps standing out like glowing embers. (Temp H –19/–28 L –25/–32, Wind — 0–5 mph. 2% chance of course change for icebergs in path of ship.)

61–80 Partial clouds cover sections of the sky, seemingly unmoving. Large waves buffet the ship attempting to carry it along with them. Wind assaults the vessel hard from the west, never wavering or letting up. Travel during the night at full sail run double risk of collision with ice. (Temp H –25/–31 L –29/–33, Wind — 25–35 mph. Characters moving on deck must succeed on a DC 6 Dexterity (Acrobatics) check each round or be knocked prone. 15% chance of course change for ice.)

80–00 Wisps of cloud move across the sky sometimes blocking the stars. The brightness of the visible stars and moon provides ample light to maneuver around the ship and perform most tasks. The ever-present wind provides enough force to keep the ship moving at optimum speed. The absence of spray from the calm waters allows for equipment to dry. (Temp H –29/–34 L –31/–35, Wind — 20–25 mph.)

EQUATORIAL

Within the Equatorial region, humidity is issue for temperature measurement. Reference to the Humidity Table will bring about a more realistic gauge for temperature; consequently, the effects of heat upon those traveling the waves should be watched closely.

RAIN/DAY

01–20 A heavy wind blows, adding a texture to the warm rain falling. Large drops patter along the deck, occasional sunshine warm the decks, quickly evaporating the rain and adding to the humidity. A sticky aspect of the air grows throughout the day as the humidity rises. Sunlight glints off the water like numerous smaller suns, blinding those not ready for the effect. Waves are large in width but not in height, rocking the ship with their passage. (Temp H 89/32 L 80/27, Wind — 30–35 mph. Characters on deck take a –1 penalty to Constitution saving throws made to maintain concentration on a spell.)

21–40 Heavy rain pummels the ship and those on board, quickly soaking all equipment and people. The waves are sedated, rarely topping 5 feet, seemingly held down with the impact of the rain. The sun tries to pierce the cloud cover with its intense glare, only succeeding in raising the temperature. Wind is non-existent, hammered to submission by the heavy rain. (Temp H 75/24 L 71/22, Wind — 0–5 mph.)

41–60 Seemingly in rhythm with the lapping waves, periodic rain drops in vast amounts, quickly soaking all surfaces and washing away loose items. Between rainfalls, the sun attempts to burn away the moisture with blistering heat, never quite successful and so leaving all with a heaviness of moisture. Waves roll languidly topping 6 feet in height but not steep enough to make more than an exaggerated rocking motion. The wind blows merrily, billowing out the sails of the ship and propelling the vessel over the large waves. (Temp H 79/27 L 71/22, Wind — 10–15 mph. Characters moving on deck during a deluge must succeed on a DC 6 Dexterity (Acrobatics) check or be knocked prone and pushed 10 feet in a random direction, and all exposed areas of the ship count as difficult terrain.)

61–80 A drizzle of rain, sometimes hard and sometimes light, falls continuously throughout the day. All surfaces are thoroughly soaked and heavy with water. The warmth of the occasional sun is diminished slightly by the cool rain, keeping it tolerable for all involved. Waves are present but pose little threat to the navigation of the ship or to the course she desires to take. The wind blows constantly, keeping the sails full but not pushing the limit of its capabilities. (Temp H 87/31 L 78/26, Wind — 15–20 mph.)

81–00 Heavy rain from unseen clouds pummels the ship and those on deck. Waves like great gray-green boulders smashing against the ship every minute. The overhead clouds have descended to a point where it seems the ship is in a large chamber. Wind hurtles against the vessel and its sail, trying to rip it free from the mast and rigging. All loose items are tossed around the decking, creating hazards for those on deck. (Temp H 80/27 L 74/24, Wind — 50–55 mph. Characters moving on deck must succeed on a DC 10 Dexterity (Acrobatics) check each round or be knocked prone and pushed 10 feet in a random direction. All exposed areas of the ship count as difficult terrain. Characters on deck also have disadvantage on Strength (Athletics) checks involving climbing and Constitution saving throws made to maintain concentration on a spell.)

RAIN/NIGHT

01–20 The humidity of the night is made comfortable by the patter of rain upon the deck. The coolness of the rain seems to steal some of the weight of the air. The thin clouds mask the presence of the stars but leave a large halo where the moon tries to shine. The waves crash against the hull as if trying to keep the ship from reaching its goal. The bounce of the ship as it passes over the waves keeps all but the soundest sleepers awake. (Temp H 80/27 L 71/22, Wind — 0–5 mph.)

21–40 Heavy rain from ebony clouds press down on the ship and those on deck. Waves can be seen in the dark like great gray-green boulders smashing against the ship every minute. The overhead clouds have descended to a point where it seems the ship is in a large chamber. Wind hurtles against the vessel and its sail, trying to rip it from the mast and rigging. All loose items on deck vie for attention from the crashing waves or the blustery wind. (Temp H 77/26 L 62/17, Wind — 20–25 mph. Characters moving on deck must succeed on a DC 10 Dexterity (Acrobatics) check each round or be knocked prone. All exposed areas of the ship are lightly obscured and count as difficult terrain. Characters on deck also have disadvantage on Strength (Athletics) checks involving climbing and Constitution saving throws made to maintain concentration on a spell.)

41–60 Seemingly in rhythm with the lapping waves, periodic rain drops in vast amounts, quickly soaking all surfaces and washing away loose materials. Waves roll languidly, topping 6 feet in height but not steep enough to make more than an exaggerated rocking motion. A light wind blows carrying a humid mist from the still warm water, visible in the intermittent moonlight. (Temp H 76/25 L 71/22, Wind — 5–10 mph. Characters moving on deck must succeed on a DC 6 Dexterity (Acrobatics) check each round or be knocked prone and pushed 10 feet in a random direction. All exposed areas of the ship are lightly obscured and count as difficult terrain.)

61–80 A drizzle of rain, sometimes hard and sometimes light, falls continuously during the nighttime hours. All surfaces are thoroughly soaked and heavy with water. The warmth of the day rapidly disappears, replaced with the humidity of the still evaporating water around the ship. The waves are smaller than normal and works with the rain to stay weak enough to be inconsequential. The wind blows constantly, keeping the sails full but not pushing the limit of its capabilities. (Temp H 80/27 L 78/26, Wind — 12–18 mph.)

81–00 A thrashing rain accompanies hurricane force winds. In the distance amid lightning flashes, water spouts can be seen reaching for the sky. Waves, the size of small mountains, rise above the vessel giving the ship a wide span of view when atop a wave, and a sense of claustrophobia when in a gully. (Temp H 79/27 L 71/22, Wind — 45–50 mph. Characters moving on deck must succeed on a DC 14 Dexterity (Acrobatics) check each round or be knocked prone and pushed 15 feet in a random direction. All exposed areas of the ship are lightly obscured and count as difficult terrain. Characters on deck also have disadvantage on Strength (Athletics) checks involving climbing.)

DRY/DAY

01–20 The large sun dominates the sky but a swift breeze keeps the temperature to a more moderate level. Spray pulled up from the many waves, capped in white froth. The horizon is marked with a large bank of gray clouds, promising rain in the next day or two. The humidity rises throughout the day adding a weight to the sun which saps the strength of those not acquainted with the Equatorial waters. (Temp H 81/28 L 75/24, Wind — 10–15 mph.)

| 21–40 | Clouds run amok along the sky, occasionally blocking the sun and its warmth. The wind seemingly growls as it tears across the water at the ship. The sail quivers, trying to keep the wind from escaping. Waves rise up and crash against the hull of the ship each impact like a bludgeon from nature itself. (Temp H 77/26 L 74/24, Wind — 60–65 mph. Characters moving on deck must succeed on a DC 10 Dexterity (Acrobatics) check each round or be knocked prone and pushed 10 feet in a random direction. All exposed areas of the ship count as difficult terrain. Characters on deck also have disadvantage on Strength (Athletics) checks involving climbing and Wisdom (Perception) checks that rely on hearing.) |

| 41–60 | A crystal clear sky magnifies the sun, directing its heat against the ship and her crew. The wind puffs slowly, not enough to extinguish a candle, let alone cool the flesh of those in the open. Waves move across the water like a herd, trying to carry the ship along in their wake, fighting the vessel should it try to turn away. The spray carries over the rail into the faces of those on deck, quickly drying to leave powdered salt. (Temp H 77/26 L 74/23, Wind — 0–5 mph.) |

| 61–80 | The thick clouds overhead threaten to release their burden, moisture released in the form of a thick palpable air. While no rain has fallen during the day, all surfaces are beaded with sweat and spray from the moisture-laced air. The moderate wind moves both the ship and the clouds, lifting the waves to heights of 10 feet, launching the spray into the air. The ship rolls with the impacts as it tips down one wave and up another, the prow having difficulty cutting through the water. (Temp H 77/26 L 75/24, Wind — 10–12 mph.) |

| 81–00 | The sky is clear, dotted with numerous small, unimposing puffs of cloud. A steady wind blows, determined to cart items away in its embrace. The sun, high overhead, seems a greater distance than usual, given the lack of heat generated. Abundant waves run to the horizon, making up for size with numbers. Churned to a gray-green, only a few feet under the surface can be seen with clarity; another indicator of the weak sun. (Temp H 79/27 L 77/26, Wind — 20–25 mph.) |

Dry/Night

| 01–20 | Clear sky provides a view of the numerous constellations and guiding stars. Wind gusts from the South West, creating a flapping staccato to match the waves breaking on the hull of the ship. White-capped waves, visible in the moonlight, reach for the sailors on board, topping 7–8 feet. A slight mist can be felt in the wind; consequently, all surfaces are slick and shiny with moisture. (Temp H 75/25 L 61/17, Wind — 15–25 mph. Characters moving on deck must succeed on a DC 6 Dexterity (Acrobatics) check each round or be knocked prone. All exposed areas of the ship count as difficult terrain. Characters on deck also take a –1 penalty to Strength (Athletics) checks involving climbing and Constitution saving throws made to maintain concentration on a spell.) |

| 21–40 | Clouds of stone gray run from horizon to horizon, extinguishing the stars and moon from view. The absence of wind allows the sails and rigging to hang listless, like cloth in a shop window. The water is unmarked, calm for many miles around the ship, waves visible in the far distance. Pressure seems build, raising the temperature over several hours to just above a comfortable level. (Temp H 76/25 L 75/24, Wind — 0–5 mph. Experienced sailors know a storm is coming. Reroll on Equatorial day–rain chart in 1d4 hours for result.) |

| 41–60 | The cool of the night is identified by the daytime heat escaping the decking, misting the moisture collected through the daylight hours. Raising the humidity to an uncomfortable level, it deadens the night sounds of creaking riggings and lapping waves. Long trenches of waves roll the ship as it moves through them like long strides of a great beast. Occasional clouds plunge the ship into darkness, allowing the moon and stars to peer through again in a few moments. (Temp H 76/25 L 69/21, Wind — 10–20 mph.) |

| 61–80 | Periodic clouds block the moon and stars, stealing their dim light and guidance. Numerous waves, about the size of a man, run the length of the water as far as the eye can see, all topped with a cone of greenish white froth. The rigging and sails have rivulets of collected water, which pools on the deck. Lines are heavy with water, and deck boards are slick and shiny, reflecting any light source. (Temp H 78/26 L 75/24, Wind — 20–25 mph. Characters moving on deck must succeed on a DC 6 Dexterity (Acrobatics) check each round or be knocked prone. All exposed areas of the ship count as difficult terrain. Characters on deck also take a –1 penalty to Strength (Athletics) checks involving climbing and Wisdom (Perception) checks that rely on sight.) |

| 81–00 | Clear ebony night overhead provides astronomers and navigators a fine view of the stars and planets. A gentle wind blows from the West, flapping the sail and nettings. Small waves lap against the side of the boat like a heartbeat, reflections of the moon on the waves stand out stark white against the black background of the water and night sky. (Temp H 79/27 L 75/24, Wind — 5–10 mph.) |

Spring

Tropical

Heat stroke is a risk for any who travel the warm regions of the world. Those exerting themselves must succeed on a DC 10 Constitution saving throw for each hour of strenuous work or gain a level of exhaustion. For each cumulative hour of strenuous work, the DC of subsequent saves increases by 1. Resting in shaded areas for 10 minutes per hour negates the +1 to the DC for that hour. Spell components run a 10% chance of spoiling in humidity, if you determine they are subject to such damage.

Rain/Day

| 01–20 | A gentle breeze blows, adding a pleasant cooling to the warm rain falling. Large drops patter along the deck, and occasional sunshine warm the deck, quickly evaporating the rain and adding to the humidity. A sticky aspect of the air grows throughout the day as the humidity rises. Sunlight sparkles off the water like numerous smaller suns, blinding those unprepared for the effect. Waves are large in width but not in height, rocking the ship with their passage. (Temp H 85/30 L 78/26, Wind — 5–10 mph. Characters on deck have disadvantage on Constitution saving throws made to maintain concentration on a spell.) |

| 21–40 | Heavy rain pummels the ship and those on board, quickly drenching all equipment and people. The waves are minimal, rarely topping 5 feet, seemingly held down with the rain. The sun tries to penetrate the cloud cover with its intense glare, only succeeding in raising the temperature. Wind is non-existent, hammered to submission by the heavy rain. (Temp H 91/33 L 88/31, Wind — 0–5 mph.) |

| 41–60 | Seemingly in rhythm with the lapping waves, periodic rain drops in vast amounts, quickly soaking all surfaces and washing away loose items. Between rainfalls the sun attempts to burn away the moisture with blistering heat. Waves roll languidly, topping 6 feet in height but not steep enough to make more than an exaggerated rocking motion. The wind blows merrily, billowing out the sails of the ship and propelling the vessel over the large waves. (Temp H 89/32 L 71/22, Wind — 10–15 mph. Characters moving on deck during a deluge must succeed on a DC 6 Dexterity (Acrobatics) check or be knocked prone and pushed 10 feet in a random direction, and all exposed areas of the ship count as difficult terrain.) |

61–80 A drizzle of rain, alternating between light and hard, falls continuously throughout the day. All surfaces are thoroughly waterlogged and heavy with water. The warmth of the occasional sun is diminished slightly by the cool rain, keeping it tolerable for all involved. Waves are present but pose no real threat to the direction of the ship or her course. The wind blows constantly, keeping the sails full but not pushing the limit of its capabilities. (Temp H 86/30 L 75/24, Wind — 30–35 mph.)

81–00 Grayish clouds dump heavy rains upon the ship and her riders. Waves like great gray-green boulders smashing against the ship every minute. The overhead clouds have descended to a point where it seems the ship is in a large chamber. Wind hurtles against the vessel and its sail, trying to rip it from the mast and rigging. All loose items on deck vie for attention from the crashing waves or the blustery wind. (Temp H 90/33 L 80/27, Wind — 20–25 mph. Characters moving on deck must succeed on a DC 10 Dexterity (Acrobatics) check each round or be knocked prone. All exposed areas of the ship are lightly obscured and count as difficult terrain. Characters on deck also have disadvantage on Strength (Athletics) checks involving climbing and Constitution saving throws made to maintain concentration on a spell.)

Rain/Night

01–20 The cool of the night is accompanied by the patter of rain upon the deck. The humidity keeps the coolness of the night from becoming comfortable. The moon makes itself known through the clouds, illuminating a portion of the night sky to milky white. The waves crash against the hull as if trying to keep the ship from reaching its goal. The bounce of the ship as it passes over the waves keeps all but the soundest sleepers awake. (Temp H 89/32 L 78/26, Winds — 0–15 mph.)

21–40 Falling rain eliminates possible viewing of any distance greater than 50 feet. Waves can be seen in the dark like great gray-green boulders smashing against the ship every minute. Wind hurtles against the vessel and its sail, trying to rip it from the mast and rigging. The strong wind tries to steal any small items from the ship through sheer determination and strength. (Temp H 87/31 L 81/27, Wind — 45–50 mph. Characters moving on deck must succeed on a DC 12 Dexterity (Acrobatics) check each round or be knocked prone and pushed 10 feet in a random direction. All exposed areas of the ship are lightly obscured and count as difficult terrain. Characters on deck also have disadvantage on Strength (Athletics) checks involving climbing and Constitution saving throws made to maintain concentration on a spell.)

41–60 The waves rock the ship in cadence to the heavy rain, quickly soaking all surfaces and washing away loose items. Waves roll languidly, topping 6 feet in height but not steep enough to make more than an exaggerated rolling motion. A light wind blows carrying mist from the still warm water, visible in the occasional moonlight. (Temp H 85/30 L 78/26, Wind — 5–10 mph. Characters moving on deck during a deluge must succeed on a DC 6 Dexterity (Acrobatics) check each round or be knocked prone and pushed 10 feet in a random direction. All exposed areas of the ship are lightly obscured and count as difficult terrain.)

61–80 A thick misting of rain keeps all items and equipment saturated. The comfort of the day rapidly disappears, replaced with the humidity of the still evaporating water around the ship. Waves are present but pose no real threat to the ship. The wind blows constantly, keeping the sails full but not pushing the limit of its capabilities. (Temp H 83/28 L 72/222, Wind — 25–30 mph.)

81–00 A continual rain falls from gray clouds overhead, keeping all within it thoroughly soaked. The wind propels the ship slowly, seemingly held back by the rain, over the large hillock-shaped waves. Occasional lightning flashes illuminate the depth of the rain, looking like iron bars for as far as the eye can see, peppering the water. (Temp H 89/32 L 85/30, Wind — 5–10 mph. All exposed areas of the ship are lightly obscured and count as difficult terrain. Characters on deck also take a –1 penalty to Strength (Athletics) checks involving climbing.)

Dry/Day

01–20 The large sun dominates the sky but a swift breeze keeps the temperature to a more moderate level. Spray is pulled up from the many waves, capped in white froth. The horizon is marked with a large bank of gray clouds promising rain in the next day or two. (Temp H 91/33 L 79/26, Wind — 20–25 mph.)

21–40 Clouds run amok along the sky, occasionally blocking the sun and its warmth. The wind seemingly howls as it tears across the water at the ship. The sail quivers, trying to keep the wind from escaping. Waves rise up and crash against the hull of the ship, each impact like a bludgeon from nature itself. (Temp H 86/30 L 79/26, Wind — 60–65 mph. Characters moving on deck must succeed on a DC 12 Dexterity (Acrobatics) check each round or be knocked prone and be pushed 10 feet in a random direction. Characters on deck also have disadvantage on Strength (Athletics) checks that rely on hearing.)

41–60 A crystal clear sky magnifies the sun, directing its heat against the ship and her crew. The wind puffs slowly, not enough to quench the heat from the flesh of those in the open. Waves move across the water like a herd, trying to carry the ship along in their wake, fighting the vessel should it try to turn away. The spray carries over the rail into the faces of those on deck, quickly drying to leave powdered salt. (Temp H 85/30 L 73/23, Wind — 0–5 mph.)

61–80 The thick clouds overhead threaten to release their burden but maintain their hold for now. The moderate wind moves both the ship and the clouds, lifting the waves to heights of 10 feet, launching the spray into the air. The ship rolls with the impacts as it tips down one wave and up another, the prow having difficulty cutting through the water. (Temp H 87/31 L 79/26, Wind — 20–25 mph.)

81–00 The sky is clear, dotted with numerous small, unimposing puffs of cloud. A steady wind blows, determined to cart items away in its embrace. The sun, high overhead, seems a greater distance than usual given the lack of heat generated. Abundant waves run to the horizon, making up for size with numbers. Churned to a gray-green, only a few feet under the surface can be seen with any clarity; another indicator of the weak sun. (Temp H 84/29 L 72/22, Wind — 18–20 mph.)

Dry/Night

01–20 Clear sky provides a view of the numerous constellations and guiding stars. Wind gusts from the North East, creating a flapping staccato to match the waves breaking on the hull of the ship. White-capped waves, visible in the moonlight, reach for the sailors on board, topping 7–8 feet. A slight mist can be felt in the wind; consequently, all surfaces are slick and shiny with moisture. (Temp H 86/30 L 75/24, Wind — 15–25 mph. Characters moving on deck must succeed on a DC 6 Dexterity (Acrobatics) check each round or be knocked prone. All exposed areas of the ship count as difficult terrain. Characters on deck also take a –1 penalty to Strength (Athletics) checks involving climbing and Wisdom (Perception) checks that rely on hearing.)

21–40 Clouds of stone gray run from horizon to horizon, extinguishing the stars and moon from view. The absence of wind allows the sails and rigging to hang listless, like cloth in a shop window. The water is unmarked, calm for many miles around the ship, waves visible in the far distance. Pressure seems to build, raising the temperature over several hours to just above a comfortable level. (Temp H 78/26 L 73/23, Wind — 0–5 mph. Experienced sailors know a storm is coming. Reroll on Tropical day–rain chart in 1d4 hours for result.)

41–60 The cool of the night is easily identified by the daytime heat escaping the decking, misting the moisture collected through the daylight hours. Raising the humidity to an uncomfortable level, it deadens the night sounds of creaking riggings and lapping waves. Long trenches of waves roll the ship as it moves through them like long strides of a great beast. Occasional clouds plunge the ship into darkness, allowing the moon and stars to peer through again in a few moments. (Temp H 88/31 L 80/27, Wind — 10–20 mph.)

61–80 Moon and gray clouds do battle overhead for dominance, sometimes plunging the world into a dark twilight or bright daylight. Numerous waves, about the size of a man, run the length of the water as far as the eye can see, all topped with a cone of grayish white froth. The rigging and sails have rivulets of collected water, which pools on the deck. Lines are heavy with water, and deck boards are slick and shiny, sometimes reflecting the occasional illumination. (Temp H 78/26 L 75/24, Wind — 20–25 mph. Characters moving on deck must succeed on a DC 6 Dexterity (Acrobatics) check each round or be knocked prone. All exposed areas of the ship count as difficult terrain. Characters on deck also take a –1 penalty to Strength (Athletics) checks involving climbing and Wisdom (Perception) checks that rely on sight.)

81–00 Clear ebony night overhead provides astronomers and navigators a fine view of the stars and planets. A gentle wind blows from the West, flapping the sail and nettings. Small waves lap against the side of the boat like a heartbeat, reflections of the moon on the waves stand out stark white against the black background of the water and night sky. (Temp H 75/24 L 72/22, Wind — 5–10 mph.)

TEMPERATE

RAIN/DAY

01–20 A gentle breeze blows, adding a slight chill to the damp air. Large drops patter along the deck, occasionally warmed by the periodic sun and quickly evaporating. Gray white clouds fill the sky from horizon to horizon, predicting a constant rainfall. Waves are large in width but not in height, rocking the ship with their passage. (Temp H 39/5 L 37/3, Wind — 5–10 mph.)

21–40 Heavy rain from ebony clouds pummel the ship and those unfortunate enough to be on deck. Waves like great grayish green hammers smashing against the ship every minute. The overhead clouds have descended to a point where they encase the ship in a large subterranean chamber. Wind plunges against the vessel and its sail, trying to tip it from the mast and rigging. All loose items on deck vie for attention from the crashing waves or the blustery wind. (Temp H 45/7 L 36/3, Wind — 35–45 mph. Characters moving on deck must succeed on a DC 10 Dexterity (Acrobatics) check each round or be knocked prone and pushed 10 feet in a random direction. All exposed areas of the ship are lightly obscured and count as difficult terrain. Characters on deck also have disadvantage on Strength (Athletics) checks involving climbing and Wisdom (Perception) checks that rely on hearing.)

41–60 The sky carries a darker shade than normal, clouds so thick they block out all trace of light. Rain is propelled horizontally with the wind, hitting like daggers and needles, reducing vision to mere feet around each person. Winds blow loose objects and people unprepared for its force off course. Waves 15–30 feet high assault the ship, blowing over the rail and soaking sailors with its frigid embrace. (Temp H 42/6 L 40/4, Wind — 45–50 mph. Characters moving on deck must succeed on a DC 14 Dexterity (Acrobatics) check each round or be knocked prone and pushed 15 feet in a random direction. All exposed areas of the ship are lightly obscured and count as difficult terrain. Characters on deck also have disadvantage on Strength (Athletics) checks involving climbing, Dexterity checks involving fine motor skills, Wisdom (Perception) checks that rely on hearing.)

61–80 A constant rain falls from gray clouds overhead, keeping all within it thoroughly soaked. The wind propels the ship slowly, seemingly held back by the rain, over the large hillock-shaped waves. Occasional lightning flashes illuminate the depth of the rain, looking like iron bars for as far as the eye can see, peppering the water. (Temp H 42/6 L 35/2, Wind — 5–10 mph. Characters moving on deck must succeed on a DC 6 Dexterity (Acrobatics) check each round or be knocked prone. All exposed areas of the ship are lightly obscured and count as difficult terrain.)

81–00 The drone of the rain on the wooden deck becomes hypnotic after a time. The wind is not strong enough to alter the vertical direction of the rain, letting the sail hang like a soaked rag from the mast. The subtle waves rock the ship almost undetectably as they move by on unseen currents. Clouds looking like an inverted mountain range press down upon the ship and crew. (Temp H 48/10 L 40/4, Wind — 5–10 mph.)

RAIN/NIGHT

01–20 Lightning-rippled clouds streak by overhead; waves lift like cliffs (6–15 feet) around the vessel. Large rain drops alternate from side-to-side and straight down with the force of a hammer blow. Rivers of water course around the deck from the rain and waves, creating treacherous footing for all on board. The sails snap and crack as it fills with the wind, dropping deluges of collected rain to the deck below. Periodically, the sky lights up with a lightning blast nearby, painting everything in shades of white and gray; all other times, the charcoal sky and water bestow a sense of isolation. (Temp H 36/3 L 26/ –3, Wind — 30–35 mph. Characters moving on deck must succeed on a DC 14 Dexterity (Acrobatics) check each round or be knocked prone and pushed 15 feet in a random direction. All exposed areas of the ship are lightly obscured and count as difficult terrain. Characters on deck also have disadvantage on Dexterity checks involving fine motor skills and Constitution saving throws made to maintain concentration on a spell.)

21–40 A constant rain falls from gray clouds overhead, keeping all within thoroughly soaked. The wind propels the ship slowly, seemingly held in check by the rain, over the large hillock-shaped waves. Occasional lightning flashes illuminate the depth of the rain, looking like fine iron bars for as far as the eye can see, peppering the water. (Temp H 43/6 L 31/0, Wind — 5–10 mph. Characters moving on deck must succeed on a DC 6 Dexterity (Acrobatics) check each round or be knocked prone. All exposed areas of the ship are lightly obscured and count as difficult terrain. Characters on deck also take a –1 penalty to Strength (Athletics) checks involving climbing.)

41–60	Thick, rolling clouds erupt continuously with thunder and rain, beating upon the wooden planks. The percussion of the rain is accented with the occasional spray of mountainous waves carried on the wind. Gusts of wind blow across the ship attempting to pull everything along in its wake. Sight is reduced to feet, distance eliminated with thick sheets of rain. (Temp H 41/5 L 38/3, Wind — 30–50 mph. Characters moving on deck must succeed on a DC 12 Dexterity (Acrobatics) check each round or be knocked prone and pushed 10 feet in a random direction. All exposed areas of the ship are heavily obscured and count as difficult terrain. Characters on deck also take a –1 penalty to Dexterity checks involving fine motor skills and Constitution saving throws made to maintain concentration on a spell.)
61–80	Hurricane force rain and winds; consequently, the ship is tossed like a child's doll. Huge waves like mountains threaten to topple the vessel and launch the sailors into the unforgiving sea. Wind blows fiercely, lifting all heavy objects or small creatures not lashed down and propelling them around and off the ship. The sky and water are undistinguishable; erasing the horizon as both are steel gray. (Temp H 35/2 L 29/–2, Wind — 80–90 mph. Characters moving on deck must succeed on a DC 15 Dexterity (Acrobatics) check each round or be knocked prone and pushed 20 feet in a random direction. All exposed areas of the ship are lightly obscured and count as difficult terrain. Characters on deck also have disadvantage on Dexterity checks and saving throws, Strength (Athletics) checks involving climbing, Wisdom (Perception) checks that rely on hearing.)
81–00	A simple rain falls, creating a drumbeat of rain on the wooden deck. The wind is not strong enough to alter the vertical direction of the rain, letting the sail hang like a soaked rag from the mast. The subtle waves rock the ship almost undetectably as they move on under currents. Clouds looking like an inverted mountain range press down upon the ship and crew. Navigation can only be done through compass or landmarks. (Temp H 37/3 L 28/–2, Wind — 5–10 mph.)

Dry/Day

01–20	The large sun governs the sky, but a swift breeze keeps the temperature to a cooler level. Spray is pulled up from the many waves, capped in white froth and thrown across the deck. The horizon is marked with a large bank of gray clouds, promising rain in the next day or two. (Temp H 47/8 L 39/4, Wind — 20–25 mph.)
21–40	The sky is clear, dotted with numerous small, unimposing puffs of cloud. A steady wind blows, determined to cart items away in its embrace. The sun, high overhead, seems a greater distance than usual given the lack of heat generated. Abundant waves run to the horizon, making up for size with numbers. Churned to a gray-green, only a few feet under the surface can be seen with any clarity; another indicator of the weak sun. (Temp H 43/6 L 33/1, Wind — 18–20 mph.)
41–60	A crystal clear sky amplifies the sun, directing its heat against the ship and her crew. The wind puffs slowly, not enough to extinguish a candle let alone cool the flesh of those warmer than usual day. Waves move across the water like a herd, trying to carry the ship along in their wake, fighting the vessel should it try to turn away. The spray carries over the rail into the faces of those on deck, quickly drying to leave traces of powdered salt. (Temp H 40/4 L 35/2, Wind — 5–10 mph. Characters on deck take a –1 penalty to Wisdom (Perception) checks that rely on sight and Constitution saving throws made to maintain concentration on a spell.)

61–80	Sun and gray clouds do battle overhead for dominance, sometimes plunging the ship into a dark twilight or bright daylight. Numerous waves, about the size of a man, run the length of the water as far as the eye can see, all topped with a cone of greenish-white froth. The wind picks this froth from each and carries it along, coating all surfaces. This cooling spray makes the trip enjoyable for most on board, even in the shade. The rigging and sails flap in the breeze, occasionally dropping additional sprays to the deck, glinting like jewels in the periodic sun. (Temp H 44/7 L 39/4, Wind — 18–20 mph.)
81–00	Gray the color of stone has been painted from horizon to horizon, plunging the day into twilight. The absence of wind allows the sails and rigging to hang lifeless, like cloth in a shop window. The water is unmarked, calm for many miles around the ship, waves visible in the far distance. Pressure seems to build, raising the temperature over several hours to a more comfortable level. (Temp H 37/3 L 32/0, Wind — 5–10 mph. Reroll in 4 game hours on the wet–day chart for the approaching storm.)

Dry/Night

01–20	Clear sky provides a view of the numerous constellations and guiding stars. Wind gusts from the East, creating a flapping staccato to match the waves breaking on the hull of the ship. White-capped waves, visible in the moonlight, reach for the sailors on board, topping 7–8 feet. A slight mist can be felt in the wind; consequently, all surfaces are slick and shiny with moisture (Temp H 38/4 L 31/0, Wind — 15–25 mph. Characters moving on deck must succeed on a DC 6 Dexterity (Acrobatics) check each round or be knocked prone. All exposed areas of the ship count as difficult terrain. Characters on deck also take a –1 penalty to Strength (Athletics) checks involving climbing and Wisdom (Perception) checks that rely on hearing.)
21–40	Clear ebony night overhead provides astronomers and navigators a fine view of the stars and planets. A gentle wind blows from the South, flapping the sail and nettings. Small waves lap against the side of the boat like a heartbeat; small white caps stand out stark against the black background of the water and night sky. (Temp H 41/5 L 36/3, Wind — 15–25 mph.)
41–60	An overcast sky blocks the view of all but the brightest stars and planets. Some navigation can still be done by experienced sailors. A breeze comes and goes, proving to be a fickle asset for the sails on the ship, waves playing tag rock the ship gently back and forth. (Temp H 42/6 L 29/–2, Wind — 5–10 mph.)
61–80	Numerous stars turn the night sky into a twilight gray, offsetting the jet black of the calm water. A steady, soft wind blows, propelling the ship along on its way. The sound of the surf being cut by the hull is seemingly alone, periodically joined by the creak of the rigging and the soft voice of a sailor. (Temp H 45/7 L 39/4, Wind — 10–15 mph.)
81–00	Gale force winds blow, threatening to rip the sail from the mast, propelling the vessel over the waves like a toy. Thick ribbons of cloud race overhead like gray gashes in the constellations. Many large waves run the length of vision, occasionally growing to such a large size (45 feet) they threaten to topple the ship like flotsam. (Temp H 37/3 L 26/–3, Wind — 65–70 mph. Characters moving on deck must succeed on a DC 8 Dexterity (Acrobatics) check each round or be knocked prone and pushed 5 feet in a random direction. Characters on deck also take a –1 penalty to Strength (Athletics) checks involving climbing and Constitution saving throws made to maintain concentration on a spell.)

ARCTIC

Wind chill is a real concern when the temperature drops below 32° F. Exposure to the wind risks frostbite for flesh. The effective temperature, for purposes of calculating potential harm caused by extreme cold, can be found in the Wind Chill Table.

RAIN/DAY

01–20	White gray clouds span from horizon to horizon, periodic deluges of snow drop upon the water and the ship. The deck is quickly covered in a blanket of white snow, making progress slow around the ship. Finding equipment is difficult for the inexperienced sailor, boxes and barrels becoming nondescript objects in the snow. The wind moves the snow in various directions as it descends, moving the sails to half full with their strongest force. (Temp H –11/–24 L –16/–27, Wind — 0–5 mph. All exposed areas of the ship count as difficult terrain. See rules above for the consequences of exposure to extreme temperatures.)
21–40	Frozen rain drops like sheets of needles upon sailors in the open. The wind drives the sleet almost horizontally across the waves. Large mountains of water move across the area, threatening to bash the vessel into submission. The steel gray sky rolls like the underside of a surf, promising many hours of attack. The rigging creaks and sails moan ominously in the barrage of the storm. Movement along the deck is perilous at best; those in the upper reaches of the vessel cling for their lives. (Temp H –15/–27 L –25/–31, Wind — 20–25 mph. Characters moving on deck must succeed on a DC 10 Dexterity (Acrobatics) check each round or be knocked prone and pushed 10 feet in a random direction. All exposed areas of the ship are lightly obscured and count as difficult terrain. Characters on deck have disadvantage on Dexterity checks involving fine motor skills, Strength (Athletics) checks, and Constitution saving throws to maintain concentration on a spell. See rules above for the consequences of exposure to extreme temperatures.)
41–60	Freezing mist falls like a cloud landing on the water. Wind is present but too weak to fill sails. Ice flows move on the sunken currents, dancing around the ship at great distances. Waves are subdued, seemingly moving in numerous directions, no pattern discernable. Ice forms on most surfaces with extended exposure, sails and rigging becoming rigid and hazardous with each passing hour. (Temp H –12/–29 L –17/–28, Wind — 0–5 mph. Characters moving on deck must succeed on a DC 8 Dexterity (Acrobatics) check each round or be knocked prone. All exposed areas of the ship are lightly obscured and count as difficult terrain. Characters on deck take a –1 penalty to Strength (Athletics) checks involving climbing. See rules above for the consequences of exposure to extreme temperatures)
61–80	Clouds pregnant with lightning streak by overhead, waves lift like cliffs (6–15 feet) around the vessel. Rain alternates from side-to-side and straight down with the force of a hammer blow. Ice coats all exposed surfaces in minutes, creating treacherous areas on the ship and rigging. The sails snap and crack as they fill with the wind, snow, and ice, dropping chunks of ice to the deck below. Periodically, the sky lights up with a lightning blast nearby, painting everything in shades of white and gray; all other times, the charcoal sky and water bestow a sense of isolation. (Temp H –19/–29 L –22/–30, Wind — 35–40 mph. Characters moving on deck must succeed on a DC 12 Dexterity (Acrobatics) check each round or be knocked prone and pushed 10 feet in a random direction. All exposed areas of the ship are lightly obscured and count as difficult terrain. Characters on deck have disadvantage on Wisdom (Perception) checks that rely on hearing and take –1 penalty on Dexterity checks involving fine motor skills, Strength (Athletics) involving climbing. See rules above for the consequences of exposure to extreme temperatures.)
81–00	The sky carries a darker shade than normal, clouds so thick they block out all trace of light. Rain is propelled horizontally with the wind, hitting like daggers and needles, reducing vision to mere feet around each person. Ice forms on all surfaces, making passage difficult on deck. Winds blow loose objects and people unprepared for its force off course. Waves 15–30 feet high assault the ship, blowing over the rail and soaking sailors with its frigid embrace. (Temp H –16/–27 L –27/–33, Wind — 27–35 mph. Characters moving on deck must succeed on a DC 10 Dexterity (Acrobatics) check each round or be knocked prone and pushed 5 feet in a random direction. All exposed areas of the ship are lightly obscured and count as difficult terrain. Characters on deck have disadvantage on Dexterity checks involving fine motor skills, Strength (Athletics) checks involving climbing, Wisdom (Perception) checks that rely on hearing.)

RAIN/NIGHT

01–20	Clouds infused with lightning fill the sky around the ship, while waves lift like cliffs (6–15 feet) around the vessel. Rain alternates from side-to-side and straight down with the force of a hammer blow. Ice coats all exposed surfaces, quickly creating treacherous areas on the ship and rigging. The sails, snap and crack as it fills with the wind, snow, and ice, dropping chunks of ice to the deck below. Periodically, the sky lights up with a lightning blast nearby, painting everything in shades of white, blue, and gray; all other times the charcoal sky and water bestow a sense of isolation. (Temp H –25/–30 L –30/–34, Wind — 50–55 mph. Characters moving on deck must succeed on a DC 12 Dexterity (Acrobatics) check each round or be knocked prone and pushed 10 feet in a random direction. All exposed areas of the ship are lightly obscured and count as difficult terrain. Characters on deck have disadvantage on Wisdom (Perception) checks that rely on hearing.)
21–40	Freezing mist falls like a cloud landing on the water. Wind is present but too weak to fill sails. Ice flows move on the sunken currents, dancing around the ship at great distances. Waves are subdued, seemingly moving in numerous directions, no pattern discernable. Ice forms on most surfaces with extended exposure, sails and rigging becoming rigid and hazardous with each passing hour. (Temp H –12/–24 L –22/–30, Wind — 0–5 mph. Characters moving on deck must succeed on a DC 8 Dexterity (Acrobatics) check each round or be knocked prone. All exposed areas of the ship are lightly obscured and count as difficult terrain. Characters on deck take a –1 penalty to Wisdom (Perception) checks that rely on hearing. See rules above for the consequences of exposure to extreme temperatures.)
41–60	The night sky carries a darker shade than normal, clouds so thick they block out all trace of light. Rain is propelled horizontally with the wind, hitting like daggers and needles, reducing vision to mere feet around each person. Ice forms on all surfaces, making passage difficult on deck. Winds blow loose objects and people unprepared for its force off course. Waves 15–30 feet high assault the ship, blowing over the rail and soaking sailors with its frigid embrace. (Temp H –17/–28 L –24/–30, Wind — 27–35 mph. Characters moving on deck must succeed on a DC 14 Dexterity (Acrobatics) check each round or be knocked prone and pushed 15 feet in a random direction. All exposed areas of the ship are heavily obscured and count as difficult terrain. Characters on deck have disadvantage on Dexterity checks involving fine motor skills, Strength (Athletics) checks involving climbing, Wisdom (Perception) checks that rely on hearing. See rules above for the consequences of exposure to extreme temperatures.)

61–80 Constant icy drizzle settles on all surfaces, turning the dark night into a dark gray, reducing vision to nearly non-existent. Frigid temperatures freeze the moisture within minutes on every surface. Travel across deck is difficult but manageable to those familiar with surroundings. Sound is subdued with the ice pellets, adding a muffling effect to conversations. Waves are unseen but can be felt hitting the ship every few seconds, occasionally bathing the deck with its spray, a testament to its height of several feet. (Temp H –16/–27 L –25/–31, Wind — 5–10 mph. Characters moving on deck must succeed on a DC 8 Dexterity (Acrobatics) check each round or be knocked prone and pushed 5 feet in a random direction. All exposed areas of the ship are heavily obscured and count as difficult terrain. Characters on deck have disadvantage on Wisdom (Perception) checks that rely on hearing. See rules above for the consequences of exposure to extreme temperatures.)

81–00 Large thick flakes drop around the ship, landing softly on the water before melting. Equipment and decking are quickly covered in a thick blanket of white snow. Waves roll languidly, topping 6 feet in height but not steep enough to make more than an exaggerated rocking motion. A light wind blows carrying the flakes on the air currents, visible in the occasional moonlight. (Temp H –20/–29 L –26/–32, Wind — 5–10 mph. Characters moving on deck must succeed on a DC 6 Dexterity (Acrobatics) check each round or be knocked prone. All exposed areas of the ship are lightly obscured and count as difficult terrain.)

Dry/Day

01–20 Clear blue sky overhead provides ample room for the bright sun to shine. Wind gusts from the North East, flapping the sail and nettings. White-capped waves, topping 7–8 feet high seem to be pushing large chunks of ice along in their grasp. (Temp H –19/–29 L –24/–31, Wind — 20–25 mph. Those working while facing the sun must succeed on a DC 10 Constitution saving throw or be blinded for 1d4 hours. Characters with a natural sensitivity to light have disadvantage on this saving throw. 10% chance of course change required for ice flow in path of ship.)

21–40 Sun and gray clouds do battle overhead for dominance, sometimes plunging the day into a gray twilight or bright daylight. Numerous waves, about the size of a man, run the length of the water as far as the eye can see, all topped with a cone of blue-white froth. The wind picks this froth from each and carries it along freezing it to any surface it covers. The rigging and sails labour under the extra weight of the ice, glinting like jewels in the periodic sun. (Temp H –21/–29 L –28/–33, Wind — 20–25 mph. Characters moving on deck must succeed on a DC 10 Dexterity (Acrobatics) check each round or be knocked prone. All exposed areas of the ship count as difficult terrain. Characters on deck also take a –1 penalty to Strength (Athletics) checks involving climbing. 12% chance of course change required for ice flow in path of ship.)

41–60 Gray the color of stone has been painted from horizon to horizon, plunging the day into twilight. The absence of wind allows the sails and rigging to hang listless, like cloth in a shop window. The water is unmarked, calm for many miles around the ship, waves visible in the far distance. Pressure seems to build, raising the temperature over several hours to a more comfortable level. Ice bergs in the distance hold steady like islands. (Temp H –18/–28 L –25/–31, Wind — 0–5 mph. Experienced sailors know a storm is coming. Reroll on Arctic day–rain chart in 1d4 hours for result. 2% chance of course change for ice bergs in path of ship.)

61–80 Streamers of billowy clouds race overhead in the wind. Large waves buffet the ship attempting to carry it along with them. Wind assaults the vessel hard from the west, never wavering or letting up. Tacking into the wind seems impossible from its vicious force while tracking with the wind runs a risk of never getting control of the ship back. (Temp H –18/–28 L –30/–34, Wind — 50–55 mph. Characters moving on deck must succeed on a DC 6 Dexterity (Acrobatics) check each round or be knocked prone and pushed 10 feet in a random direction.)

81–00 The air burns with the wind chill, crusting ice all over the ship, the sun adding no aid to the frigid temperature. Clouds are non-existent in the sky, collecting only on the horizons. While filling the sails, the wind steals the breath from those on deck, freezing exposed flesh in minutes. (Temp H –16/–27 L –29/–34, Wind — 45–50 mph S. Characters moving on deck must succeed on a DC 8 Dexterity (Acrobatics) check each round or be knocked prone and pushed 10 feet in a random direction. All exposed areas of the ship count as difficult terrain. Characters on deck take a –1 penalty on Dexterity checks involving fine motor skills and Strength (Athletics) checks involving climbing.)

Dry/Night

01–20 Clear ebony night overhead provides astronomers and navigators a fine view of the stars and planets. A gentle wind blows from the South, flapping the sail and nettings. Small waves lap against the side of the boat like a heartbeat, ice bergs stand out stark white against the black background of the water and night sky. (Temp H –20/–29 L –27/–33, Wind — 5–10 mph. 10% chance of course changes required for ice flow in path of ship. No change to skills.)

21–40 Large clouds move overhead, blocking the stars and moon with their bulk. The ship rolls gently on the waves as it rides through the water. Occasionally larger waves provide a small drop for the vessel as it is carried over the lip of the wave. The strong wind takes the ship along with it, filling the sails and pulling at cloaks of those on board. (Temp H –17/–28 L –25/–31, Wind — 40–45 mph. Characters on deck take a –1 penalty on Wisdom (Perception) checks that rely on hearing.)

41–60 Clouds block all stars and only hint at the location of the moon, adding a claustrophobic feel to the trip. The absence of wind allows the sails and rigging to hang listless, like cloth in a shop window. The ebony water ripples in the soft breeze, white caps standing out like glowing embers. (Temp H –14/–26 L –28/–33, Wind — 0–5 mph. 2% chance of course change for ice bergs in path of ship.)

61–80 Partial clouds cover sections of the sky, seemingly unmoving. Large waves buffet the ship attempting to bear it along with them. Wind assaults the vessel hard from the west, never wavering or letting up. Travel during the night at full sail runs a double risk of collision with ice. (Temp H –19/–29 L –25/–31, Wind — 45–50 mph. Characters moving on deck must succeed on a DC 6 Dexterity (Acrobatics) check each round or be knocked prone and pushed 10 feet in a random direction. 15% chance of course change for ice.)

81–00 Wisps of cloud move across the sky, sometimes blocking the stars. The brightness of the visible stars and moon provides ample light to maneuver around the ship and perform most tasks. The ever-present wind provides enough force to keep the ship moving at optimum speed. The absence of spray from the calm waters allows for equipment to remain cold but dry. (Temp H –25/–31 L –35/–37, Wind — 10–15 mph.)

EQUATORIAL

Within the Equatorial region, humidity is issue for temperature measurement. Reference to the Humidity Table will bring about a more realistic gauge for temperature; consequently, the effects of heat upon those traveling the waves should be watched closely.

RAIN/DAY

01–20	A heavy wind blows, adding a texture to the warm rain falling. Large drops patter along the deck, occasional sunshine warms the deck, quickly evaporating the rain and adding to the humidity. A sticky aspect of the air grows throughout the day as the humidity rises. Sunlight glints off the water like numerous smaller suns, blinding those not ready for the effect. Waves are large in width but not in height, rocking the ship with their passage. (Temp H 75/24 L 58/15, Wind — 20–25 mph. Characters on deck take a –1 penalty to Constitution saving throws made to maintain concentration on a spell.)
21–40	Driving rain pummels the ship and those on board, quickly soaking all equipment and people. The waves are sedated, rarely topping 5 feet, seemingly held down with the impact of the rain. The sun tries to pierce the cloud cover with its intense glare, only succeeding in raising the temperature. Wind is non-existent, hammered to submission by the heavy rain. (Temp H 77/25 L 63/17, Wind — 0–5 mph.)
41–60	Seemingly in rhythm with the lapping waves, periodic rain drops in vast amounts, quickly soaking all surfaces and washing away loose items. Between rainfalls, the sun attempts to burn away the moisture with blistering heat, never quite successful and so leaving all with a heaviness of moisture. Waves roll languidly, topping 6 feet in height but not steep enough to make more than an exaggerated rocking motion. The wind blows merrily, billowing out the sails of the ship and propelling the vessel over the large waves. (Temp H 79/27 L 71/22, Wind — 10–15 mph. Characters moving on deck during a deluge must succeed on a DC 6 Dexterity (Acrobatics) check or be knocked prone and pushed 10 feet in a random direction, and all exposed areas of the ship as difficult terrain.)
61–80	A drizzle of rain, sometimes hard and sometimes light, falls throughout the day. All surfaces are thoroughly soaked and heavy with water. The warmth of the occasional sun is diminished slightly by the cool rain, keeping it tolerable for all involved. Waves are present but pose no threat to the navigation of the ship or to the course she desires to take. The wind blows constantly, keeping the sails full but not pushing the limit of its capabilities. (Temp H 76/25 L 66/19, Wind — 30–35 mph.)
81–00	Rain drops like a swarm of arrows carried at a velocity that actually inflicts pain on exposed skin. Waves like great gray-green boulders smashing against the ship every minute. The overhead clouds have descended to a point where it seems the ship is in a large chamber. Wind hurtles against the vessel and its sail, trying to rip it free from the mast and rigging. All loose items are tossed around the decking, creating hazards for those on deck. (Temp H 73/22 L 62/17, Wind — 60–65 mph. Characters moving on deck must succeed on a DC 12 Dexterity (Acrobatics) check each round or be knocked prone and pushed 10 feet in a random direction. All exposed areas of the ship count as difficult terrain. Characters on deck have disadvantage on Strength (Athletics) checks involving climbing and take a –1 penalty to Constitution saving throws made to maintain concentration on a spell.)

RAIN/NIGHT

01–20	The humidity of the night is made comfortable by the patter of rain upon the deck. The coolness of the rain seems to steal some of the thickness in the air. The thin clouds mask the presence of the stars but leave a large halo where the moon tries to shine. The waves crash against the hull as if trying to keep the ship from reaching its goal. The bounce of the ship as it passes over the waves keeps all but the soundest sleepers awake. (Temp H 73/22 L 57/14, Wind — 0–5 mph.)
21–40	Heavy rain from ebony clouds press down on the ship and those on deck. Waves can be seen in the dark like great gray-green boulders smashing against the ship every minute. The overhead clouds have descended to a point where it seems the ship is in a large gray bubble. Wind hurtles against the vessel and its sail, trying to rip it from the mast and rigging. All loose items on deck vie for attention from the crashing waves or the blustery wind. (Temp H 71/21 L 68/20, Wind — 50–60 mph. Characters moving on deck must succeed on a DC 8 Dexterity (Acrobatics) check each round or be knocked prone and pushed 10 feet in a random direction. All exposed areas of the ship are lightly obscured and count as difficult terrain. Characters on deck have disadvantage on Strength (Athletics) checks involving climbing and take –1 penalty to Constitution saving throws made to maintain concentration on a spell.)
41–60	Seemingly in rhythm with the lapping waves, periodic rain drops in vast amounts, quickly soaking all surfaces and washing away loose materials. Waves roll languidly, topping 6 feet in height but not steep enough to make more than an exaggerated rocking motion. A light wind blows, carrying a humid mist from the still warm water, visible in the intermittent moonlight. (Temp H 72/22 L 65/15, Wind — 5–10 mph. Characters moving on deck must succeed on a DC 6 Dexterity (Acrobatics) check each round or be knocked prone. All exposed areas of the ship are lightly obscured and count as difficult terrain.)
61–80	A drizzle of rain, sometimes hard and sometimes light, falls continuously throughout during the nighttime hours. All surfaces are thoroughly soaked and heavy with water. The warmth of the day rapidly disappears replaced with the humidity of the still evaporating water around the ship. The waves are smaller than normal and works with the rain to stay weak enough to be inconsequential. The wind blows constantly, keeping the sails full but not pushing the limit of its capabilities. (Temp H 71/21 L 66/19, Wind — 20–25 mph.)
81–00	A thrashing rain accompanies hurricane force winds. In the distance amid lightning flashes, water spouts can be seen reaching for the sky. Waves, the size of small mountains, rise above the vessel, giving the ship a wide span of view when atop a wave, and a sense of claustrophobia when in a gully. (Temp H 74/24 L 64/18, Wind — 70–75 mph. Characters moving on deck must succeed on a DC 14 Dexterity (Acrobatics) check each round or be knocked prone and pushed 15 feet in a random direction. All exposed areas of the ship are lightly obscured and count as difficult terrain. Characters on deck have disadvantage on Dexterity checks and saving throws, Strength (Athletics) checks involving climbing, Wisdom (Perception) checks that rely on hearing.)

DRY/DAY

01–20	The large sun dominates the sky, but a swift breeze keeps the temperature to a more moderate level. Spray pulled up from the many waves, capped in white froth. The horizon is marked with a large range of gray clouds, promising rain in the next day or two. The humidity rises throughout the day, adding a weight to the sun, which saps the strength of those not acquainted with the Equatorial waters. (Temp H 76/25 L 64/18, Wind — 30–35 mph.)
21–40	Clouds run amok along the sky, occasionally blocking the sun and its warmth. The wind seemingly growls as it tears across the water at the ship. The sail quivers, trying to keep the wind from escaping. Waves rise up and crash against the hull of the ship, each impact like a bludgeon from nature itself. (Temp H 77/26 L 74/24, Wind — 25–35 mph. Characters moving on a deck must succeed on a DC 6 Dexterity (Acrobatics) check each round or be knocked prone. All exposed areas of the ship are lightly obscured and count as difficult terrain. Characters on deck also have disadvantage on Strength (Athletics) checks involving climbing and take a –1 penalty to Wisdom (Perception) checks that rely on hearing.)

41–60	A crystal clear sky seems to enlarge the sun, directing its heat against the ship and her crew. The wind puffs slowly, not enough to extinguish a candle, let alone cool the flesh of those in the open. Waves move across the water like a herd, trying to carry the ship along in their wake, fighting the vessel should it try to turn away. The spray carries over the rail into the faces of those on deck, quickly drying to leave powdered salt. (Temp H 77/26 L 70/21, Wind — 0–5 mph.)
61–80	The thick clouds overhead threaten to release their burden, moisture released in the form of a thick, palpable air. While no rain has fallen during the day, all surfaces are beaded with sweat and spray from the moisture-laced air. The moderate wind moves both the ship and the clouds, lifting the waves to heights of 10 feet, launching the spray into the air. The ship rolls with the impact as it tips down one wave and up another, the prow having difficulty cutting through the water. (Temp H 71/21 L 58/15, Wind — 10–15 mph.)
81–00	The sky is clear, dotted with numerous small, unimposing puffs of cloud. A steady wind blows, determined to cart items away in its embrace. The sun, high overhead, seems a greater distance than usual given the lack of heat generated. Abundant waves run to the horizon, making up for size with numbers. Churned to a gray-green only a few feet under the surface can be seen with any clarity; another indicator of the weak sun. (Temp H 73/22 L 67/19, Wind — 25–30 mph.)

DRY/NIGHT

01–20	Clear expanse provides a view of the numerous constellations and guiding stars. Wind gusts from the South, creating a flapping staccato to match the waves breaking on the hull of the ship. White-capped waves, visible in the moonlight reach for the sailors on board, topping 7–8 feet. A slight mist can be felt in the wind; consequently, all surfaces are slick and shiny with moisture. (Temp H 75/25 L 64/18, Wind — 15–25 mph. Characters moving on deck must succeed on a DC 6 Dexterity (Acrobatics) check each round or be knocked prone. All exposed areas of the ship count as difficult terrain. Characters on deck also take a –1 penalty to Strength (Athletics) checks involving climbing and Wisdom (Perception) checks that rely on hearing.)
21–40	Clouds of stone gray run from horizon to horizon, extinguishing the stars and moon from view. The absence of wind allows the sails and rigging to hang listless, like cloth in a shop window. The water is unmarked, calm for many miles around the ship, waves visible in the far distance. Pressure seems to build, raising the temperature over several hours to just above a comfortable level. (Temp H 77/25 L 58/15, Wind — 0–5 mph. Experienced sailors know a storm is coming. Reroll on Equatorial day–rain chart in 1d4 hours for result.)
41–60	The cool of the night is identified by the daytime heat escaping the decking, misting the moisture collected through the daylight hours. Raising the humidity to an uncomfortable level, it deadens the night sounds of creaking riggings and lapping waves. Long trenches of waves roll the ship as it moves through them like long strides of a great beast. Occasional clouds plunge the ship into darkness, allowing the moon and stars to peer through again in a few moments. (Temp H 73/22 L 65/18, Wind — 10–20 mph.)
61–80	Stars and gray clouds do battle overhead for control, sometimes plunging the world into a dark twilight or bright moonlight. Numerous waves, about the size of a man, run the length of the water as far as the eye can see, all topped with a small cone of greenish white froth. The rigging and sails have rivulets of collected water, which pools on the deck. Lines are heavy with water, and deck boards are slick and shiny, sometimes reflecting the occasional moonlight. (Temp H 74/24 L 56/14, Wind — 20–25 mph. Characters moving on deck must succeed on a DC 6 Dexterity (Acrobatics) check each round or be knocked prone. All exposed areas of the ship count as difficult terrain. Characters on deck also take a –1 penalty to Strength (Athletics) checks involving climbing and Wisdom (Perception) checks that rely on sight.)

81–00	Clear ebony night overhead provides astronomers and navigators a fine view of the stars and planets. A gentle wind blows form the South South-East, flapping the sail and nettings. Small waves lap against the side of the boat like a heartbeat, reflections of the moon on the waves stand out stark white against the black background of the water and night sky. (Temp H 78/25 L 67/19, Wind — 5–10 mph.)

AUTUMN

TROPICAL

Heat stroke is a risk for any who travel the warm regions of the world. Those exerting themselves must succeed on a DC 10 Constitution saving throw for each hour of strenuous work or gain a level of exhaustion. For each cumulative hour of strenuous work, the DC of subsequent saves increases by 1. Resting in shaded areas for 10 minutes per hour negates the +1 to the DC for that hour. Spell components run a 10% chance of spoiling in humidity, if you determine they are subject to such damage.

RAIN/DAY

01–20	A gentle breeze blows, adding a pleasant cooling to the warm rain falling. Large drops patter along the deck and occasional sunshine warms the deck, quickly evaporating the rain and adding to the humidity. A sticky aspect of the air grows throughout the day as the humidity rises. Sunlight glints off the water like numerous smaller suns, blinding those not ready for the effect. Waves are large in width but not in height, rocking the ship with their passage. (Temp H 90/33 L 78/26, Wind — 10–15 mph. Characters on deck take a –1 penalty to Constitution saving throws made to maintain concentration on a spell.)
21–40	Severe rain pummels the ships and those on board, quickly soaking all equipment and people. The waves are sedated, rarely topping 5 feet seemingly held down with the rain. The sun tries to pierce the cloud cover with its intense glare, only succeeding in raising the temperature. Wind is non-existent, hammered to submission by the heavy rain. (Temp H 89/32 L 84/30, Wind — 0–5 mph.)
41–60	Seemingly in rhythm with the lapping waves, periodic rain drops in large amounts, quickly soaking all surfaces and washing away loose items. Between rainfalls the sun attempts to burn away the moisture with searing heat. Waves roll languidly, topping 6 feet in height but not steep enough to make more than an exaggerated rocking motion. The wind blows merrily, billowing out the sails of the ship and propelling the vessel over the large waves. (Temp H 88/32 L 74/24, Wind — 20–25 mph. Characters moving on deck during a deluge must succeed on a DC 6 Dexterity (Acrobatics) check each round or be knocked prone and pushed 10 feet in a random direction. All exposed areas of the ship count as difficult terrain.)
61–80	A drizzle of rain, sometimes hard and sometimes light, falls continuously throughout the day. All surfaces are thoroughly soaked and heavy with water. The warmth of the occasional sun is diminished slightly by the cool rain, keeping it tolerable for all involved. The wind blows constantly, keeping the sails full but not pushing the limit of its capabilities. (Temp H 86/31 L 79/27, Wind — 30–35 mph.)

81–00 Rain from imposing clouds strike the ship and those on deck. Waves like great gray-green boulders smashing against the ship every minute or so. The overhead clouds have descended to a point where it seems the ship is in a large chamber. Wind hurtles against the vessel and its sail, trying to rip it from the mast and rigging. All loose items on deck vie for attention from the crashing waves or the blustery wind. (Temp H 85/30 L 75/25, Wind — 45–50 mph. Characters moving on deck must succeed on a DC 10 Dexterity (Acrobatics) check each round or be knocked prone and pushed 10 feet in a random direction. All exposed areas of the ship are lightly obscured and count as difficult terrain. Characters on deck take a –1 penalty to Constitution saving throws made to maintain concentration on a spell and have disadvantage on Strength (Athletics) checks involving climbing and Wisdom (Perception) checks that rely on hearing.)

Rain/Night

01–20 The cool of the night is accompanied by the patter of rain upon the deck. The humidity keeps the coolness of the night from becoming entirely comfortable. The moon makes itself known through the clouds, illuminating a portion of the night sky to milky white. The waves crash against the hull as if trying to keep the ship from reaching its goal. The bounce of the ship as it passes over the waves keeps all but the soundest sleepers awake. (Temp H 84/30 L 74/24, Wind — 15–20 mph. Characters on deck take a –1 penalty to Constitution saving throws made to maintain concentration on a spell.)

21–40 Steady rainfall beats at the ship with determination normally reserved for the cursed. Waves can be seen in the dark like a herd of turquoise animals, smashing against the ship every minute. Wind plunges against the vessel and its sails, trying to rip it from its bindings. All loose items and small creatures on deck vie for attention from the crashing waves or the blustery wind. (Temp H 87/31 L 81/28, Wind — 60–65 mph. Characters moving on deck must succeed on a DC 10 Dexterity (Acrobatics) check each round or be knocked prone and pushed 10 feet in a random direction. All exposed areas of the ship are lightly obscured and count as difficult terrain. Characters on deck have disadvantage on and Strength (Athletics) checks involving climbing, Wisdom (Perception) checks that rely on hearing, and Constitution saving throws made to maintain concentration on a spell.)

41–60 Sheets of rain drop upon the water and the unfortunate sea-going vessel, completely waterlogging the ship and her crew. Occasionally easing off in intensity, the rain soon begins again, ramping up its strength. Waves roll languidly, topping 6 feet in height but not steep enough to make a difference in any ships course should they attempt to climb its expanse. A light wind blows, carrying mist from the still warm water, visible in the occasional moonlight. (Temp H 83/29 L 79/27, Wind — 5–10 mph. Characters moving on deck during a deluge must succeed on a DC 6 Dexterity (Acrobatics) check each round or be knocked prone and pushed 10 feet in a random direction. All exposed areas of the ship are lightly obscured and count as difficult terrain.)

61–80 A light drizzle of rain falls from gray clouds overhead, keeping all within it thoroughly soaked. The wind propels the ship slowly, seemingly held back by the rain, over the large hillock-shaped waves. Occasional lightning flashes illuminate the depth of the rain, looking like iron bars for as far as the eye can see, peppering the water. (Temp H 77/26 L 68/21, Wind — 15–20 mph.)

81–00 A continual rain falls from gray clouds overhead, keeping all within it thoroughly soaked. The wind propels the ship slowly, seemingly held back by the rain, over the large hillock-shaped waves. Occasional lightning flashes illuminate the depth of the rain, looking like iron bars for as far as the eye can see, peppering the water. (Temp H 77/26 L 68/21, Wind — 15–20 mph. Characters moving on deck must succeed on a DC 6 Dexterity (Acrobatics) check each round or be knocked prone. All exposed areas of the ship are lightly obscured and count as difficult terrain. Characters on deck take a –1 penalty to Dexterity saving throws and Strength (Athletics) checks involving climbing.)

Dry/Day

01–20 The large sun dominates the sky, but a swift breeze keeps the temperature to a more moderate level. Spray is pulled up from the many waves, capped in white froth and tossed upon the ship and anything on deck. The horizon is marked with a large bank of gray clouds, promising rain in the next day or two. (Temp H 88/32 L 75/24, Wind — 20–25 mph.)

21–40 Clouds run amok along the sky, occasionally blocking the sun and its warmth. The wind seemingly growls as it tears across the water at the ship. The sail quivers, trying to keep the wind from escaping. Waves rise up and crash against the hull of the ship, each impact like a bludgeon from nature itself. (Temp H 86/31 L 79/27, Wind — 25–35 mph. Characters on deck have disadvantage on Strength (Athletics) checks involving climbing and take a –1 penalty to Wisdom (Perception) checks that rely on hearing.)

41–60 A crystal clear sky magnifies the sun, directing its heat against the ship and her crew. The wind puffs slowly, not enough to extinguish a candle, let alone cool the flesh of those in the open. Waves move across the water like a herd, trying to carry the ship along in their wake, fighting the vessel should it try to turn away. The spray carries over the rail into the faces of those on deck, quickly drying to leave powdered salt. (Temp H 90/33 L 84/30, Wind — 0–5 mph.)

61–80 The thick clouds overhead threaten to release their burden but maintain their hold for now. The moderate wind moves both the ship and the clouds, lifting waves to heights of 10 feet, launching the spray into the air. The ship rolls with the impacts as it tips down one wave and up another, the prow having difficulty cutting through the water. (Temp H 84/30 L 79/27, Wind — 15–20 mph.)

81–00 The sky is clear, dotted with numerous small, unimposing puffs of cloud. A steady wind blows, determined to cart items away in its embrace. The sun, high overhead, seems a greater distance than usual, given the lack of heat generated. Abundant waves run to the horizon, making up for size with numbers. Churned to a gray-green, only a few feet under the surface can be seen with any clarity; another indicator of the weak sun. (Temp H 79/27 L 77/26, Wind — 30–35 mph.)

Dry/Night

01–20 Clear sky provides a view of the numerous constellations and guiding stars. Wind gusts from the North East, creating a flapping staccato to match the waves breaking on the hull of the ship. White-capped waves, visible in the moonlight, reach for the sailors on board, topping 7–8 feet. A slight mist can be felt in the wind; consequently, all surfaces are slick and shiny with moisture. (Temp H 80/27 L 79/27, Wind — 15–25 mph. Characters on deck take a –1 penalty to Strength (Athletics) checks involving climbing and Wisdom (Perception) checks that rely on hearing.)

21–40	Clouds of stone gray run from horizon to horizon, extinguishing the stars and moon from view. The absence of wind allows the sails and rigging to hang listless, like cloth in a shop window. The water is unmarked, calm for many miles around the ship, waves visible in the far distance. Pressure seems to build, raising the temperature over several hours to just above a comfortable level. (Temp H 81/28 L 77/26, Wind — 0–5 mph. Experienced sailors know a storm is coming. Reroll on Tropical day–rain chart in 1d4 hours for result.)
41–60	The cool of the night is easily identified by the daytime heat escaping the decking, misting the moisture collected through the daylight hours. Raising the humidity to an uncomfortable level, it deadens the night sounds of creaking riggings and lapping waves. Long trenches of water roll the ship as it moves through them like long strides of a great beast. Occasional clouds plunge the ship into darkness, allowing the moon and stars to peer through again in a few moments. (Temp H 85/30 L 83/29, Wind — 10–20 mph.)
61–80	Alternating cloud cover keeps the world in either the pitch dark or the luminescent twilight. Numerous waves, about the size of a large horse (8 feet), run the length of the water and far as the eye can see, all topped with a cone of greenish white froth. The rigging and sails have rivulets of collected water, which pools on the deck. Lines are heavy with water and deck boards are slick and shiny, sometimes reflecting the occasional moonlight. (Temp H 78/26 L 75/24, Wind — 20–25 mph. Characters on deck take a –1 penalty to Dexterity saving throws, Strength (Athletics) checks involving climbing, and Wisdom (Perception) checks that rely on sight.
81–00	Clear ebony night overhead provides astronomers and navigators a fine view of the stars and planets. A gentle wind blows from the West, flapping the sail and nettings. Small waves lap against the side of the boat like a heartbeat, reflections of the moon on the waves stand out stark white against the black background of the water and night sky. (Temp H 82/29 L 80/28, Wind — 5–10 mph.

TEMPERATE

RAIN/DAY

| 01–20 | A placid breeze blows, adding a slight chill to the damp air. Large drops patter along the deck, occasionally warmed by the periodic sun and quickly evaporating. Gray white clouds fill the sky from horizon to horizon, predicting a constant rainfall. Waves are large in width but not in height, rocking the ship with their passage. (Temp H 75/25 L 63/18, Wind — 5–10 mph.) |
| 21–40 | Heavy rain from ebony clouds attack the ship and those on unfortunate enough to be on deck. Waves like great gray-green hammers smashing against the ship every minute. The overhead clouds have descended to a point where they encase the ship in a world of twilight. Wind hurtles against the vessel and its sail, trying to rip it from the mast and rigging. All loose items on deck vie for attention from the crashing waves or the blustery wind. (Temp H 82/29 L 69/21, Wind — 50–60 mph. Characters moving on deck must succeed on a DC 10 Dexterity (Acrobatics) check each round or be knocked prone and pushed 10 feet in a random direction. All exposed areas of the ship and count as difficult terrain. Characters on deck also have disadvantage on Strength (Athletics) checks involving climbing, Wisdom (Perception) checks that rely on hearing, and Constitution saving throws made to maintain concentration on a spell.) |

41–60	The sky carries a darker shade than normal, clouds so thick they block out all trace of light. Rain is propelled horizontally with the wind, hitting like daggers and needles, reducing vision to mere feet around each person. Winds blow loose objects and people unprepared for its force off course. Waves 15–30 feet high assault the ship, blowing over the rail and soaking sailors with its frigid embrace. (Temp H 79/27 L 75/24, Wind — 45–50 mph NE. Characters moving on deck must succeed on a DC 10 Dexterity (Acrobatics) check each round or be knocked prone and pushed 5 feet in a random direction. All exposed areas of the ship are lightly obscured and count as difficult terrain. Characters on deck have disadvantage on Dexterity checks involving fine motor skills, Strength (Athletics) checks involving climbing, Wisdom (Perception) checks that rely on hearing, and Constitution saving throws made to maintain concentration on a spell.)
61–80	A constant rain falls from gray clouds overhead, keeping all within it thoroughly soaked. The wind propels the ship slowly, seemingly afraid to let its fury loose. Waves remain small and inconsequential providing no hindrance to navigation or speed. Occasional lightning flashes illuminate the depth of the rain, looking like iron bars for as far as the eye can see, peppering the water. (Temp H 76/25 L 65/19, Wind — 5–10 mph. All exposed areas of the ship are lightly obscured and count as difficult terrain. Characters on deck take a –1 penalty to Dexterity saving throws and Strength (Athletics) checks involving climbing.)
81–00	A simple rain falls, creating a constant drone of rain on the wooden deck. The wind is not strong enough to alter the vertical direction of the rain, letting the sail hang like a soaked rag from the mist. The subtle waves rock the ship almost undetectably as they move by on unseen currents. Clouds looking like an inverted mountain range press down upon the ship and crew. (Temp H 82/29 L 63/18, Wind — 5–10 mph.)

RAIN/NIGHT

| 01–20 | Lightning-rippled clouds streak by overhead as waves lift like cliffs (6–15 feet) around the vessel. Rain alternates from side-to-side and straight down with the force of a hammer blow. Rivers of water course around the deck from the rain and waves, creating treacherous footing for all on board. The sails snap and crack as they fill with wind, dropping deluges of collected rain to the deck below. Periodically, the sky lights up with a lightning blast nearby, painting everything in shades of white, blue, and gray; all other times, the charcoal sky and water bestow a sense of isolation. (Temp H 75/25 L 74/24, Wind — 20–25 mph. Characters moving on deck must succeed on a DC 14 Dexterity (Acrobatics) check each round or be knocked prone and pushed 5 feet in a random direction. All exposed areas of the ship are lightly obscured and count as difficult terrain. Characters on deck have disadvantage on Dexterity checks involving fine motor skills and Constitution saving throws made to maintain concentration on a spell.) |
| 21–40 | Rain constantly falls from gray clouds overhead, keeping all within it thoroughly soaked. The wind propels the ship slowly, seemingly held back by the rain, over the large hillock-shaped waves. Occasional lightning flashes illuminate the depth of the rain, looking like iron bars for as far as the eye can see, peppering the water. (Temp H 78/26 L 69/21, Wind — 5–10 mph. All exposed areas of the ship are lightly obscured and count as difficult terrain. Characters on deck take a –1 penalty to Dexterity saving throws and Strength (Athletics) checks involving climbing.) |

41–60

Thick, rolling clouds erupt constantly with thunder and rain, beating upon the wooden planks. The percussion of the rain is accented with the occasional spray of enormous waves carried on the wind. Gusts of wind blow across the ship, attempting to pull everything along in its wake. Sight is reduced to feet, while seeing into the distance is eliminated with the thick sheets of rain. (Temp H 76/25 L 63/18, Wind — 35–45 mph. Characters moving on deck must succeed on a DC 12 Dexterity (Acrobatics) check each round or be knocked prone and pushed 5 feet in a random direction. All exposed areas of the ship are heavily obscured and count as difficult terrain. Characters on deck have disadvantage on Dexterity saving throws and Strength (Athletics) checks involving climbing and take a –1 penalty to Dexterity checks involving fine motor skills and Constitution saving throws made to maintain concentration on a spell.)

61–80

Hurricane force rain and winds; consequently, the ship is tossed like a doll during a child's tantrum. Huge waves like mountains threaten to topple the vessel and launch the sailors into the unforgiving sea. Wind blows fiercely, lifting all heavy objects or small creatures not lashed down and propelling them around and off the ship. The sky and water are indistinguishable, erasing the horizon and any gauge for distance. (Temp H 69/21 L 61/17, Wind — 55–60 mph. Characters moving on deck must succeed on a DC 14 Dexterity (Acrobatics) check each round or be knocked prone and pushed 10 feet in a random direction. All exposed areas of the ship count as difficult terrain. Characters on deck have disadvantage on Strength (Athletics) checks involving climbing, Dexterity checks and saving throws, and Constitution saving throws made to maintain concentration on a spell.)

81–00

A simple rain falls, creating a constant drumming of rain on the wooden deck. The wind is not strong enough to alter the vertical direction of the rain, letting the sail hang like a soaked rag from the mast. The waves rock the ship almost lovingly as they move past, propelled by unseen currents. Clouds looking like an inverted mountain range press down upon the ship and crew. Navigation can only be done through compass or landmarks. (Temp H 74/124 L 68/21, Wind — 5–10 mph E.)

Dry/Day

01–20

The enormous sun dominates the sky, but a swift breeze keeps the temperature to a cooler level. Spray pulled up from the many waves, capped in white froth and thrown across the deck. The horizon is marked with a large bank of gray clouds, promising rain in the next day or two. (Temp H 78/26 L 70/22, Wind — 30–35 mph.)

21–40

The sky is clear, dotted with numerous small unimposing puffs of cloud. A solid wind blows, determined to cart items away in its embrace. The sun, high overhead, seems a greater distance than usual given the lack of heat generated. Abundant waves run to the horizon, making up for size with numbers. Churned to a gray-green, only a few feet under the surface can be seen with any clarity; another indicator of the weak sun. (Temp H 76/25 L 69/21, Wind — 25–30 mph.)

41–60

A crystal clear sky magnifies the sun, directing its heat against the ship and her crew. The wind puffs slowly, not enough to extinguish a candle let alone cool the flesh of those caught in the sun's angry flare. Waves move across the water like a herd, trying to carry the ship along in their wake, fighting the vessel should it try to turn away. The spray carries over the rail into the faces of those on deck, quickly drying to leave traces of powdered salt. (Temp H 82/29 L 74/24, Wind — 5–10 mph. Sun stroke in 3d8 rounds unless properly attired for the sun. Characters on deck take a –1 penalty to Wisdom (Perception) checks that rely on sight and Constitution saving throws made to maintain concentration on a spell.)

61–80

Sun and gray clouds do battle overhead for supremacy, sometimes plunging the water into a dark twilight or bright daylight. Numerous waves, about the size of a man, run the length of the water as far as the eye can see, all topped with a cone of white froth. The wind picks this froth from each and carries it along, coating all surfaces. This cooling spray makes the trip enjoyable for most on board, even in the shade. The rigging and sails labour, flapping in the breeze, occasionally dropping additional sprays to the deck, glinting like jewels in the periodic sun. (Temp H 75/25 L 67/20, Wind — 18–20 mph N.)

81–00

The sky resembles a great slab of granite from horizon to horizon, plunging the day into twilight. The absence of wind allows the sails and rigging to hang listless, like robes on a wizard. The water is unmarked, calm for many miles around the ship, waves visible in the far distance. Pressure seems to build, raising the temperature over several hours to a more comfortable level. (Temp H 71/22 L 66/19, Wind — 5–10 mph. Reroll in 4 game hours on the wet–day chart for the approaching storm.)

Dry/Night

01–20

Clear sky provides a view of the numerous constellations and guiding stars. Wind gusts from the West to create a flapping staccato to match the waves breaking on the hull of the ship. White-capped waves, visible in the moonlight, reach for the sailors on board, topping 7–8 feet. A slight mist can be felt in the wind; consequently, all surfaces are slick and shiny with moisture. (Temp H 78/26 L 63/18, Wind — 15–25 mph. Characters on deck take a –1 penalty to Strength (Athletics) checks involving climbing and Wisdom (Perception) checks that rely on hearing.)

21–40

Clear ebony night overhead provides astronomers and navigators a fine view of the stars and planets. A gentle wind blows from the South, flapping the sail and nettings. Small waves lap against the side of the boat like a heartbeat; small white caps stand out stark against the black background of the water and night sky. (Temp H 80/28 L 66/19, Wind — 15–25 mph.)

41–60

An overcast sky blocks the view of all but the brightest stars and planets. Some navigation can still be done by experienced sailors. A breeze comes and goes, proving to be a fickle asset for the sails on the ship, waves playing tag rock the ship gently back and forth. (Temp H 79/27 L 75/24, Wind — 5–10 mph.)

61–80

Numerous stars turn the onyx sky into a twilight gray, offsetting the jet black of the calm water. A steady, soft wind blows, propelling the ship along on its way. The sound of the surf being cut by the hull is seemingly alone, periodically joined by the creak of the rigging and the soft voice of a sailor. (Temp H 70/22 L 66/19, Wind — 10–15 mph. Characters proficient in the use of navigator's tools have advantage on Wisdom (Survival) checks made to use those tools.)

81–00

A severe wind blows, threatening to rip the sail from the mast, propelling the vessel over the waves like a plaything. Thick ribbons of cloud race overhead like gray gashes in the constellations. Many large waves run the length of the vision, occasionally growing to such a large size (45 feet) they threaten to topple the ship like flotsam. (Temp H 69/21 L 61/17, Wind — 15–25 mph. Characters on deck take a –1 penalty to Strength (Athletics) checks involving climbing and Constitution saving throws made to maintain concentration on a spell.)

ARCTIC

Wind chill is a real concern when the temperature drops below 32° F. Exposure to the wind risks frostbite for flesh. The effective temperature, for purposes of calculating potential harm caused by extreme cold, can be found in the Wind Chill Table.

RAIN/DAY

01–20	White gray clouds span from horizon to horizon, periodic deluges of snow drop upon the water and the ship. The deck is quickly covered in a blanket of white snow, making progress slow around the ship. Finding equipment is difficult for the inexperienced sailor, boxes and barrels becoming nondescript objects in the snow. The wind moves the snow in various directions as it descends, moving the sails to half full with their strongest force. (Temp H 29/–2 L 21/–6, Wind — 10–15 mph. All exposed areas of the ship count as difficult terrain. Characters on deck take a –1 penalty to Dexterity checks involving fine motor skills.)
21–40	Sleet drops like sheets of needles upon sailors in the open. The wind drives the sleet almost horizontally across the waves. Large mountains of water move across the area, threatening to bash the vessel into submission. The steel gray sky rolls like the underside of a surf, promising many hours of attack. The rigging creaks and sails moan ominously in the barrage of the storm. Movement along the deck is perilous at best; those in the upper reaches of the vessel cling for their lives. (Temp H 23/–5 L 20/–4, Wind — 35–40 mph. Characters moving on deck must succeed on a DC 10 Dexterity (Acrobatics) check each round or be knocked prone and pushed 10 feet in a random direction. All exposed areas of the ship are lightly obscured and count as difficult terrain. Characters on deck also have disadvantage on Wisdom (Perception) checks that rely on hearing and Constitution saving throws made to maintain concentration on a spell, and take a –1 penalty to Dexterity checks involving fine motor skills and Strength (Athletics) checks involving climbing.)
41–60	Freezing mist falls like a cloud landing on the water. Wind is present but too weak to fill sails. Ice flows move on the sunken currents, dancing around the ship at great distances. Waves are subdued, seemingly moving in numerous directions with no pattern discernable. Ice forms on most surfaces with extended exposure, sails and rigging becoming rigid and hazardous with each passing hour. (Temp H 28/–3 L 21/–6 Wind — 0–5 mph. Characters moving on deck must succeed on a DC 6 Dexterity (Acrobatics) check each round or be knocked prone. All exposed areas of the ship are lightly obscured and count as difficult terrain. Characters on deck also take a –1 penalty to Wisdom (Perception) checks that rely on hearing.)
61–80	Crimson lightning tears through the clouds, streaking by overhead, and waves lift like cliffs (6–15 feet) around the vessel. Rain alternates from side-to-side and straight down with the force of a hammer blow. Ice coats all exposed surfaces in minutes, creating treacherous areas on the ship and rigging. The sails snap and crack as it fills with the wind, snow, and ice, dropping chunks of ice to the deck below. Periodically the sky lights up with a lightning blast nearby painting everything with in shades of white and black, all other times the charcoal sky and water bestow a sense of isolation. (Temp H 31/0 L 23/–4, Wind — 50–55 mph. Characters moving on deck must succeed on a DC 10 Dexterity (Acrobatics) check each round or be knocked prone and pushed 10 feet in a random direction. All exposed areas of the ship are lightly obscured and count as difficult terrain. Characters on deck also have disadvantage on Wisdom (Perception) checks that rely on hearing and take a –1 penalty to Dexterity saving throws. 10% chances of course change required for ice formation in path of ship.)
81–00	The sky carries a darker shade than normal, clouds so thick they block out all trace of light. Hail is propelled horizontally with the wind, hitting like daggers and needles, reducing vision to mere feet around each person. Ice forms on all surfaces, making passage difficult on deck. Winds blow loose objects and people unprepared for its force off course. Waves 15–30 feet high assault the ship, blowing over the rail and soaking sailors with its frigid embrace. (Temp H 33/1 L 27/–2, Wind — 35–40 mph. Characters moving on deck must succeed on a DC 12 Dexterity (Acrobatics) check each round or be knocked prone and pushed 10 feet in a random direction. All exposed areas of the ship count as difficult terrain. Characters on deck also have disadvantage on Dexterity checks involving fine motor skills, Strength (Athletics) checks involving climbing, Wisdom (Perception) checks that rely on hearing, and Constitution saving throws made to maintain concentration on a spell.)

RAIN/NIGHT

01–20	Lightning-rippled clouds streak by overhead. Waves lift like cliffs (6–15 feet) around the vessel as rain attacks side-to-side and straight down with the force of a hammer blow. Ice coats all exposed surfaces quickly, creating treacherous areas on the ship and rigging. The sails, resounding with snaps and cracks as it fills with the wind, snow, and ice, dropping chunks of ice to the deck below. Periodically the sky lights up with a violet or crimson lightning blast nearby, painting everything with shades of white; all other times, the charcoal sky and water bestow a sense of isolation. (Temp H 28/–2 L 21/–6, Wind — 25–35 mph. Characters moving on deck must succeed on a DC 10 Dexterity (Acrobatics) check each round or be knocked prone and pushed 5 feet in a random direction. All exposed areas of the ship count as difficult terrain. Characters on deck also have disadvantage on Wisdom (Perception) checks that rely on hearing or sight, and take a –1 penalty to Dexterity saving throws. 10% chance of course change required for ice formation in path of ship.)
21–40	Icy mist falls like a cloud, landing on the water. Wind is present but too weak to fill sails. Ice flows move on the sunken currents, dancing around the ship like predators at great distances. Waves are subdued, seemingly moving in numerous directions, no pattern discernable. Ice forms on most surfaces with extended exposure, sails and rigging becoming rigid and hazardous with each passing hour. (Temp H 30/–1 L 23/–5, Wind — 0–5 mph. Characters moving on deck must succeed on a DC 8 Dexterity (Acrobatics) check each round or be knocked prone. All exposed areas of the ship are lightly obscured and count as difficult terrain. Characters on deck also take a –1 penalty to Wisdom (Perception) checks that rely on hearing.)
41–60	The night sky carries a shade darker than normal, clouds so thick they block out all trace of light. Rain is propelled horizontally with the wind, hitting like daggers and needles, reducing vision to mere feet around each person. Ice forms on all surfaces, making passage dangerous on deck and in the lines above. Winds blow loose objects and people unprepared for its force off course. Waves 15–30 feet high assault the ship, blowing over the rail and soaking sailors with its frigid embrace. (Temp H 33/1 L 23/–5, Wind — 27–35 mph. Characters moving on deck must succeed on a DC 12 Dexterity (Acrobatics) check each round or be knocked prone and pushed 10 feet in a random direction. All exposed areas of the ship are heavily obscured and count as difficult terrain. Characters on deck also have disadvantage on Dexterity checks involving fine motor skills, Strength (Athletics) checks involving climbing, Wisdom (Perception) checks that rely on hearing, and Constitution saving throws made to maintain concentration on a spell.)

61–80 Constant sub-zero drizzle settles on all surfaces, turning the dark night into a dark gray, reducing vision to nearly non-existent. Frigid temperatures freeze the moisture within minutes on every surface. Travel across deck is difficult but manageable to those familiar with surroundings. Sound is subdued with the ice pellets, adding a muffling effect to conversations. Waves are unseen but can be felt hitting the ship every few seconds, occasionally bathing the deck with its spray, a testament to its height of several feet. (Temp H 28/–2 L 21/–6, Wind — 5–10 mph. Characters moving on deck must succeed on a DC 12 Dexterity (Acrobatics) check each round or be knocked prone and pushed 10 feet in a random direction. All exposed areas of the ship are heavily obscured and count as difficult terrain. Characters on deck also take a –1 penalty to Wisdom (Perception) checks that rely on hearing.)

81–00 Large thick flakes drop around the ship, landing softly on the water before melting. Equipment and decking are quickly covered in a thick blanket of white snow. Waves roll languidly, topping 6 feet in height but not steep enough to make more than an exaggerated rocking motion. A light wind blows carrying the flakes on the air currents, visible in the occasional moonlight. (Temp H 33/1 L 26/–3, Wind — 5–10 mph. Characters moving on deck must succeed on a DC 8 Dexterity (Acrobatics) check each round or be knocked prone. All exposed areas of the ship are lightly obscured and count as difficult terrain.)

DRY/DAY

01–20 Clear blue sky overhead provides ample room for the bright sun to shine. Wind gusts from the North East, flapping the sail and nettings. White-capped waves, topping 7–8 feet high, seem to be pushing large chunks of ice along in their grasp. (Temp H 30/–1 L –26–3, Wind — 10–15 mph. Those working while facing the sun must succeed on a DC 10 Constitution saving throw or be blinded for 1d4 hours. Characters with a natural sensitivity to light have disadvantage on this saving throw. 10% chance of course changed required for ice flow in path of ship.)

21–40 Sun and gray clouds do battle overhead for power, sometimes plunging the water into a dark twilight or bright daylight. Numerous waves, about the size of a man, run the length of the water as far as the eye can see, all topped with a cone of blue-white froth. The wind picks this froth from each and carries it along, freezing it to any surface it covers. The rigging and sails labour under the extra weight of the ice, glinting like jewels in the periodic sun. (Temp H 29/–2 L 21/–6, Wind — 20–25 mph. Characters moving on deck must succeed on a DC 10 Dexterity (Acrobatics) check each round or be knocked prone. All exposed areas of the ship count as difficult terrain. Characters on deck take a –1 penalty to Dexterity saving throws, Strength (Athletics) checks involving climbing, and Wisdom (Perception) checks that rely on sight. 12% chance of course change required for ice flow in path of ship.)

41–60 A wide bank of clouds have blotted out the sun; consequently, the diluted light colors the world in tints of twilight gray. The absence of wind allows the sails and rigging to hang listless, like cloth in a shop window. The water is unmarked, calm for many miles around the ship, waves visible in the far distance. Pressure seems to build, raising the temperature over several hours to a more comfortable level. Ice bergs in the distance hold steady like islands. (Temp H 32/0 L 28/–2, Wind — 0–5 mph. Experienced sailors know a storm is coming. Reroll on Arctic day–rain chart in 1d4 hours for result. 2% chance of course change for ice bergs in path of ship.)

61–80 Streamers of billowy clouds race overhead in the wind. Large waves buffet the ship, attempting to carry it along with them. Wind assaults the vessel hard from the west, never wavering or letting up. Tacking into the wind seems impossible from its vicious force while tacking with the wind runs a risk of never getting control of the ship back. (Temp H 23/–5 L 18/–8, Wind — 25–35 mph. Characters on deck take a –1 penalty to Dexterity checks and saving throws.)

81–00 The air burns with the wind chill crusting ice all over the ship, the sun adding no aid to the frigid temperature. Clouds are non-existent in the sky, collecting only on the horizons. While filling the sails, the wind steals the breath from those on deck freezing exposed flesh in minutes. (Temp H 22/–5 L 15/–10, Wind — 35–40 mph. Characters moving on deck must succeed on a DC 6 Dexterity (Acrobatics) check each round or be knocked prone. All exposed areas of the ship count as difficult terrain. Characters on deck take a –1 penalty to Dexterity checks involving fine motor skills.)

DRY/NIGHT

01–20 Clear ebony sky overhead provides astronomers and navigators a fine view of the stars and planets. A gentle wind blows from the South, flapping the sail and nettings. Small waves lap against the side of the boat like a heartbeat; ice bergs stand out stark white against the black background of the water and night sky. (Temp H 32/0 L 25/–4, Wind — 5–10 mph. 2% chance of course changes required for ice flow in path of ship.)

21–40 Large clouds move overhead, blocking the stars and moon with their bulk. The ship rolls gently on the waves as it rides through the water. Occasionally larger waves provide a small drop for the vessel as it is carried over the lip of the wave. The strong wind takes the ship along with it, filling the sails and pulling at cloaks of those on board. (Temp H 29/–2 L 24/–4, Wind — 10–15 mph. Characters on deck take a –1 penalty to Wisdom (Perception) checks that rely on hearing.)

41–60 Clouds block all stars and only hint at the location of the moon, adding a claustrophobic feel to the trip. The absence of wind allows the sails and rigging to hang listless, like cloth in a shop window. The ebony water ripples in the soft breeze, white caps standing out like glowing embers. (Temp H 31/0 L 26/–3, Wind — 0–5 mph. 2% chance of course change for ice bergs in path of ship).

61–80 Partial clouds covers sections of the sky, seemingly unmoving. Large waves buffet the ship, attempting to carry it along with them. Wind assaults the vessel hard from the west, never wavering or letting up. Travel during the night at full sail run double risk of collision with ice. (Temp H 30/–1 L 22/–5, Wind — 25–35 mph. Characters on deck take a –1 penalty to Dexterity checks and saving throws. 15% chance of course change for ice).

81–00 Wisps of cloud move across the sky, sometimes blocking the stars. The brightness of the visible stars and moon provides ample light to maneuver around the ship and perform most tasks. The ever-present wind provides enough force to keep the ship moving at optimum speed. The absence of spray from the calm waters allows for equipment to dry. (Temp H 30/–1 L 26/–3, Wind — 10–15 mph.)

EQUATORIAL

Within the Equatorial region humidity is an issue for temperature measurement. Reference to the Humidity Table will bring about a more realistic gauge for temperature; consequently, the effects of heat upon those traveling the waves should be watched closely.

RAIN/DAY

01–20	A strong wind blows, adding a texture to the warm rain falling. The occasional rain mists on the warm deck, adding more humidity to the air. A sticky aspect of the air grows throughout the day as the humidity rises. Bright sun reflects off all wet and shiny surfaces, creating a glare from all directions. Waves are large in width but not in height, rocking the ship with their passage. (Temp H 79/27 L 65/19, Wind — 10–15 mph. Characters on deck take a –1 penalty to Constitution saving throws made to maintain concentration on a spell.)
21–40	Heavy rain pummels the ship and those on board, drenching all equipment and passengers. The waves are sedated, rarely topping 8 feet, seemingly held down with the impact of the rain. The sun tries to pierce the cloud cover with its intense glare, only succeeding in raising the temperature. Wind is non-existent hammered to submission by the heavy rain. (Temp H 75/24 L 71/22, Wind — 0–5 mph.)
41–60	Seemingly in rhythm with the lapping waves, periodic rain drops in vast amounts, quickly soaking all surfaces and washing away loose items. Between rainfalls, the sun attempts to burn away the moisture with blistering heat, never quite successful and so leaving all with a heaviness of moisture. Waves roll languidly, topping 6 feet in height but not steep enough to make more than an exaggerated rocking motion. The wind blows merrily, billowing out the sails of the ship and propelling the vessel over the large waves. (Temp H 79/27 L 71/22, Wind — 20–25 mph. Characters moving on deck during a deluge must succeed on a DC 8 Dexterity (Acrobatics) check each round or be knocked prone and pushed 5 feet in a random direction. All exposed areas of the ship count as difficult terrain.)
61–80	A drizzle of rain, sporadically hard and light, falls throughout the day. All surfaces is thoroughly soaked and heavy with water. The warmth of the occasional sun is diminished slightly by the cool rain, keeping it tolerable for all involved. The wind blows constantly, keeping the sails full but not pushing the limit of its capabilities. (Temp H 81/28 L 77/26, Wind — 25–30 mph.)
81–00	Heavy rain from unseen clouds pummels the ship and those on deck. Waves like great green battering rams smashing against the ship every minute. The overhead clouds have descended to a point where it seems the ship is in a large chamber. Wind hurtles against the vessel and its sail, trying to rip it free from the mast and rigging. All loose items are tossed around the decking creating hazards for those on deck. (Temp H 80/27 L 74/24, Wind — 25–30 mph. Characters moving on deck must succeed on a DC 10 Dexterity (Acrobatics) check each round or be knocked prone and pushed 5 feet in a random direction. All exposed areas of the ship count as difficult terrain. Characters on deck also have disadvantage on Strength (Athletics) checks involving climbing and take a –1 penalty to Constitution saving throws made to maintain concentration on a spell.)

RAIN/NIGHT

01–20	The humidity of the night is made comfortable by the patter of rain upon the deck. The coolness of the rain seems to steal some of the thickness in the air. The thin clouds mask the presence of the stars but leave a large halo where the moon tries to shine. The waves crash against the hull as if trying to keep the ship from reaching its goal. The bounce of the ship as it passes over the waves keeps all but the soundest sleepers awake. (Temp H 80/27 L 70/22, Wind — 0–5 mph.)
21–40	Heavy rain from ebony clouds press down on the ship and those on deck. Waves can be seen in the dark like great gray-green boulders smashing against the ship every minute. The overhead clouds have descended to a point where it seems the ship is in a large chamber. Wind hurtles against the vessel and its sail, trying to rip it from the mast and rigging. All loose items and small creatures on deck vie for attention from the crashing waves or the blustery wind. (Temp H 77/26 L 62/17, Wind — 20–25 mph. Characters moving on deck must succeed on a DC 10 Dexterity (Acrobatics) check each round or be knocked prone. All exposed areas of the ship are lightly obscured and count as difficult terrain. Characters on deck also have disadvantage on Strength (Athletics) checks involving climbing and Wisdom (Perception) checks that rely on hearing, and take a –1 penalty to Constitution saving throws made to maintain concentration on a spell.)
41–60	Seemingly in rhythm with the lapping waves, periodic rain drops in vast amounts, quickly soaking all surfaces and washing away loose materials. Waves roll languidly, topping 6 feet in height but not steep enough to make more than an exaggerated rocking motion. A light wind blows carrying a humid mist from the still warm water, visible in the intermittent moonlight. (Temp H 76/25 L 71/22, Wind — 5–10 mph. Characters moving on deck must succeed on a DC 6 Dexterity (Acrobatics) check each round or be knocked prone. All exposed areas of the ship are lightly obscured and count as difficult terrain.)
61–80	A drizzle of rain, sometimes hard and sometimes light, falls continuously throughout during the nighttime hours. All surfaces are thoroughly soaked and heavy with water. The warmth of the day rapidly disappears replaced with the humidity of the still evaporating water around the ship. The waves are smaller than normal and works with the rain to stay weak enough to be inconsequential. The wind blows constantly, keeping the sails full but not pushing the limit of its capabilities. (Temp H 80/27 L 78/26, Wind — 312–18 mph.)
81–00	A thrashing rain accompanies hurricane force winds. In the distance amid lightning flashes water spouts can be seen reaching for the sky. Waves, the size of small mountains, rise above the vessel giving the ship a wide span of view when atop a wave, and a sense of claustrophobia when in a gully. (Temp H 79/27 L 71/22, Wind — 80–85 mph. Characters moving on deck must succeed on a DC 14 Dexterity (Acrobatics) check each round or be knocked prone and pushed 15 feet in a random direction. All exposed areas of the ship are lightly obscured and count as difficult terrain. Characters on deck also have disadvantage on Dexterity checks and saving throws, Strength (Athletics) checks involving climbing, and Constitution saving throws made to maintain concentration on a spell.)

DRY/DAY

01–20	The incessant sun is offset by a breeze, keeping the temperature to a seemingly more moderate level. Spray flies up in the wind, fed by the many white-capped waves sprinting past the ship. The horizon is marked with a large bank of gray clouds, promising rain in the next day or two. The humidity rises throughout the day, adding a weight to the sun which saps the strength of those not acquainted with the Equatorial waters. (Temp H 81/28 L 75/24, Wind — 20–25 mph.)
21–40	Clouds run amok along the sky, occasionally blocking the sun and its warmth. The wind seemingly growls as it tears across the water at the ship. The sail quivers, trying to keep the wind from escaping. Waves rise up and crash against the hull of the ship, each impact like a bludgeon from nature itself. (Temp H 77/26 L 69/21, Wind — 25–35 mph. Characters on deck have disadvantage on Strength (Athletics) checks involving climbing and take a –1 penalty to Dexterity saving throws and Wisdom (Perception) checks that rely on hearing.)

41–60	A crystal clear sky magnifies the sun, aiming its heat against the ship and her crew. The wind puffs slowly, not enough to cool the flesh of those in the open or ruffle the sails. Waves move across the water like a herd, trying to carry the ship along in their wake, fighting the vessel should it try to turn away. The spray carries over the rail into the faces of those on deck, quickly drying to leave powdered salt. (Temp H 77/26 L 65/19, Wind — 0–5 mph. Characters on deck take a –1 penalty to Strength checks and Constitution saving throws made to maintain concentration on a spell.)
61–80	The thick clouds overhead threaten to release their load, moisture currently released in the form of a thick palpable air. While no rain has fallen during the day, all surfaces are beaded with sweat and spray from the humidity-laced air. The moderate wind moves both the ship and the clouds, lifting the waves to heights of 10 feet, launching the spray into the air. The ship rolls with the impacts as it tips down one wave and up another, the prow having difficulty cutting through the water. (Temp H 77/26 L 70/22, Wind — 25–30 mph.)
81–00	The sky is clear, dotted with the occasional cloud. A steady wind blows determined to cart items away in its embrace. The weak sun cannot raise the temperature, regardless of its steady glare. Abundant waves run to the horizon, making up for size with numbers. Churned to a gray-green only a few feet under the surface can be seen with any clarity; another indicator of the weak sun. (Temp H 75/25 L 64/18, Wind — 35–40 mph.)

Dry/Night

01–20	Clear sky provides a view of the numerous constellations and guiding stars. Wind gusts from the North East, creating a flapping staccato to match the waves breaking on the hull of the ship. White-capped waves, visible in the moonlight reach for the sailors on board, topping 7–8 feet. A slight mist can be felt in the wind; consequently, all surfaces are slick and shiny with moisture. (Temp H 75/25 L 61/17, Wind — 15–25 mph. Characters on deck take a –1 penalty to Strength (Athletics) checks involving climbing and Wisdom (Perception) checks that rely on hearing.)
21–40	Clouds of stone gray run from horizon to horizon, extinguishing the stars and moon from view. The absence of wind allows the sails and rigging to hang listless, like cloth in a shop window. The water is like unmarked, calm for many miles around the ship, waves visible in the far distance. Pressure seems to build, raising the temperature over several hours to just above a comfortable level. (Temp H 76/25 L 63/18, Wind — 0–5 mph. Experienced sailors know a storm is coming. Reroll on Equatorial day- rain chart in 1d4 hours for result.)
41–60	The cool of the night is identified by the daytime heat escaping the decking, misting the moisture collected through the daylight hours. Raising the humidity to an uncomfortable level, it deadens the night sounds of creaking riggings and lapping waves. Long trenches of waves roll the ship as it moves through them like long strides of a great beast. Occasional clouds plunge the world into darkness, allowing the moon and stars to peer through again in a few moments. (Temp H 74/24 L 69/21, Wind — 10–20 mph.)
61–80	Lines of clouds run the length of the night sky. The bright moon hides behind this occasional cover, sometimes plunging the world into a dark twilight or bright moonlight. Numerous waves, about the size of a man, run the length of the water as far as the eye can see, all topped with a cone of greenish white froth. The rigging and sails have rivulets of collected water which pools on the deck. Lines are heavy with water and deck boards are slick and shiny, sometimes reflecting the occasional sunlight. (Temp H 78/26 75/24, Wind — 20–25 mph. Characters on deck take a –1 penalty to Dexterity saving throws, Strength (Athletics) checks involving climbing, and Wisdom (Perception) checks that rely on sight.)

81–00	Clear ebony night overhead provides astronomers and navigators a fine view of the stars and planets. A gentle wind blows from the West, flapping the sail and nettings. Small waves lap against the side of the boat like a heartbeat; reflections of the moon on the waves stand out stark white against the black background of the water and night sky. (Temp H 79/27 L 67/20, Wind — 5–10 mph.)

Winter

Tropical

Rain/Day

01–20	A gentle breeze blows, adding a pleasant cooling to the warm rain falling. Large drops patter along the deck, quickly evaporating the rain and adding to the humidity. A sticky aspect of the air grows throughout the day as the humidity rises. Sunlight glints off the water like numerous smaller suns, blinding those not ready for the effect. Waves are large in width but not in height, rocking the ship with their passage. (Temp H 88/32 L 75/25, Wind — 10–15 mph. Characters on deck take a –1 penalty to Constitution saving throws made to maintain concentration on a spell.)
21–40	Steady rainfall descends upon the ship and those on board, quickly soaking all equipment and people. The waves are sedated, rarely topping 5 feet seemingly held down with the rain. The sun tries to pierce the cloud cover with its intense glare, only succeeding in raising the temperature. Wind is non-existent hammered to submission by the heavy rain (Temp H 83/29 L 78/26, Wind — 0–5 mph.)
41–60	Waves brush against the ship in counter point to the periodic rain, falling in vast amounts, quickly water logging everything. Between rainfalls the sun attempts to burn away the moisture with blistering heat. Waves roll, languidly topping 6 feet in height but not steep enough to make more than an exaggerated rocking motion. The wind blows merrily, billowing out the sails of the ship and propelling the vessel over the large waves. (Temp H 89/23 L 76/ 25, Wind — 20–25 mph. Characters moving on deck must succeed on a DC 6 Dexterity (Acrobatics) check each round or be knocked prone and pushed 10 feet in a random direction. All exposed areas of the ship count as difficult terrain.)
61–80	Rain falls continuously through the day, varying between hard and soft, keeping all items and surfaces heavy with moisture. The warmth of the occasional sun is diminished slightly by the cool rain, keeping it tolerable for all involved. The wind blows constantly, keeping the sails full but not pushing the limit of its capabilities. (Temp H 83/29 L 70/22, Wind — 25–30 mph.)
81–00	Blankets of water fall from the sky, creating a deluge which threatens to wash away all on deck. Waves like great gray-green boulders smashing against the ship every minute. The overhead clouds have descended to a point where it seems the ship is in a large chamber. Wind hurtles against the vessel and its sail, trying to rip it from the mast and rigging. (Temp H 87/32 L 74/24, Wind — 20–25 mph. Characters moving on deck must succeed on a DC 8 Dexterity (Acrobatics) check each round or be knocked prone and pushed 10 feet in a random direction. All exposed areas of the ship are lightly obscured and count as difficult terrain. Characters on deck also have disadvantage on Strength (Athletics) checks involving climbing and take a –1 penalty to Wisdom (Perception) checks that rely on hearing and Constitution saving throws made to maintain concentration on a spell.)

Rain/Night

01–20
While cool, the night remains uncomfortable due to the humidity carried on the air. The moon makes itself known through the clouds, illuminating a portion of the night sky to milky white. The waves crash against the hull as if trying to keep the ship from reaching its goal. The bounce of the ship as it passes over the waves keeps all but the soundest sleepers awake. (Temp H 86/31 L 79/27, Wind — 0–5 mph. Characters on deck take a –1 penalty to Constitution saving throws made to maintain concentration on a spell.)

21–40
Heavy rain from substantial clouds pummel the ship and those on deck. Waves can be seen in the dark like great gray-green boulders smashing against the ship every minute. The overhead clouds have descended to a point where it seems the ship is in a large chamber. Wind hurtles against the vessel and its sail, trying to rip it from the mast and rigging. All loose items and small creatures on deck vie for attention from the crashing waves or the blustery wind. (Temp H 85/30 L 79/27, Wind — 50–55 mph. Characters moving on deck must succeed on a DC 6 Dexterity (Acrobatics) check each round or be knocked prone. All exposed areas of the ship are lightly obscured and count as difficult terrain. Characters on deck also have disadvantage on Strength (Athletics) checks involving climbing and Wisdom (Perception) checks that rely on hearing, and take a –1 penalty to Constitution saving throws made to maintain concentration on a spell.)

41–60
Seemingly in rhythm with the lapping waves, periodic rain drops in vast amounts, quickly soaking all surfaces and washing away loose items. Waves roll languidly, topping 6 feet in height but not steep enough to make more than an exaggerated rocking motion. A light wind blows carrying mist from the still warm water, visible in the occasional moonlight. (Temp H 87/31 L 77/26, Wind — 5–10 mph. All exposed areas of the ship are lightly obscured. Characters on deck take a –1 penalty to Strength (Athletics) checks involving climbing.)

61–80
A drizzle of rain falls endlessly throughout during the nighttime hours. All surfaces are thoroughly soaked and heavy with water. The warmth of the day rapidly disappears replaced with the humidity of the still evaporating water around the ship. Waves are present but pose no real threat to the direction of the ship or her course. The wind blows constantly, keeping the sails full but not pushing the limit of its capabilities. (Temp H 83/29 L 77/26, Wind — 12–18 mph.)

81–00
A constant rain falls from gray clouds overhead keeping all within it thoroughly soaked. The wind propels the ship slowly, seemingly held back by the rain, over the large hillock shaped waves. Occasional lightning flashes illuminate the depth of the rain, looking like iron bars for as far as the eye can see, peppering the water. (Temp H 79/27 L 71/22, Wind — 5–10 mph. All exposed areas of the ship are lightly obscured. Characters on deck take a –1 penalty to Dexterity saving throws, Strength (Athletics) checks involving climbing and Wisdom (Perception) checks that rely on sight.)

Dry/Day

01–20
The large sun dominates the sky but a swift breeze keeps the temperature to a more moderate level. Spray pulled up from the many waves, capped in white froth. The horizon is marked with a large bank of gray clouds promising rain in the next day or two. (Temp H 85/30 L 72/23, Wind — 20–25 mph.)

21–40
Clouds run riot along the sky, occasionally blocking the sun and its warmth. The wind seemingly growls as it tears across the water at the ship. The sail quivers trying to keep the wind from escaping. Waves rise up and crash against the hull of the ship each impact like a bludgeon from nature itself. (Temp H 86/31 L 75/ 25, Wind — 25–35 mph. Characters on deck have disadvantage on Strength (Athletics) checks involving climbing and take a –1 penalty to Wisdom (Perception) checks that rely on hearing.)

41–60
A crystal clear sky magnifies the sun directing its heat against the ship and her crew. The wind puffs slowly, not enough to extinguish a candle let alone cool the flesh of those in the open. Waves move across the water like a herd, trying to carry the ship along in their wake, fighting the vessel should it try to turn away. The spray carries over the rail into the faces of those on deck, quickly drying to leave powdered salt. (Temp H 84/29 L 77/26, Wind — 0–5 mph.)

61–80
The thick clouds overhead threaten to release their burden but maintain their hold for now. The moderate wind moves both the ship and the clouds, lifting the waves to heights of 10 feet, launching the spray into the air. The ship rolls with the impacts as it tips down one wave and up another, the prow having difficulty cutting through the water. (Temp H 89/32 L 82/29, Wind — 25–30 mph.)

81–00
The sky is clear, dotted with numerous small mediocre puffs of cloud. A steady wind blows determined to cart items away in its embrace. The sun, high overhead seems a greater distance than usual given the lack of heat generated. Abundant waves run to the horizon, making up for size with numbers. Churned to a gray green only a few feet under the surface can be seen with any clarity; another indicator of the weak sun. (Temp H 88/32 L 80/28, Wind — 20–25 mph.)

Dry/Night

01–20
Clear sky provides a view of the innumerous constellations and guiding stars. Wind gusts from the South creating a flapping staccato to match the waves breaking on the hull of the ship. White-capped waves, visible in the moonlight reach for the sailors on board, topping 10 feet. A slight mist can be felt in the wind; consequently, all surfaces are slick and shiny with moisture. (Temp H 87/31 L 81/28, Wind — 30–35 mph. Characters on deck take a –1 penalty to Strength (Athletics) checks involving climbing and Wisdom (Perception) checks that rely on hearing.)

21–40
Clouds of dull steel run from horizon to horizon, extinguishing the stars and moon from view. The lack of wind allows the sails and rigging to hang listless, like cloth in a shop window. The water is unmarked, tranquil for many miles around the ship, waves visible in the far distance. Pressure seems to build, raising the temperature over several hours to just above a comfortable level. (Temp H 86/31 L 80/28, Wind — 0–5 mph. Experienced sailors know a storm is coming. Reroll on Tropical day-rain chart in 1d4 hours for result.)

41–60
The cool of the night is acknowledged by the daytime heat escaping the decking, misting the moisture collected through the daylight hours. Raising the humidity to an uncomfortable level it deadens the night sounds of creaking riggings and lapping waves. Troughs of water roll the ship as it moves through them like long strides of a great beast. Occasional clouds steal the minimal light, allowing the moon and stars to pear through again in a few moments. (Temp H 90/33 L 84/29, Wind — 10–20 mph.)

61–80
The clouds battle with the moon overhead for supremacy, plunging the world into pitch dark or muted twilight. Numerous waves, about the size of a man run the length of the water as far as the eye can see, all topped with a cone of greenish white froth. The rigging and sails have rivulets of collected water which pools on the deck. Lines are heavy with water and deck boards are slick and shiny, sometimes reflecting the occasional moonlight. (Temp H 83/29 L 74/24, Wind — 20–25 mph. Characters on deck take a –1 penalty to Dexterity saving throws, Strength (Athletics) checks involving climbing, and Wisdom (Perception) checks that rely on sight.)

81–00
Clear ebony night overhead provides astronomers and navigators a fine view of the stars and planets. A gentle wind blows from the West flapping the sail and nettings. Small waves lap against the side of the boat like a heartbeat, reflections of the moon on the waves stand out stark white against the black background of the water and night sky. (Temp H 83/29 L 78/26, Wind — 10–15 mph.)

Temperate

Rain/Day

01–20 A gentle breeze blows, adding a slight chill to the damp air. Large drops patter along the deck, occasionally warmed by the periodic sun and quickly evaporated. Gray white clouds fill the sky from horizon to horizon predicting a constant rainfall. Waves are large in width but not in height, rocking the ship with their passage (Temp H 46/9 L 35/2, Wind — 5–10 mph.)

21–40 Rain from onyx clouds thrash the ship and those on unfortunate enough to be on deck. Waves like great gray-green behemoths smashing against the ship every few minutes. The overhead clouds have descended gathering the ship in its embrace. Wind hurtles against the vessel and its sail, trying to rip it from the mast and rigging. The clouds of mist streak by carried on the fierce wind presenting the illusion of even greater speed. All loose items on deck vie for attention from the crashing waves or the blustery wind. (Temp H 54/13 L 42/6, Wind — 55–60 mph. Characters moving on deck must succeed on a DC 6 Dexterity (Acrobatics) check each round or be knocked prone. All exposed areas of the ship are lightly obscured and count as difficult terrain. Characters on deck also have disadvantage on Strength (Athletics) checks involving climbing and Wisdom (Perception) checks that rely on hearing, and take a –1 penalty to Constitution saving throws made to maintain concentration on a spell.)

41–60 The sky carries a darker shade than normal, clouds so thick they block out all trace of light. Rain is propelled horizontally with the wind, hitting like daggers and needles, reducing vision to mere feet around each person. Winds blow loose objects and people unprepared for its force off course. Waves 15–30 feet high assault the ship, blowing over the rail and soaking sailors with its frigid embrace. (Temp H 44/8 L 37/3, Wind — 40–45 mph NE. Characters moving on deck must succeed on a DC 8 Dexterity (Acrobatics) check each round or be knocked prone and pushed 5 feet in a random direction. All exposed areas of the ship are lightly obscured and count as difficult terrain. Characters on deck also have disadvantage on Dexterity checks involving fine motor skills, Wisdom (Perception) checks that rely on hearing, and Constitution saving throws made to maintain concentration on a spell.)

61–80 A constant rain falls from gray clouds overhead keeping all within it thoroughly soaked. The wind propels the ship slowly, seemingly held back by the rain, over the large hillock shaped waves. Occasional lightning flashes illuminate the depth of the rain, looking like iron bars for as far as the eye can see, peppering the water. (Temp H 50/11 L 40/5, Wind — 5–10 mph NE. All exposed areas of the ship are lightly obscured. Characters on deck take a –1 penalty to Dexterity saving throws and Strength (Athletics) checks involving climbing.)

81–00 A simple rain falls creating a constant drone of rain on the wooden deck. The wind is not strong enough to alter the vertical direction of the rain letting the sail hang like a soaked rag from the mast. The subtle waves rock the ship almost undetectably as they move by on unseen currents. Clouds looking like an inverted mountain range press down upon the ship and crew. (Temp H 44/8 L 33/1, Wind — 10–15 mph.)

Rain/Night

01–20 Clouds brimming with lightning streak by overhead as waves lift like cliffs (6–15 feet) around the vessel. Rain alternates from side to side and straight down with the force of a hammer blow. Rivers of water course around the deck from the rain and waves creating treacherous footing for all on board. The sails snap and crack as it fills with the wind, dropping deluges of collected rain to the deck below. Periodically the sky lights up with a lightning blast nearby painting everything with in shades of white, blue and gray, all other times the charcoal sky and water bestow a sense of isolation. (Temp H 47/9 L 41/6, Wind — 20–25 mph. Characters moving on deck must succeed on a DC 10 Dexterity (Acrobatics) check each round or be knocked prone and pushed 5 feet in a random direction. All exposed areas of the ship are lightly obscured and count as difficult terrain. Characters on deck also have disadvantage on Dexterity checks involving fine motor skills, Strength (Athletics) checks involving climbing, and Constitution saving throws made to maintain concentration on a spell.)

21–40 A constant rain falls from gray clouds overhead keeping all within it thoroughly soaked. The wind propels the ship slowly, seemingly held back by the rain, over the large hillock shaped waves. Occasional lightning flashes illuminate the depth of the rain, looking like iron bars for as far as the eye can see, peppering the water. (Temp H 45/8 L 38/4, Wind — 5–10 mph. All exposed areas of the ship are lightly obscured. Characters on deck take a –1 penalty to Dexterity saving throws and Strength (Athletics) checks involving climbing.)

41–60 Thick rolling clouds erupt constantly with thunder and rain beating upon the wooden planks. The percussion of the rain is accented with the occasional spray of mountainous waves carried on the wind. Gusts of wind blow across the ship attempting to pull everything along in its wake. Sight is reduced to feet, distance eliminated with the thick sheets of rain. (Temp H 50/11 L 43/7, Wind — 15–20 mph. Characters moving on deck must succeed on a DC 8 Dexterity (Acrobatics) check each round or be knocked prone. All exposed areas of the ship are heavily obscured and count as difficult terrain. Characters on deck also have disadvantage on Dexterity saving throws, and take a –1 penalty to Dexterity checks involving fine motor skills and Constitution saving throws made to maintain concentration on a spell.)

61–80 Hurricane force rain and wind, the ship is tossed like a child's doll. Huge waves like mountains threaten to topple the vessel and launch the sailors into the unforgiving sea. Wind blows fiercely lifting all heavy objects not lashed down and propelling them around and off the ship. The sky and water are undistinguishable, erasing the horizon as both are steel gray. (Temp H 39/4 L 31/0, Wind — 75–80 mph NNW. Characters moving on deck must succeed on a DC 14 Dexterity (Acrobatics) check each round or be knocked prone and pushed 15 feet in a random direction. All exposed areas of the ship count as difficult terrain. Characters on deck also have disadvantage on Dexterity checks and saving throws, Strength (Athletics) checks involving climbing, and Constitution saving throws made to maintain concentration on a spell.)

81–00 A simple rain falls creating a constant drone of rain on the wooden deck. The wind is not strong enough to alter the vertical direction of the rain letting the sail hang like a soaked rag from the mast. The faint waves rock the ship almost indiscernibly as they move on underwater currents. Clouds looking like an inverted mountain range press down upon the ship and crew. Navigation can only be done through compass or landmarks. (Temp H 60/16 L 52/12, Wind — 5–10 mph E.)

Dry/Day

01–20 The large sun governs the sky but a swift breeze keeps the temperature to a cooler level. Spray pulled up from the many waves, capped in white froth and thrown across the deck. The horizon is marked with a large bank of gray clouds promising rain in the next day or two. (Temp H 56/14 L 44/8, Wind — 20–25 mph.)

21–40	The sky is clear, dotted with numerous small unimposing puffs of cloud. A steady wind blows determined to cart items away in its embrace. The sun, high overhead seems a greater distance than usual given the lack of heat generated. Abundant waves run to the horizon, making up for size with numbers. Churned to a gray-green only a few feet under the surface can be seen with any clarity; another indicator of the weak sun. (Temp H 58/15 L 49/10, Wind — 15–20 mph.)
41–60	A crystal clear sky magnifies the sun directing its heat against the ship and her crew. The wind puffs slowly, not enough to extinguish a candle let alone cool the flesh of those warmer than usual day. Waves move across the water like a herd, trying to carry the ship along in their wake, fighting the vessel should it try to turn away. The spray carries over the rail into the faces of those on deck, quickly drying to leave traces of powdered salt. (Temp H 60/16 L 52/12, Wind — 5–10 mph. Sun stroke in 3d8 rounds unless properly attired for the sun. Sunburn may be a risk. Characters on deck take a –1 penalty to Wisdom (Perception) checks that rely on sight and Constitution saving throws made to maintain concentration on a spell.)
61–80	Sun and gray clouds do battle overhead for dominance, sometimes plunging the water into a dark twilight or bright daylight. Numerous waves, about the size of a man run the length of the water as far as the eye can see, all topped with a cone of white froth. The wind picks this froth from each and carries it along and coats all surfaces. This cooling spray makes the trip enjoyable for most on board, even in the shade. The rigging and sails labour flap in the breeze, occasionally dropping additional sprays to the deck, glinting like jewels in the periodic sun. (Temp H 45/8 L 36/3, Wind — 18–20 mph N.)
81–00	Gray the colour of stone has been painted from horizon to horizon, plunging the day into twilight. The absence of wind allows the sails and rigging to hang listless, like cloth in a shop window. The water is unmarked, calm for many miles around the ship, waves visible in the far distance. Pressure seems to build, raising the temperature over several hours to a more comfortable level. (Temp H 55/13 L 46/9, Wind — 5–10 mph. Re-roll in 4 game hours on the wet-day chart for the approaching storm.)

Dry/Night

01–20	Clear sky provides a view of the numerous constellations and guiding stars. Wind gusts from the West, creating a flapping staccato to match the waves breaking on the hull of the ship. White capped waves, visible in the moonlight reach for the sailors on board, topping 7-8 feet. A slight mist can be felt in the wind; consequently, all surfaces are slick and shiny with moisture (Temp H 39/5 L 32/0, Wind — 15–25 mph. Characters on deck take a –1 penalty to Dexterity saving throws, Strength (Athletics) checks involving climbing, and Wisdom (Perception) checks that rely on hearing.)
21–40	Clear jet black night overhead provides astronomers and navigators a fine view of the stars and planets. A gentle wind blows from the South flapping the sail and nettings. Small waves lap against the side of the boat like a heartbeat; small white caps stand out stark against the black background of the water and night sky. (Temp H 58/15 L 44/8, Wind — 15–25 mph.)
41–60	An overcast sky blocks the view of all but the brightest stars and planets. Some navigation can still be done by experienced sailors. A breeze comes and goes, proving to be a fickle asset for the sails on the ship, waves playing tag rock the ship gently back and forth. (Temp H 49/10 L 43/7, Wind — 15–20 mph.)

61–80	Numerous stars turn the night sky into a twilight gray, offsetting the onyx of the calm water. A steady soft wind blows propelling the ship along on its way. The sound of the surf being cut by the hull is seemingly alone, periodically joined by the creak of the rigging and the soft voice of a sailor. (Temp H 55/13 L 44/8, Wind — 20–25 mph. Characters proficient in the use of navigator's tools have advantage on Wisdom (Survival) checks made to use those tools.)
81–00	A severe wind blows threatening to rip the sail from the mast, propelling the vessel over the waves like a toy. Thick ribbons of cloud race overhead like gray gashes in the constellations. Many large waves run the length of vision, occasionally growing to such a large size (45 feet) they threaten to topple the ship like flotsam. (Temp H 52/12 L 45/8, Wind 15–25 mph. Characters on deck take a –1 penalty to Strength (Athletics) checks involving climbing and Constitution saving throws made to maintain concentration on a spell.)

Arctic

Wind chill is a real concern when the temperature drops below 32° F. Exposure to the wind risks frostbite for flesh. The effective temperature, for purposes of calculating potential harm caused by extreme cold, can be found in the Wind Chill Table.

Rain/Day

01–20	White gray clouds span from horizon to horizon, periodic deluges of snow drop upon the water and the ship. The deck is quickly covered in a white blanket of snow making progress slow around the ship. Finding equipment is difficult for the inexperienced sailor, boxes and barrels becoming nondescript objects in the snow. The wind moves the snow in various directions as it descends, moving the sails to half full with their strongest force. (Temp H –15/–26 L –20/–29, Wind — 15–20 mph. All exposed areas of the ship count as difficult terrain.)
21–40	Sleet drops like sheets of needles upon sailors in the open. The wind drives the sleet almost horizontally across the waves. Large mountains of water move across the area threatening to bash the vessel into submission. The steel gray sky rolls like the underside of a surf promising many hours of attack. The rigging creaks and sails moan ominously in the barrage of the storm. Movement along the deck is perilous at best; those in the upper reaches of the vessel cling for their lives. (Temp H –12/–25 L –23/–30, Wind — 20–25 mph. Characters moving on deck must succeed on a DC 10 Dexterity (Acrobatics) check each round or be knocked prone. All exposed areas of the ship are lightly obscured and count as difficult terrain. Characters on deck also have disadvantage on Wisdom (Perception) checks that rely on hearing, and Constitution saving throws made to maintain concentration on a spell, and take a –1 penalty to Dexterity checks involving fine motor skills and Strength (Athletics) checks involving climbing.)
41–60	Freezing mist falls, landing like a blanket upon the water. Wind is present but too weak to fill sails. Ice flows move on the sunken currents, dancing around the ship at great distances. Waves are subdued, seemingly moving in numerous directions with no pattern discernable. Ice forms on most surfaces with extended exposure, sails and rigging becoming rigid and hazardous with each passing hour. (Temp H –14/–26 L –19/p–28, Wind — 0–5 mph. Characters moving on deck must succeed on a DC 6 Dexterity (Acrobatics) check each round or be knocked prone. All exposed areas of the ship are lightly obscured and count as difficult terrain.)

61–80 Clouds explode with lightning and thunder as waves lift like cliffs (6–15 feet) around the vessel. Rain alternates from side to side and straight down with the force of a hammer blow. Ice coats all exposed surfaces in minutes creating treacherous areas on the ship and rigging. The sails snap and crack as it fills with the wind, snow and ice, dropping chunks of ice to the deck below. Periodically the sky lights up with a lightning blast nearby painting everything with in shades of white and black, all other times the charcoal sky and water bestow a sense of isolation. (Temp H –16/–27 L –25/–31, Wind — 25–35 mph. Characters moving on deck must succeed on a DC 8 Dexterity (Acrobatics) check each round or be knocked prone. All exposed areas of the ship are lightly obscured and count as difficult terrain. Characters on deck also have disadvantage on Wisdom (Perception) checks that rely on hearing and take a –1 penalty to Dexterity saving throws. 10% chance of course change required for ice formation in path of ship.)

81–00 The sky carries a darker shade than normal, clouds so thick they block out all trace of light. Rain is propelled horizontally with the wind, hitting like daggers and needles reducing vision to mere feet around each person. Ice forms on all surfaces making passage difficult on deck. Winds blow loose objects and people unprepared for its force off course. Waves 15–30 feet high assault the ship, blowing over the rail and soaking sailors with its frigid embrace. (Temp: H -20/ -29 L -25/ -31 Wind 40- 45 mph. Characters moving on deck must succeed on a DC 12 Dexterity (Acrobatics) check each round or be knocked prone and pushed 5 feet in a random direction. All exposed areas of the ship are heaviliy obscured and count as difficult terrain. Characters on deck also have disadvantage on Dexterity checks involving fine motor skills, Strength (Athletics) checks involving climbing, Wisdom (Perception) checks that rely on hearing, and Constitution saving throws made to maintain concentration on a spell.)

Rain/Night

01–20 Bulbous clouds promise a tremendous storm front. Waves lift like cliffs (20–30 feet) around the vessel as rain attacks side-to-side and straight down with the force of a hammer blow. Ice coats all exposed surfaces in minutes, creating treacherous areas on the ship and rigging. The sails snap and crack as it fills with the wind, snow and ice, dropping chunks of ice to the deck below. Periodically the sky lights up with a lightning blast nearby painting everything with in shades of white, all other times the charcoal sky and water bestow a sense of isolation. (Temp H –17/–27 L –24/–31, Wind — 25–35 mph. Characters moving on deck must succeed on a DC 12 Dexterity (Acrobatics) check each round or be knocked prone and pushed 5 feet in a random direction. All exposed areas of the ship are lightly obscured and count as difficult terrain. Characters on deck also have disadvantage on Wisdom (Perception) checks that rely on hearing and take a –1 penalty to Dexterity saving throws. 10% chance of course change required for ice formation in path of ship.)

21–40 Freezing mist falls like a cloud landing on the water. Wind is present but too weak to fill sails. Ice flows move on the sunken currents, dancing around the ship at great distances. Waves are subdued, seemingly moving in numerous directions, no pattern discernable. Ice forms on most surfaces with extended exposure, sails and rigging becoming rigid and hazardous with each passing hour. (Temp H –18/–28 L –22/–30, Wind — 0–5 mph. Characters moving on deck must succeed on a DC 6 Dexterity (Acrobatics) check each round or be knocked prone. All exposed areas of the ship count as difficult terrain. Characters on deck also take a –1 penalty to Wisdom (Perception) checks that rely on sight.)

41–60 The night sky carries a shade darker than normal, clouds so thick they block out all trace of light. Rain is propelled horizontally with the wind, hitting like daggers and needles, reducing vision to mere feet around each person. Ice forms on all surfaces making passage dangerous on deck and in the lines above. Winds blow loose objects and people unprepared for its force off course. Waves 15–30 feet high assault the ship, blowing over the rail and soaking sailors with its frigid embrace. (Temp H –16/–27 L –18/–28, Wind — 40–45 mph. Characters moving on deck must succeed on a DC 12 Dexterity (Acrobatics) check each round or be knocked prone and pushed 10 feet in a random direction. All exposed areas of the ship are heavily obscured and count as difficult terrain. Characters on deck also have disadvantage on Dexterity checks involving fine motor skills, Strength (Athletics) checks involving climbing, Wisdom (Perception) checks that rely on hearing, and Constitution saving throws made to maintain concentration on a spell.)

61–80 Constant icy drizzle settles on all surfaces, turning the dark night into a dark gray, reducing vision to nearly non-existent. Frigid temperatures freeze the moisture within minutes on every surface. Travel across deck is difficult but manageable to those familiar with surroundings. Sound is subdued with the ice pellets, adding a muffling effect to conversations. Waves are unseen but can be felt hitting the ship every few seconds, occasionally bathing the deck with its spray, a testament to its height of several feet. (Temp H –15/–26 L –20/–29, Wind — 5–10 mph. Characters moving on deck must succeed on a DC 10 Dexterity (Acrobatics) check each round or be knocked prone and pushed 10 feet in a random direction. All exposed areas of the ship are lightly obscured and count as difficult terrain.)

81–00 Large thick flakes drop around the ship, landing softly on the water before melting. Equipment and decking are quickly covered in a thick blanket of white snow. Waves roll languidly, topping 6 feet in height but not steep enough to make more than an exaggerated rocking motion. A light wind blows carrying the flakes on the air currents, visible in the occasional moonlight. (Temp H –11/–24 L –19/–28, Wind — 5–10 mph. Characters moving on deck must succeed on a DC 6 Dexterity (Acrobatics) check each round or be knocked prone. All exposed areas of the ship are lightly obscured and count as difficult terrain.)

Dry/Day

01–20 Clear blue sky overhead provides ample room for the bright sun to shine. Wind gusts from the West, flapping the sail and nettings. White-capped waves, topping 7–8 feet high seem to be pushing large chunks of ice along in their grasp. (Temp H –12/–25 L –17/–27, Wind — 10–15 mph. Those working while facing the sun must succeed on a DC 10 Constitution saving throw or be blinded for 1d4 hours. Characters with a natural sensitivity to light have disadvantage on this saving throw. 10% chance of course changed required for ice flow in path of ship.)

21–40 Sun and gray clouds do battle overhead for power, sometimes plunging the water into a dark twilight or bright daylight. Numerous waves, about the size of a man, run the length of the water as far as the eye can see, all topped with a cone of white froth. The wind picks this froth from each and carries it along freezing it to any surface it covers. The rigging and sails labour under the extra weight of the ice, glinting like jewels in the periodic sun. (Temp H –16/–27 L –22/–30, Wind — 20–25 mph. Characters moving on deck must succeed on a DC 6 Dexterity (Acrobatics) check each round or be knocked prone. All exposed areas of the ship count as difficult terrain. Characters on deck also take a –1 penalty to Dexterity saving throws, Strength (Athletics) checks involving climbing, and Wisdom (Perception) checks that rely on sight. 12% chance of course change required for ice flow in path of ship.)

41–60	Gray the colour of stone has been painted from horizon to horizon, plunging the day into twilight. The absence of wind allows the sails and rigging to hang listless, like cloth in a shop window. The water is unmarked, calm for many miles around the ship, waves visible in the far distance. Pressure seems to build, raising the temperature over several hours to a more comfortable level. Ice bergs in the distance hold steady like islands. (Temp H –17/–27 L –26/–32, Wind — 0–5 mph. Experienced sailors know a storm is coming. Reroll on Arctic day–rain chart in 1d4 hours for result. 2% chance of course change for ice bergs in path of ship).
61–80	Streamers of billowy clouds race overhead in the wind. Large waves buffet the ship attempting to carry it along with them. Wind assaults the vessel hard from the west, never wavering or letting up. Tacking into the wind seems impossible from its vicious force while tacking with the wind runs a risk of never getting control of the ship back. (Temp H –19/–28 L –25/–31, Wind — 30–35 mph. Characters on windward side of deck take a –1 penalty to Dexterity checks and saving throws.)
81–00	The air burns with the wind chill crusting ice all over the ship, the sun adding no aid to the frigid temperature. Clouds are non-existent in the sky, collecting only on the horizons. While filling the sails, the wind steals the breath from those on deck freezing exposed flesh in minutes. (Temp H –18/–28 L –23/–30, Wind — 25–30 mph. Characters moving on deck must succeed on a DC 6 Dexterity (Acrobatics) check each round or be knocked prone. All exposed areas of the ship count as difficult terrain. Characters on deck take a –1 penalty to Dexterity checks involving fine motor skills and Strength (Athletics) checks involving climbing.)

DRY/NIGHT

01–20	Untouched sky overhead provides astronomers and navigators a fine view of the stars and planets. A gentle wind blows from the South, flapping the sail and nettings. Small waves lap against the side of the boat like a heartbeat, ice bergs stand out stark white against the black background of the water and night sky. (Temp H –20/–29 L –25/–32, Wind — 5–10 mph. 10% chance of course changes required for ice flow in path of ship.)
21–40	Large clouds move overhead, blocking the stars and moon with their bulk. The ship rolls gently on the waves as it rides through the water. Occasionally larger waves provide a small drop for the vessel as it is carried over the lip of the wave. The strong wind takes the ship along with it, filling the sails and pulling at cloaks of those on board. (Temp H –13/–21 L –21/–30, Wind — 45–50 mph. Characters on deck take a –1 penalty to Wisdom (Perception) checks that rely on hearing.)
41–60	Clouds block all stars and only hint at the location of the moon, adding a claustrophobic feel to the trip. The absence of wind allows the sails and rigging to hang listless, like cloth in a shop window. The ebony water ripples in the soft breeze, white caps standing out like glowing embers. (Temp H –19/–28 L –25/–32, Wind — 0–5 mph. 2% chance of course change for ice bergs in path of ship.)
61–80	Partial clouds covers sections of the sky, seemingly unmoving. Large waves buffet the ship attempting to carry it along with them. Wind assaults the vessel hard from the west, never wavering or letting up. Travel during the night at full sail run double risk of collision with ice. (Temp H –23/–30 L –29/–33, Wind — 55–60 mph. Characters on deck take a –1 penalty to Dexterity checks and saving throws. 15% chance of course change for ice.)
81–00	Wisps of cloud move across the sky sometimes blocking the stars. The brightness of the visible stars and moon provides ample light to maneuver around the ship and perform most tasks. The ever-present wind provides enough force to keep the ship moving at optimum speed. The absence of spray from the calm waters allows for equipment to dry. (Temp H –19/–28 L –21/–29, Wind — 30–35 mph.)

EQUATORIAL

Within the Equatorial region humidity is an issue for temperature measurement. Reference to the Humidity Table will bring about a more realistic gauge for temperature; consequently, the effects of heat upon those traveling the waves should be watched closely.

RAIN/DAY

01–20	A fierce wind blows, adding a texture to the warm rain falling. Large drops patter along the deck, occasional sunshine warms the deck, quickly evaporating the rain and adding to the humidity. A sticky aspect of the air grows throughout the day as the humidity rises. Sunlight glints off the water like numerous smaller suns, blinding those not ready for the effect. Waves are large in width but not in height, rocking the ship with their passage. (Temp H 73/22 L 65/18, Wind — 35–40 mph. Characters on deck take a –1 penalty to Constitution saving throws made to maintain concentration on a spell.)
21–40	Heavy rain pummels the ship and those on board, quickly soaking everything on deck. The waves are sedated, rarely topping 5 feet, seemingly held down with the impact of the rain. The sun tries to pierce the cloud cover with its intense glare, only succeeding in raising the temperature. Wind is non-existent hammered to submission by the heavy rain. (Temp H 70/21 L 62/17, Wind — 0–5 mph.)
41–60	Seemingly in rhythm with the lapping waves, periodic rain drops in vast amounts, quickly soaking all on board and washing away loose items. Between rainfalls the sun attempts to burn away the moisture with blistering heat, never quite successful and so leaving all with a heaviness of moisture. Waves roll languidly, topping 6 feet in height but not steep enough to make more than an exaggerated rocking motion. The wind blows merrily, billowing out the sails of the ship and propelling the vessel over the large waves. (Temp H 67/19 L 58/15, Wind — 10–15 mph. Characters moving on deck during a deluge must succeed on a DC 8 Dexterity (Acrobatics) check each round or be knocked prone and pushed 10 feet in a random direction.)
61–80	A drizzle of rain, sometimes hard and sometimes light, falls throughout the day. All equipment is thoroughly soaked and heavy with water. The warmth of the occasional sun is diminished slightly by the cool rain, keeping it tolerable for all involved. The wind blows constantly, keeping the sails full but not pushing the limit of its capabilities. Waves rise from the water to knock the ship with thundering impacts every few minutes. (Temp H 73/22 L 66/19, Wind — 20–25 mph.)
81–00	Thick rains from gargantuan clouds clobber the ship and those on deck. Waves like great green battering rams smashing against the ship every few minutes. The overhead clouds have descended to a point where it seems the ship is in a large chamber. Wind hurtles against the vessel and its sail, trying to rip it free from the mast and rigging. All loose items are tossed around the decking creating hazards for those on deck. (Temp H 67/19 L 59/15, Wind — 50–55 mph. Characters moving on deck must succeed on a DC 10 Dexterity (Acrobatics) check each round or be knocked prone and pushed 10 feet in a random direction. All exposed areas of the ship count as difficult terrain. Characters on deck also have disadvantage on Strength (Athletics) checks involving climbing and take a –1 penalty to Constitution saving throws made to maintain concentration on a spell.)

RAIN/NIGHT

01–20	The humidity of the night is made comfortable by the patter of rain upon the deck, the coolness of the rain stealing some of the heat. The thin clouds mask the presence of the stars but leave a large halo where the moon tries to shine. The waves crash against the hull as if trying to keep the ship from reaching its goal. The bounce of the ship as it passes over the waves keeps all but the soundest sleepers awake. (Temp H 74/24 L 64/18, Wind — 0–5 mph.)

21–40	A deluge of rain from ebony clouds press down on the ship and those on deck. Waves can be seen in the dark like great gray-green boulders smashing against the ship every minute. The overhead clouds have descended to a point where it seems the ship is in a large chamber. Wind hurtles against the vessel and its sail, trying to rip it from the mast and rigging. All loose items and small creatures on deck vie for attention from the crashing waves or the blustery wind. (Temp H 71/21 L 62/17, Wind — 45–50 mph. Characters have disadvantage on Strength (Athletics), Wisdom (Perception), and Concentration checks.)
41–60	Seemingly in rhythm with the lapping waves, periodic rain drops in vast amounts, quickly soaking all surfaces and washing away loose materials. Waves roll languidly, topping 6 feet in height but not steep enough to make more than an exaggerated rocking motion. A light wind blows carrying a humid mist from the still warm water, visible in the intermittent moonlight. (Temp H 75/24 L 66/19, Wind — 15–20 mph. Characters moving on deck during a deluge must succeed on a DC 8 Dexterity (Acrobatics) check each round or be knocked prone and pushed 10 feet in a random direction. All exposed areas of the ship are lightly obscured and count as difficult terrain.)
61–80	A drizzle of rain, flip-flopping between hard and light, falls continuously throughout during the nighttime hours. All surfaces are thoroughly soaked and heavy with water. The warmth of the day rapidly disappears replaced with the humidity of the still evaporating water around the ship. The waves are smaller than normal and work with the rain to stay weak enough to be inconsequential. The wind blows constantly, keeping the sails full but not pushing the limit of its capabilities. (Temp H 78/25 L 71/21, Wind — 30–35 mph.)
81–00	A thrashing rain accompanies hurricane force winds. In the distance amid lightning flashes, water spouts can be seen reaching for the sky. Waves, the size of small mountains, rise above the vessel giving the ship a wide span of view when atop a wave, and a sense of claustrophobia when in a gully. (Temp H 72/22 L 68/20, Wind — 75–85 mph. Characters moving on deck must succeed on a DC 14 Dexterity (Acrobatics) check each round or be knocked prone and pushed 15 feet in a random direction. All exposed areas of the ship are lightly obscured and count as difficult terrain. Characters on deck also have disadvantage on Dexterity checks and saving throws, Strength (Athletics) checks involving climbing, Wisdom (Perception) checks that rely on hearing, and Constitution saving throws made to maintain concentration on a spell.)

Dry/Day

01–20	The large sun dominates the sky but a swift breeze keeps the temperature to a more moderate level. Spray is pulled up from the many waves, capped in white froth. The horizon is marked with a large bank of gray clouds promising rain in the next day or two. The humidity rises throughout the day adding a weight to the sun which saps the strength of those not acquainted with the Equatorial waters. (Temp H 79/26 L 72/22, Wind — 10–15 mph.)
21–40	Clouds run amok along the sky, occasionally blocking the sun and its warmth. The wind seemingly growls as it tears across the water at the ship. The sail quivers trying to keep the wind from escaping. Waves rise up and crash against the hull of the ship each impact like a bludgeon from nature itself. (Temp H 75/24 L 65/15, Wind — 45–50 mph. Characters on deck have disadvantage on Strength (Athletics) checks involving climbing and take a –1 penalty to Dexterity saving throws and Wisdom (Perception) checks that rely on hearing.)
41–60	A crystal clear sky allows the sun to direct its heat against the ship and her crew. The wind breathes slowly, not enough to extinguish a candle let alone cool the flesh of those in the open. Waves move across the water like a herd, trying to carry the ship along in their wake, fighting the vessel should it try to turn away. The spray carries over the rail into the faces of those on deck, quickly drying to leave powdered salt. (Temp H 74/24 L 69/20, Wind — 0–5 mph.)

61–80	The turbulent clouds overhead threaten to release their load, allowing the moisture to be released in the form of a thick palpable air. While no rain has fallen during the day, all surfaces are beaded with sweat and spray from the moisture laced air. The moderate wind moves both the ship and the clouds, lifting the waves to heights of 10 feet, launching the spray into the air. The ship rolls with the impacts as it tips down one wave and up another, the prow having difficulty cutting through the water. (Temp H 68/20 L 60/10 Wind — 20–25 mph.)
81–00	The sky is clear, dotted with numerous small unimposing collections of cloud. A steady wind blows determined to cart items away in its embrace. The sun, high overhead seems a greater distance than usual given the lack of heat generated. Abundant waves run to the horizon, making up for size with numbers. Churned to a gray-green only a few feet under the surface can be seen with any clarity; another indicator of the weak sun. (Temp H 75/24 L 71/21, Wind — 20–25 mph.)

Dry/Night

01–20	An open sky provides a view of the numerous constellations and guiding stars. Wind gusts from the North East, creating a flapping staccato to match the waves breaking on the hull of the ship. White-capped waves, visible in the moonlight reach for the sailors on board, topping 7–8 feet. A slight mist can be felt in the wind; consequently, all surfaces are slick and shiny with moisture. (Temp H 74/24 L 67/19, Wind — 20–35 mph. Characters on deck take a –1 penalty to Strength (Athletics) checks involving climbing and Wisdom (Perception) checks that rely on hearing.)
21–40	Clouds, reminiscent of the underside of gray crashing surf, run from horizon to horizon, extinguishing the stars and moon from view. The absence of wind allows the sails and rigging to hang listless, like cloth in a shop window. The water is like glass, calm for many miles around the ship, waves visible in the far distance. Pressure seems to build, raising the temperature over several hours to just above a comfortable level. (Temp H 70/21 L 61/16, Wind — 0–5 mph. Experienced sailors know a storm is coming. Reroll on Equatorial day–rain chart in 1d4 hours for result.)
41–60	The cool of the night is identified by the daytime heat escaping the decking, misting the moisture collected through the daylight hours. Raising the humidity to an uncomfortable level, it deadens the night sounds of creaking riggings and lapping waves. Long trenches of waves roll the ship as it moves through them like long strides of a great beast. Occasional clouds plunge the world into darkness, allowing the moon and stars to pear through again in a few moments. (Temp H 76/25 L 69/21, Wind — 10–20 mph.)
61–80	Thin clouds attempt to block the bright moonlight, only muting the brilliance periodically. Rain falls lightly from unseen sources slowly drenching the ship and equipment. Numerous waves, about 10 feet tall run the length of the water as far as the eye can see, all topped with a cone of greenish white froth. The rigging and sails have rivulets of collected water which pools on the deck. Lines are heavy with water and deck boards are slick and shiny, sometimes reflecting the occasional sunlight. (Temp H 62/17 58/15, Wind — 20–25 mph. Characters on deck take a –1 penalty to Strength (Athletics) checks involving climbing, Dexterity saving throws, and Wisdom (Perception) checks that rely on sight.)
81–00	A clear night overhead provides astronomers and navigators a fine view of the stars and planets. A gentle wind blows from the South, flapping the sail and nettings. Small waves lap against the side of the boat like a heartbeat, reflections of the moon on the waves stand out stark white against the black background of the water and night sky. (Temp H 67/19 L 61/16, Wind — 5–10 mph.)

Chapter 4: New Spells

Most of these spells deal with water-related events, ships, sailing, the ocean, or the weather, while some are used in the creation of certain sea-based magic items or constructs, namely the glass whale.

Spell Lists

Bard Spells

1st Level
Anchor
Buoyancy
Detect Current
Detect Land
Unseen Pilot

2nd Level
Ballast
Navigator's Eye
Protection from Pressure

3rd Level
Cause Bends

4th Level
Farvision
Ironrope

Cleric Spells

1st Level
Anchor
Control Fog
Detect Current
Detect Land

3rd Level
Cause Bends
Glassiron

4th Level
Farvision
Ironrope

5th Level
Land Sail

Druid Spells

Cantrips (0 Level)
Hard Water Blast

1st Level
Control Fog
Detect Current
Detect Fish
Detect Land

2nd Level
Ballast
Fill the Sails
Hard Water Weapon
Protection from Pressure
Undertow

3rd Level
Cause Bends
Strangling Seaweed

4th Level
Lunar Glare
Stonehull

5th Level
Air Sphere
Create Iceberg
Split Ice

9th Level
Create Island

Ranger Spells

1st Level
Detect Current
Detect Fish
Detect Land

2nd Level
Ballast
Hard Water Weapon
Protection from Pressure

3rd Level
Strangling Seaweed

4th Level
Stonehull

5th Level
Air Sphere

Sorcerer Spells

Cantrips (0 Level)
Hard Water Blast

1st Level
Anchor
Buoyancy
Detect Current
Detect Land

2nd Level
Ballast
Boarding Plank
Fill the Sails
Hard Water Weapon
Protection from Pressure
Spectral Sail
Undertow
Water Web

3rd Level
Glassiron

4th Level
Desail
Farvision
Ironrope
Lunar Glare
Scalding Sea
Stonehull

5th Level
Air Sphere
Create Iceberg
Land Sail
Split Ice

8th Level
Raise Shipwreck

9th Level
Create Island

Warlock Spells

1st Level
Unseen Pilot

3rd Level
Cause Bends

4th Level
Farvision
Lunar Glare

9th Level
Curse of the Ancient Mariner

Wizard Spells

Cantrips (0 Level)
Hard Water Blast

1st Level
Anchor
Buoyancy
Control Fog
Detect Current
Detect Fish
Detect Land
Unseen Pilot

2nd Level
Ballast
Boarding Plank
Fill the Sails
Hard Water Weapon
Navigator's Eye
Protection from Pressure
Spectral Sail
Undertow
Water Web

3rd Level
Cause Bends
Glassiron
Strangling Seaweed

4th Level
Desail
Farvision
Ironrope
Lunar Glare
Scalding Sea
Stonehull

5th Level
Air Sphere
Create Iceberg
Land Sail
Split Ice

8th Level
Raise Shipwreck

9th Level
Create Island
Curse of the Ancient Mariner

AIR SPHERE

5th-level transmutation
Casting Time: 1 action
Range: Self (5-foot-radius)
Components: V, S, M (a metal wire bent into a loop)
Duration: Concentration, up to 10 minutes

A bubble of pure, fresh air extends out from you in a 5-foot radius, lifting you a few inches off the ground, and moves with you, remaining centered on you. Until this spell ends, your speed is 0, and the bubble provides you and those in the area with fresh, breathable air, no matter the conditions outside the bubble. If underwater, the bubble also protects those in the area from the drawbacks caused by being in a deep, underwater environment. The bubble doesn't prevent attacks or spells from passing through it, but creatures inside the bubble have advantage on saving throws against noxious or poisonous gases, such as from the *stinking cloud* spell or burnt othur fumes.

When you cast this spell and as a bonus action on your turn, you can move yourself up to 20 feet in any direction. Willing creatures within the bubble move with you. An unwilling creature that succeeds on a Constitution saving throw is unaffected. If this movement would cause a creature within the bubble to provoke an opportunity attack by moving out of an enemy's reach, that enemy has disadvantage on the opportunity attack to hit the creature.

A creature no longer affected by this spell, either by moving out of the bubble or by the spell ending, floats gently to the ground if it is aloft.

At Higher Levels. When you cast this spell using a spell slot of 6th or 7th level, you can maintain your concentration on the spell for up to 1 hour. When you use a spell slot of 8th level or higher, you can maintain your concentration on the spell for up to 8 hours.

ANCHOR

1st-level abjuration
Casting Time: 1 action
Range: Touch
Components: V, S, M (a small bit of iron and a piece of string)
Duration: 24 hours

You touch a boat or ship, bringing it to a gentle halt. Until the spell ends, the vessel can't be moved by any means. You can use an action to touch the vessel again and end the effect.

BALLAST

2nd-level transmutation
Casting Time: 1 action
Range: Touch
Components: S
Duration: Concentration, up to 1 minute

This spell causes an object or creature that is no larger than Medium sized to be either neutrally buoyant or positively buoyant (your choice). If the object or creature is neutrally buoyant, it floats at its current depths. If it is a creature, it can then make ability checks to swim without suffering from the effects of wearing armor. If the object or creature becomes positively buoyant, it rises 30 feet at the end of each of its turns until it reaches a solid object that stops its progress or the surface of the body of water, whichever comes first.

At Higher Levels. For each spell slot above 2nd, increase the size of the object or creature you can affect with this spell, up to 5th level.

BOARDING PLANK

2nd-level evocation
Casting Time: 1 action
Range: 60 feet
Components: V, S, M (a splinter of wood)
Duration: Concentration, up to 10 minutes

An invisible plank of force springs into existence at a point you choose within range. The plank appears in a horizontal orientation or at an angle no greater than 45 degrees. If the plank isn't anchored on or between two solid masses (such as boats, walls, or trees), it collapses on itself, and the spell ends at the start of your next turn. The plank is 5 feet wide and can be up to 30 feet long. It is 1/4 inch thick, and it lasts for the duration.

Nothing can physically pass through the plank. It is immune to all damage and can't be dispelled by *dispel magic*. A *disintegrate* spell destroys the plank instantly, however. The plank also extends into the Ethereal Plane, blocking ethereal travel through the plank.

BUOYANCY

1st-level transmutation
Casting Time: 1 reaction, which you take when you or a creature within 60 feet of you begins sinking or suffocating while underwater
Range: 60 feet
Components: S, M (a small pumice stone)
Duration: 5 minutes

Choose up to five sinking or suffocating creatures within range. A sinking or suffocating creature ascends to the surface of the water at a rate of 10 feet per round until the spell ends. If a creature reaches the surface before the spell ends, it floats on the surface until the spell ends. An unwilling creature that succeeds on a Constitution saving throw is unaffected.

CAUSE BENDS

3rd-level necromancy
Casting Time: 1 action
Range: Touch
Components: V, S
Duration: Concentration, up to 1 minute

Your touch forces high-pressure gas bubbles into the bloodstream of a creature, causing it great pain, especially while in water. Make a melee spell attack against a creature within your reach. On a hit, you afflict the creature with a cursed version of the bends. While afflicted with the bends, its speed is halved, and it is incapacitated if it is submerged in water.

The target can make a Constitution saving throw at the end of each of its turns. On a success, the spell ends. Alternatively, a *remove curse* spell ends the effect.

This spell has no effect on undead, constructs, or creatures that ignore the drawbacks caused by being in a deep, underwater environment.

At Higher Levels. If you cast this spell using a spell slot of 4th level or higher, the duration is concentration, up to 10 minutes. If you use a spell slot of 5th level or higher, the duration is 8 hours. If you use a spell slot of 7th level or higher, the duration is 24 hours. If you use a 9th level spell slot, the spell lasts until it is dispelled. Using a spell slot of 5th level or higher grants a duration that doesn't require concentration.

CONTROL FOG

1st-level transmutation
Casting Time: 1 action
Range: 120 feet
Components: V, S, M (a small horn)
Duration: Concentration, up to 1 hour

Until the spell ends, you control any freestanding fog within range inside an area you choose that is a cube up to 20 feet on a side. You can choose from any of the following effects when you cast this spell. As an action on your turn, you can repeat the same effect or choose a different one.

Thin. You can cause the fog in the area to thin. If the fog's area is heavily obscured, it becomes lightly obscured. If the fog's area is lightly obscured, it no longer obscures vision. The fog remains thinned in this way until the spell ends or you choose a different effect.

Thick. You can cause the fog in the area to thicken. If the fog's area is lightly obscured, it becomes heavily obscured. If there is no fog in the area, you create fog in the area. This fog spreads around corners, and its area is lightly obscured.

At Higher Levels. When you cast this spell using a spell slot of 2nd level or higher, the area of fog you can control increases by 10 feet for each slot level above 1st.

CREATE ICEBERG

5th-level evocation
Casting Time: 1 action
Range: 120 feet
Components: V, S, M (a small piece of glass)
Duration: Instantaneous

You create an iceberg up to 60 feet in diameter in an area of saltwater you can see within range. It must be in an area with enough saltwater to support an iceberg of its size. The iceberg can have any shape you desire, though it can't occupy the same space as a creature or object. If the iceberg cuts through a creature's space when it appears, the creature is pushed directly away from the center of the iceberg.

The iceberg is an object that can be damaged. It has AC 12 and 60 hit points, and it is vulnerable to fire damage. If created in a non-arctic climate, the iceberg takes 1d4 fire damage at the start of each of your turns.

CREATE ISLAND

9th-level conjuration
Casting Time: 10 minutes
Range: Sight
Components: V, S, M (pearl dust worth at least 1,000 gp, which the spell consumes)
Duration: 30 days

You create an island of bare stone up to 1 mile in diameter in an area of saltwater you can see within range that is big enough to hold the island. The island isn't connected to the seafloor, but it remains stationary in the location you create it. The island can have any shape you desire.

Because the island's creation occurs slowly, creatures in the area can't usually be trapped or injured by the creation. Similarly, this spell doesn't directly affect plant growth in the area, and plants in the area either move with the island's creation or are pushed directly away from its center, at the GM's discretion.

You can create a permanent island by casting this spell in the same location every month for one year.

CURSE OF THE ANCIENT MARINER

9th-level necromancy
Casting Time: 1 minute
Range: Touch
Components: V, S, M (an albatross made of diamond, worth at least 500 gp per Hit Die of the target, which embeds in the target's flesh while the spell lasts)
Duration: Until dispelled

You create a magical curse on a creature you touch. The target must succeed on a Wisdom saving throw or be cursed by this spell; if it succeeds, it is immune to this spell if you cast it again. While cursed by this spell, the target brings bad luck onto any water-bound vessel it rides or captains. The bad luck manifests itself in a variety of ways, usually minor at first, such as the crew failing basic navigation checks, then progressing to major, such as the wind steering the vessel into an oncoming storm, and finally ending in catastrophic events, such as a mighty sea monster attacking the vessel and sinking it. The bad luck's manifestation is at the GM's discretion, and GMs are encouraged to make the curse's effects both gradual and severely punishing. In all cases, the curse eventually leads to the vessel's destruction, though the cursed target always, sometimes miraculously, survives.

The curse can be ended only with a *wish* spell, which causes the albatross embedded in the target's skin to disintegrate.

DESAIL

4th-level transmutation
Casting Time: 1 action
Range: 300 feet
Components: V, S, M (a tiny candle)
Duration: Concentration, up to 10 minutes

You cause the sails of a vessel within range to shrink. If the vessel is wind-powered, its speed is halved for the duration. If the vessel is both wind and oar-powered, its speed is reduced by one quarter instead. This spell can't target a vessel that doesn't have sails.

DETECT CURRENT

1st-level divination (ritual)
Casting Time: 1 action
Range: Self
Components: V, S
Duration: Concentration, up to 10 minutes

For the duration, you can sense the presence of currents within 1 mile of you. You know the location of the current, the direction it is moving, and its speed.

The spell can penetrate most barriers, but it is blocked by 1 foot of stone, 1 inch of common metal, a thin sheet of lead, or 3 feet of wood or dirt.

DETECT FISH

1st-level divination (ritual)
Casting Time: 1 action
Range: Self
Components: V, S, M (a fish scale)
Duration: Concentration, up to 10 minutes

For the duration, you can sense the presence and location of beasts with an Intelligence of 2 or lower that have the Amphibious or Water Breathing traits within 60 feet of you. You can also identify the kind of beast, such as crab, reef shark, or tuna fish, and its general health, such as injured, suffering from an illness, or healthy.

DETECT LAND

1st-level divination (ritual)
Casting Time: 1 action
Range: Self
Components: V, S
Duration: Concentration, up to 10 minutes

For the duration, you can sense the presence of land, such as islands or a continent, within 5 miles of you. You know the direction to the land, but not its size or other features, such as terrain type. You detect only land that is above the surface of the water.

The spell can penetrate most barriers, but it is blocked by 1 foot of stone, 1 inch of common metal, a thin sheet of lead, or 3 feet of wood or dirt.

FARVISION

4th-level transmutation
Casting Time: 1 action
Range: Touch
Components: V, S, M (a glass or crystal eye and a pinch of high-quality sand)
Duration: 8 hours

You touch a transparent object such as glass spectacles, a glass monocle, a crystal spyglass, or similar object and imbue it with magic. For the duration, a creature can use a bonus action to place the object over at least one of its eyes, gaining darkvision out to a range of 90 feet until the object is removed from its eye.

Casting this spell on the same object every day for a year makes this effect permanent.

FILL THE SAILS

2nd-level transmutation
Casting Time: 1 minute
Range: 30 feet
Components: V, S, M (a feather from a seabird)
Duration: Concentration, up to 1 hour

You fill the sails of a vessel within range with swift-moving air. For the duration, the vessel's speed increases by half. For example, a vessel with a speed of 2 miles per hour moves 3 miles per hour when affected by this spell. This spell can't target a vessel that doesn't have sails.

At Higher Levels. When you cast this spell using a spell slot of 3rd or 4th level, you can maintain concentration on the spell for up to 8 hours. When you use a spell slot of 5th level or higher, you can maintain your concentration on the spell for up to 24 hours.

GLASSIRON

3rd-level transmutation
Casting Time: 1 action
Range: Touch
Components: V, S
Duration: Concentration, up to 1 hour

You touch a nonmagical object made of glass, crystal, metal, or stone or a creature made of glass, crystal, metal, or stone. For the duration, the target has resistance to thunder damage and has immunity to the special effects of spells and effects with drawbacks specific to nonmagical objects made of glass, crystal, metal, or stone, such as the drawback for inorganic materials in the *shatter* spell or a rust monster's Rust Metal trait or Antennae action.

At Higher Levels. When you cast this spell using a spell slot of 6th level or higher, the spell lasts until dispelled, without requiring your concentration.

HARD WATER BLAST

Evocation cantrip
Casting Time: 1 action
Range: 60 feet
Components: V, S
Duration: Instantaneous

A stream of water streaks out from your palm toward a creature within range. Make a ranged spell attack against the target. On a hit, it takes 1d4 bludgeoning damage, and it is pushed 5 feet away from you. The target can't be pushed into damaging terrain such as lava or a pit, a solid object such as a wall, or another creature.

The spell's damage increases by 1d4 when you reach 5th level (2d4), 11th level (3d4), and 17th level (4d4).

HARD WATER WEAPON

2nd-level conjuration
Casting Time: 1 bonus action
Range: Self
Components: V, S
Duration: Concentration, up to 1 minute

You create a weapon of solidified water in your hand. It takes the shape of any one-handed simple or martial weapon, and you are proficient with it. When you hit with it, the weapon deals normal damage for a weapon of its type plus an extra 1d6 cold damage.

At Higher Levels. When you cast this spell using a spell slot of 3rd level or higher, the damage increases by 1d6 for every two slot levels above 2nd.

IRONROPE

4th-level transmutation
Casting Time: 1 action
Range: Touch
Components: V, S, M (a pinch of powdered iron)
Duration: 24 hours

You touch a length of rope that is up to 100 feet long and make it as tough as iron. The rope's AC increases to19, it has 20 hit points, it has a damage threshold of 5, and it has resistance to fire damage. A creature must succeed on a Strength saving throw to bend or manipulate the rope.

Alternatively, you can touch a single sail tied with rope. A vessel with a sail enchanted with this spell has advantage on saving throws and ability checks against strong winds, storms, and other effects that would move the vessel against the pilot's will.

At Higher Levels. When you cast this spell using a spell slot of 5th level or higher, the length of rope you can affect with this spell increases by 50 feet for each slot level above 5th.

LAND SAIL

5th-level transmutation (ritual)
Casting Time: 1 action
Range: 60 feet
Components: V, S, M (three seabird feathers fastened to the hull of the target vessel)
Duration: 8 hours

This spell grants a vessel within range the ability to move across any solid surface—such as dirt, ice, or rock—as if it were harmless water (vessels crossing damaging terrain can still take damage from moving through the area, such as an area of ground covered by the *spike growth* spell). The vessel's movement through the solid surface leaves a narrow trench no wider or deeper than the vessel's keel in the surface as the vessel moves, the majority of its bulk gliding above the surface.

Though this spell allows a vessel to move across a solid surface, the vessel must still have a method of propulsion. A sailing vessel needs wind to sail across a solid surface just as it does in water, and an oar-powered vessel must be poled along the ground.

If you target a beached vessel, the vessel rights itself and can be moved by its method of propulsion; however, this spell doesn't repair damage to the hull or guarantee that the vessel will be seaworthy once returned to the water. Unless supported or returned to water, the vessel grinds to a halt and falls over when the spell ends.

LUNA'S GLARE
4th-level illusion
Casting Time: 10 minutes
Range: 300 feet
Components: V, S, M (a small white or silver pearl worth 100 gp)
Duration: 8 hours

You create a false moon that is visible within 5 miles of you for the duration. You must be outdoors at night to cast this spell.

A shapechanger that can see the moon must succeed on a Constitution saving throw or instantly revert to its original form. It can't assume a different form until it leaves the moon's light, such as by stepping around a shadowed corner or into a building.

Tidal water within 5 miles of the moon rise to high tide gradually as you cast the spell. The tide remains high for the duration. Because the water's movement occurs slowly, creatures in the tidal water can't be trapped or injured by the water's movement, and objects in the water that aren't being worn or carried and plants floating in the water are carried along with the water's movement. Moored and anchored boats rise with the water's level but are otherwise unaffected by the water's movement.

NAVIGATOR'S EYE
2nd-level conjuration
Casting Time: 1 minute
Range: 30 feet
Components: V, S
Duration: 24 hours

You create a set of navigator's tools in a space or on a surface within range. Choose up to two creatures within range. Each target has proficiency with the navigator's tools you created for the duration. After 24 hours, the tools crumble to dust.

RAISE SHIPWRECK
8th-level transmutation
Casting Time: 1 minute
Range: Sight
Components: V, S
Duration: Concentration, up to 1 hour

One sunken vessel of your choice that you can see within range rises vertically 20 feet per round until it reaches the water's surface. It floats on the surface for the duration. If the vessel is in multiple pieces, you must choose which piece to raise to the surface.

When the spell ends, the vessel sinks gently to the seafloor unless it was made seaworthy before the end of the spell.

At Higher Levels. When you cast this spell using a spell slot of 9th level, the duration is 24 hours and doesn't require your concentration.

PROTECTION FROM PRESSURE
2nd-level abjuration
Casting Time: 1 action
Range: Touch
Components: S, M (a hard shell)
Duration: 8 hours

This spell greatly increases a creature's resistance to the pressure of depths. One creature you touch multiplies their maximum depth rating by your spellcasting ability score.

At Higher Levels. For each spell slot above 2nd, you can extend the benefits of this spell to another creature within range.

SCALDING SEA
4th-level conjuration
Casting Time: 1 action
Range: 120 feet
Components: V, S
Duration: Concentration, up to 1 minute

You create a 20-foot-radis sphere of steam on a point within range on the surface of a body of water. The steam spreads around corners, and its area is lightly obscured. It lasts for the duration or until a wind of moderate or greater speed (at least 10 miles per hour) disperses it.

When you cast this spell and as an action on a later turn, you can superheat the steam, burning the creatures in the area. Each creature in the steam must make a Constitution saving throw. The creature takes 3d6 fire damage on a failed save, or half as much damage on a successful one. After you superheat the steam three times, the spell ends.

At Higher Levels. When you cast this spell using a spell slot of 5th level or higher, the radius of the cloud increases by 10 feet for each slot level above 4th.

SPECTRAL SAIL
2nd-level conjuration
Casting Time: 1 action
Range: 60 feet
Components: V, S, M (a small swatch of canvas)
Duration: 8 hours

You create a spectral sail on the mast of a sailing vessel that has lost its sail or that has a sail that is tied or otherwise incapable of catching the wind to propel the vessel. For the duration, you can change the direction of the spectral sail as a bonus action on each of your turns. The spectral sail is invisible and made of force, but it otherwise acts like a canvas sail.

At Higher Levels. When you cast this spell using a spell slot of 4th level or higher, the duration is 24 hours.

SPLIT ICE
5th-level transmutation
Casting Time: 10 minutes
Range: Self (200-foot line)
Components: V, S, M (a miniature field plow)
Duration: Concentration, up to 8 hours

Sea-bound ice in a 200-foot line extending in front of and behind you parts in a trench that is 30 feet wide and 15 feet deep. The parted ice forms walls on either side of you. The trench moves with you, creating a passageway in front of and behind you for seafaring vessels. As you move away from an area that was parted, the ice slowly recombines over the course of the next round until it is restored to the way it was before you cast this spell.

The ice's splitting occurs slowly, and creatures in the area can't usually be trapped or injured by the ice's movement. Similarly, this spell doesn't directly affect plant growth. The moved ice carries any plants and creatures along with it as it splits and reforms with your passing. An unwilling creature must make a Dexterity saving throw to avoid being moved with the ice, though it might find itself falling into the water of the trench created by this spell unless it is capable of flying.

This spell can target only nonmagical ice and can't harm or destroy ice created by spells or effects, such as the *wall of ice* spell or an ice devil's Wall of Ice action.

STONEHULL

4th-level abjuration
Casting Time: 1 action
Range: 60 feet
Components: V, S, M (diamond dust worth 250 gp, which the spell consumes)
Duration: Concentration, up to 1 hour

This spell turns the hull of a vessel within range as hard as stone. Until the spell ends, the target vessel has resistance to nonmagical bludgeoning, piercing, and slashing damage.

STRANGLING SEAWEED

3rd-level conjuration
Casting Time: 1 action
Range: 90 feet
Components: V, S, M (a piece of seaweed)
Duration: Concentration, up to 10 minutes

Squirming, green seaweed fills a 10-foot-radius sphere on a point in the water that you can see within range. The area becomes difficult terrain for the duration.

When a creature enters the area for the first time on a turn or starts its turn there, the creature must succeed on a Dexterity saving throw or be restrained. Until this restraint ends, the creature is suffocating. A creature that starts its turn in the area and is already restrained by the seaweed takes 2d6 bludgeoning damage. A creature, including a restrained creature, can use its action to make a Strength or Dexterity check (its choice) against your spell save DC. On a success, it frees the restrained creature.

A boat or ship 60 feet long or shorter that enters the area of seaweed stops moving, held in place by the seaweed. The vessel's pilot can use its action to make an Intelligence or Wisdom check (its choice) using navigator's tools against your spell save DC. On a success, the pilot frees the vessel.

The growth of the seaweed is camouflaged to look natural. Any creature that can't see the area at the time the spell is cast must make a Wisdom (Perception) check against your spell save DC to recognize the water as hazardous before entering it.

UNDERTOW

2nd-level evocation
Casting Time: 1 action
Range: Self (60-foot line)
Components: V, S
Duration: Concentration, up to 1 minute

While underwater, a line of fast-moving water 60 feet long and 10 feet wide blasts from you in a direction you choose for the spell's duration. Each creature that starts its turn in the line must succeed on a Strength saving throw or be pushed 15 feet away from you in a direction following the line. If a creature on the surface of the water fails the saving throw, it is also pulled beneath the surface of the water and begins suffocating unless it can breathe underwater.

Any creature in the line must spend 2 feet of movement for every 1 foot it moves when moving closer to you.

As a bonus action on each of your turns before the spell ends, you can change the direction in which the line blasts from you.

At the GM's discretion, the undertow can push current-driven seafaring vessels in a direction following the line, and a vessel's pilot can resist the push by succeeding on a Strength saving throw.

UNSEEN PILOT

1st-level conjuration (ritual)
Casting Time: 1 action
Range: 100 feet
Components: V, S, M (a piece of string and a bit of wood)
Duration: 8 hours

This spell creates an invisible, mindless, shapeless force that pilots and navigates a vehicle, such as a ship or wagon, in the direction of your choice until the spell ends. The pilot springs into existence in an unoccupied space near a vehicle's wheel or primary controls within range. It has AC 10, 1 hit point, and a Strength of 2, and it can't attack. If it drops to 0 hit points, the spell ends.

Once on each of your turns as a bonus action, you can mentally command the pilot to change the direction it is steering the vehicle or stop the vehicle. The pilot knows basic directions and how to navigate the vehicle in most normal conditions and terrain, but it can't navigate a vehicle in uncertain or chaotic situations, such as through a storm or on a chariot chase through crowded city streets. The pilot doesn't know specific locations, nor can it read a map. and can steer the vehicle only in the direction you indicate.

The pilot drives and navigates the vehicle, but it doesn't power the vehicle. A vehicle powered by oars, wind, horses, or the like must still have its power source for the pilot to successfully navigate the vehicle. The pilot is stationary at the primary controls of the vehicle, and, if you move more than 100 feet away from it, the spell ends.

WATER WEB

2nd-level conjuration
Casting Time: 1 action
Range: 60 feet
Components: V, S, M (a bit of rope from a net)
Duration: Concentration, up to 1 hour

You conjure a mass of tangled rope at a point underwater within range. The rope fills a 20-foot cube from that point for the duration. The rope is difficult terrain and lightly obscures the area.

Each creature that starts its turn in the rope or that enters the rope-filled area during its turn must make a Dexterity saving throw. On a failed save, the creature is restrained as long as it remains in the rope or until it breaks free.

A creature restrained by the rope can use its action to make a Strength check against your spell save DC. If it succeeds, it is no longer restrained.

Any 5-foot cube of rope above the surface of the water frays and fades away in 1 round, releasing any creature restrained in that section.

Chapter 5: New Magic Items

Many new magical objects make their debut in this book. They are described below.

Anchor of Weighing
Wondrous item, rare

When you use an action to speak the command word, this ornate, pocket-sized, wooden anchor becomes a full-sized anchor. While full-sized on a boat or ship, the anchor prevents the vessel from being moved by any means for up to 24 hours. Using an action to speak the command word again ends this effect. Once used, this feature can't be used again until the next dawn.

Apparatus of the Crab, Scouting
Wondrous item, legendary

This version of the *apparatus of the crab* is more lightweight and compact than its larger cousin. It can seat only one Medium or smaller creature, and its compartment holds enough air for 6 hours of breathing. It includes two additional levers.

Grasping Claws. This lever extends (up) and retracts (down) a pair of grasping claws, which can pick up and hold objects weighing up to 20 pounds within 20 feet of the *apparatus*. These claws can't be used to make attacks.

Magnet. This lever activates (up) and deactivates (down) a magnet on the front of the *apparatus*. When activated, metal objects that aren't being worn or carried within 10 feet of the *apparatus* move to it and stick to the front of the *apparatus*. Each creature within 10 feet of the *apparatus* must succeed on a DC 17 Strength saving throw or the metal items worn or carried by it stick to the front of the *apparatus*. A creature that is wearing metal armor that fails the saving throw is pulled toward the *apparatus* and restrained as it sticks to the front of the *apparatus*. A creature can use its action to remove itself or a stuck object from the front of the *apparatus* by succeeding on a DC 17 Strength check.

The *scouting apparatus of the crab* is a Large object with the following statistics:

Armor Class: 15
Hit Points: 100
Speed: 30 ft., swim 60 ft. (or 0 ft. for both if the legs and tail aren't extended)
Damage Immunities: poison, psychic

Other than the listed changes, the *scouting apparatus of the crab* functions the same as the *apparatus of the crab*.

Aquascope of the Kuah-Lij
Wondrous item, uncommon

This item is two lanterns bound by a thin, silken rope. While holding at least one of the lanterns, you can speak its command word and extend the rope from 100 feet to 500 feet.

While one of the lanterns is in water and you are holding the other, you can speak another command word as an action to peer into your lantern. If you do, the lantern you are holding displays what the other lantern sees. The lantern in the water has darkvision with a radius of 120 feet and can be rotated by rotating the lantern you are holding.

If you drop the lantern into an area with cramped confines such as a ship wreckage or coral reef, there is a 25 percent chance that it becomes tangled. This chance increases to 50 percent if you are moving along the surface of the water and pulling the underwater lantern with you. To untangle it, a creature must dive down and physically remove the lantern from the confines.

Ballasts of Buoyancy
Wondrous item, very rare

These barrels come in a set of four. While all four barrels are affixed to a larger ship (a ship requiring a crew of 20 or more to function), an officer of the ship can use an action to speak its command word, reducing the ship's draft by 50 percent).

Bamboo Skiff
Wondrous item, uncommon

This object is a small skiff made from linked bamboo poles. It is 10 feet long, 4 feet wide, and 2 feet deep and can hold up to four Medium or smaller creatures. You can use an action to speak its command word while grasping the tiller, causing the skiff to move up to 60 feet in a direction of your choice. While within 3 miles of a coast or reef, the skiff can't be capsized, no matter how violent the weather or movement of its occupants.

Boots of the Waves
Wondrous item, uncommon (requires attunement)

While you wear these calf-high boots, you have advantage on ability checks and saving throws against being pushed, pulled, or knocked prone by strong winds and waves or the movement of a ship at sea. In addition, you have advantage on saving throws against spells or features that push, pull, or knock prone by creating or manipulating wind or water, such as the *control water, gust of wind,* or *sleet storm* spells or a water elemental's Whelm action.

Bottled Cloud
Wondrous item, uncommon

This clear crystal bottle swirls with white, fluffy clouds and weighs 1 pound. When you use an action to remove the stopper, a cloud up to 40 feet long, up to 10 feet wide, and 1 foot thick appears. It flows along the ground out of the bottle, forming a solid, but fluffy, surface after 1 round. It stays together even over openings in the ground, allowing it to form a bridge across a pit or chasm as long as at least 5 feet of the cloud is on a solid surface. Once formed, the cloud is immobile and can support up to 500 pounds, and a creature that moves across it has advantage on Dexterity (Stealth) checks.

You can use an action to speak its command word while touching the bottle to the cloud to bring the cloud back into the bottle. If you don't collect the cloud, it disperses after 1 hour. It can't be dispersed early by wind unless the wind is at least a strong wind (21 or more miles per hour), which disperses the cloud after 1 minute. Once used, the cloud can't be summoned again until dawn of the next cloudy day.

Brooch of the Desert
Wondrous item, common

While wearing this brooch, you and your equipment remain dry even in the heaviest of storms. This brooch doesn't keep you dry while immersed in water, but it dries you and your equipment 1 round after you are no longer immersed.

BROOCH OF THE DOLPHIN

Wondrous item, uncommon

While wearing this dolphin-shaped brooch, you can hold your breath for up to 30 minutes, and you have blindsight out to a range of 30 feet while underwater. Your blindsight is echolocation, and you can't use it while deafened.

CAPTAIN'S HORN

Wondrous item, very rare

These small, gold hoop earrings come in a set of ten: one captain pair and four officer pairs. While you are wearing one pair of the earrings, you can communicate telepathically with any creature within 60 feet of you that is wearing one of the pairs of earrings in this set. While you are wearing the captain pair of earrings, you can send a single, telepathic message to all of the creatures within 60 feet of you that are wearing pairs of the officer earrings.

If the captain's pair of earrings is destroyed, all of the pairs of earrings become nonmagical.

CASTER'S BONES

Wondrous item, uncommon (requires attunement by a spellcaster)

As a bonus action, you rattle or drop these rune-etched animal bones and choose whether to target yourself or a creature within 60 feet of you with the bones' magic. If you target yourself, you have advantage on your next spell attack roll. If you target another creature, the creature must succeed on a DC 15 Wisdom saving throw or have disadvantage on its saving throw against the next spell of 3rd level or lower that you cast with the creature as the target. Once you use the bones, they can't be used again until the next dawn.

CORAL ARMOR

Armor (medium or heavy, but not hide), uncommon

This suit of armor is crafted out of coral by the songchangers. While you're wearing it, you have a swimming speed of 10 feet.

CORAL LUNG

Wondrous item, uncommon

This hollow tube of coral is about 1 foot long with a mouthpiece at one end. While underwater, you can hold the tube in your mouth and breathe air for 1 hour. Once emptied, the tube's reservoir of air can be refilled by holding it above water for 1 minute.

CORAL SWORD

Weapon (any sword), uncommon

You gain a +1 bonus to attack and damage rolls made with this magic weapon. In addition, when you attack with this magic sword while underwater, you don't have disadvantage on the attack roll from attacking underwater without a swimming speed.

COMPASS OF PELORA

Wondrous item, rare (requires attunement)

While holding this compass, you can use an action to target a creature you can see within 120 feet of you. The compass points in the direction of the targeted creature, regardless of distance, as long as the two of you are on the same plane of existence. It points to the creature's physical body whether living or dead, and it points in the direction of that target until you use an action to target a new creature.

DEEP SUIT OF THE KUAH-LIJ

Wondrous item, rare (requires attunement)

This wet suit is light, flexible, and comes with an attached cowl. It can be worn under normal clothes. While wearing this wet suit with its cowl up, you can breathe underwater, and you have a swimming speed equal to your walking speed. In addition, you have resistance to cold damage while immersed in water, and you ignore any drawbacks from being in a deep, underwater environment. Pulling the cowl up or down requires an action.

Some variations of the wet suit come with a *light* spell enchanted on the top of the cowl, which can be activated by speaking its command word.

DERELICT'S CHARTBOOK

Wondrous item, rare

This large chartbook contains maps, charts, and notes penned ages ago by sailors since lost to time. It is waterproof, suffering no ill effects from being submerged or stored in a humid location. If a page is damaged, destroyed, or removed, it is magically repaired by the next dawn. If you reference this book while navigating a ship, you have advantage on the ability check.

Control Weather. You can use an action to cast *control weather* from the chartbook. The duration is 8 hours without requiring concentration, but, after the initial casting, you can't change the weather more often than once each hour. Once you use this feature, you can't use it again until 7 days have passed.

DISSENSION'S DIGIT

Wondrous item, artifact (requires attunement)

Castagil was a great captain of the piratical sort. Aboard the mighty galleon *The Sea Wench*, he and his crew plundered the seas for nearly a decade. Castagil was a nautical genius and a practicing hydromancer. His skills of captaining and his command of water were outshone only by his lust for gold.

Night had fallen on the 45th day of an unrelenting search for the gold of Captain Moritire Nightshade, famed pirate captain ages gone. The crew was weary, the provision barrels were empty, and the ship wasn't a league closer to the famed treasure. That night as a storm brewed in the north, mutiny brewed in the barracks. The crew took Castagil in his sleep, beat him, and bound him in the cargo hold.

The next day, the ship set anchor near a small uncharted island. The quartermaster and six others dragged Castagil to shore, intending to maroon him with nothing more than a dirk. In the distance they heard a rumbling, and ash flitted through the air. They marched Castagil no more than a hundred yards into the jungle and came upon a trembling volcano. With their cutlasses they prodded their former captain up to the rim, and pushed him in. As he plummeted toward the lava, he summoned all his magic into one curse. When he hit the lava, the volcano erupted so violently that boulders the size of wagons crashed into the hull of the ship, sinking it. As the dust and ash settled, it was revealed that the entire island had been razed. The only thing that remained was a small, glowing sphere.

The *dissension's digit* is a red crystal globe about 2 inches in diameter. When used, it glows with the oozing, red light of lava.

Random Properties. The *dissension's digit* has the following random properties:
- 2 minor beneficial properties
- 1 minor detrimental property

Forged in Fire. While attuned to the globe, you are immune to fire damage.

Spells. The globe has 5 charges and regains 1d4 + 1 expended charges daily at dawn. If you are attuned to the globe, you can use an action and expend one or more charges to cast one of the following spells (save DC 18) from it: *flame strike* (2 charges), *locate object* (must be an object made of gold or other precious substance, 1 charge), *protection from energy* (1 charge), or *teleport* (3 charges).

Curse. Castagil's greed curses this item and attuning to the *dissension's digit* extends the curse to you. Each time you are within 30 feet of an object worth 100 gp or more, you must succeed on a DC 20 Wisdom saving throw or do everything in your power to hold and possess the object. You are unwilling to part with objects worth 100 gp or more unless it leads to possessing an even more valuable item. You are unwilling to part with the *dissension's digit* unless you are targeted by the *remove curse* spell or similar magic.

Destroying the Globe. The *dissension's digit* can be destroyed only by a good-aligned spellcaster casting *remove curse* on the item twice then throwing it into an active volcano.

Exile's Wood
Wondrous item, uncommon

This 3-foot-long plank of wood has three pairs of leather loops, and it never sinks, no matter the weather or water conditions, as long as it doesn't support more than 1,000 pounds of weight.

Guide Stone
Wondrous item, rare

This Medium gray, oval stone is the saving grace of many guilds with merchants traveling in dangerous weather. Each stone has up to four smaller, fragment stones tied to it. While holding one of these fragments, you feel a gentle tugging in the direction of the *guide stone* if you are within 250 miles of it.

Hospitality's Hammock
Wondrous item, uncommon

This hammock is spun of the finest spider silk. When you spend a long rest in this hammock, you recover from one disease or one blinded, deafened, paralyzed, or poisoned condition afflicting you. In addition, you regain 1 extra spent Hit Dice after finishing a long rest in this hammock.

Lung Leaf
Wondrous item, rare

This large leaf is a deep, rich blue with silver veins running through it. For 8 hours after you consume this leaf, you can breathe underwater, and you have a swimming speed equal to your walking speed.

Mariner's Eyepatch
Wondrous item, uncommon

This eyepatch is heavily encrusted with jewels and arcane writing. While wearing this eyepatch, you can use an action to cast the *comprehend languages* spell or the *see invisibility* spell with it. The eyepatch can't be used this way again until the next dawn.

Mercy's Mandolin
Wondrous item, rare

The face of this balsa wood mandolin is inlaid with mother-of-pearl. The neck has been carved to resemble the jumping form of a porpoise. You must be proficient with string instruments to use this mandolin. You can use this mandolin to create soothing music to help revitalize your wounded allies during a short rest. If you or up to six friendly creatures of your choice who can hear your performance regain hit points at the end of the short rest, each of those creatures regains an extra 1d4 hit points.

If you are a bard and use this mandolin as part of your Song of Rest feature, each creature affected by your Song of Rest regains 1d4 hit points in addition to the hit points it regains from your Song of Rest.

Moonsilver Orb
Wondrous item, artifact (requires attunement)

When the Yalts, now called the Coralites, first arrived at their current home, they found a quiet coral reef that was pounded by surf and often wracked by tropical storms. For many centuries, the Coralites huddled together in island caves as they watched their homes sweep away with the wind.

With the advent of the songchangers, the creations of the Coralites became more sophisticated and increasingly infused with magic. The *Moonsilver Orb* was conceived to bring the same peace to nature that the Coralites had achieved in society. Calm winds and placid seas were the result.

The *Moonsilver Orb* is composed of sand from the ocean floor, silver from the Elemental Plane of Earth, and moonlight gathered on a moonless night. The orb is a silver, glass sphere about 4 inches in diameter with mist swirling inside it.

Random Properties. The *Moonsilver Orb* has the following random properties:

- 1 minor beneficial property
- 1 major beneficial property
- 2 minor detrimental properties

Denizen of the Deep. While attuned to the orb, you can speak Aquan, you can breathe underwater, you have a swimming speed of 60 feet, and you can ignore the drawbacks caused by a deep, underwater environment.

Eye of the Storm. While attuned to the orb and at sea, the weather within 1 mile of you is warm with light clouds and a moderate wind, no matter the weather conditions outside of that mile.

Spells. The orb has 7 charges and regains 1d4 + 3 expended charges daily at dawn. If you are attuned to the orb, you can use an action and expend one or more charges to cast one of the following spells (save DC 18) from it: *conjure animals* (water-based animals only, 2 charges), *conjure minor elementals* (water only, 2 charges), or *conjure elemental* (water only, 3 charges).

Whirlpool. You can use an action to create a whirlpool on a point of water you can see within 1 mile of you. Each creature that starts its turn in the water within 100 feet of that point must succeed on a DC 20 Strength saving throw or be pulled 30 feet closer to the center of the whirlpool. A creature that starts its turn in the center of the whirlpool must succeed on a DC 22 Strength saving throw or be pulled underwater and begin suffocating if it can't breathe underwater. In addition, a creature that starts its turn underwater in the center of the whirlpool must make a DC 18 Constitution saving throw, taking 21 (6d6) cold damage on a failed save, or half as much damage on a successful one. Any object that is not being worn or carried automatically fails the saving throw. A ship that starts its turn on the water within 100 feet of the point you chose automatically fails the saving throw unless its pilot succeeds on a DC 18 Dexterity or Wisdom check using navigator's tools. On initiative count 20 (losing initiative ties), the whirlpool moves 1d100 feet in a random direction. The whirlpool lasts for up to 1 minute, until your concentration ends (as if concentrating on a spell), or until the whirlpool moves into water that is less than 20 feet deep. The *Moonsilver Orb* can't be used in this way again until 7 days have passed.

Destroying the Orb. The only way to destroy the *Moonsilver Orb* is to cast the *shatter* spell on it while it is on the Elemental Plane of Earth. The remains of the orb must then be consumed by an earth elemental within 1 minute or the *Moonsilver Orb* reforms within 1 hour in a random body of water on the Material Plane.

PORTRAIT OF SELF-EXAMINATION
Wondrous item, rare

This portrait of a woman with penetrating eyes is charged with magic. If you spend 24 hours over a period of 3 days or fewer studying and contemplating the portrait, the colors swirl and shift to reflect you, and you learn some deep, inner truth about yourself. At the end of the 24 hours, you must make a DC 15 Wisdom saving throw. On a success, you accept the deep, inner truth the portrait reveals to you, and your Wisdom score increases by 1. On a failure, the portrait's revelation shakes your confidence in yourself and your abilities, and your Charisma score decreases by 1.

PRESERVED HEARTS
Wondrous item, rarity by heart

A *preserved heart* is the magically-preserved heart from a humanoid. Different types of hearts exist, each with a different single-use effect. To activate the heart's magic, you must use an action to consume it.

Courtesan (uncommon). This heart once belonged to a courtesan slain by a competitor. When you consume it, you gain the ability to cast the *friends* cantrip for 24 hours. In addition, you can cast the *charm person* spell once for the next 24 hours. Your spell save DC for these spells is equal to 8 + your proficiency bonus + your Constitution modifier.

Shaman (rare). This heart once belonged to the shaman of a nomadic tribe. When you consume it, you gain 20 temporary hit points for 24 hours.

Shark Hunter (very rare). This heart once belonged to a great shark-hunting warrior who died of old age. When you consume it, you gain a swimming speed equal to your walking speed for 24 hours. In addition, severed body members (fingers, legs, tails, and so on), if any, are restored after 2 minutes. If you have the severed part and hold it to the stump, consuming the heart also causes the limb to instantaneously knit to the stump.

Slave (uncommon). This heart once belonged to an escaped slave. When you consume it, your walking speed increases by 10 feet for 24 hours.

Warrior (rare). This heart once belonged to great warrior who died after defeating overwhelming odds. When you consume it, you are immune to the charmed and frightened conditions, and you have advantage on Strength checks and Strength saving throws for 24 hours.

Witch Doctor (uncommon). This heart once belonged to a witch doctor whose heart was removed while the witch doctor was still breathing. When you consume it, you gain the ability to cast one cleric cantrip and one wizard cantrip of your choice for 24 hours. Your spell save DC for these spells is equal to 8 + your proficiency bonus + your Constitution modifier.

Youth (very rare). This heart once belonged to a wrongfully-accused youth who was punished and slain for a crime. When you consume it, your body reverses some of its aging, reducing your age by 7 years. The magic of this heart can't reduce your age to less than 7 years old.

ROD OF AIR AND WATER MASTERY
Rod, very rare (requires attunement)

This rod has two glass orbs affixed to either end. One is filled with water and the other is filled with murky, white air. It has the following properties.

Of Air and Water. While underwater and holding the rod, you have a swimming speed equal to your walking speed. While exposed to air and holding the rod, you have advantage on ability checks and saving throws against being pushed or shoved by wind, such as by a strong storm or the *gust of wind* spell.

Spells. While holding the rod, you can use an action to cast one of the following spells from it: *feather fall*, *fog cloud*, *water breathing*, or *water walk*.

Of Ice and Wind. While holding the rod, you can use an action to cast *wall of ice* or *wind wall*. The spell save DC for these spells is 17. This feature can't be used again until the next dawn.

SAHUAGIN'S DISMAY
Wondrous item, very rare

This tattered, green flag bears the image of a red trident. While this flag flies on the mast of a ship, the ship and its crew are protected from nonmagical extreme weather. The temperature on the ship is always cool, wind speeds never go higher than strong, and precipitation that falls on the ship is never heavier than a steady mist. The flag also protects the ship from begin swamped by even the largest waves, though strong currents still affect the ship. The flag doesn't protect the ship from predation by sea creatures or from being capsized or sunk by such creatures.

SEXTANT OF SEEMING
Wondrous item, very rare

While holding this sextant inside a seafaring vessel, you can use an action to cast *mirage arcane* on the vessel. The illusion lasts for up to 24 hours or until you use an action to dismiss it. Once you use this feature, you can't use it again until the next dawn.

SHUDDERER'S COWL
Wondrous item, rare (requires attunement)

While wearing this cloak in bright or dim light, you have resistance to cold damage.

Curse. Once you don this cursed cloak, you can't remove it unless you are targeted by the *remove curse* spell or similar magic. While wearing this cloak in darkness, you have vulnerability to cold damage, and you have disadvantage on saving throws against being frightened.

SPECTACLES OF THE SAHUAGIN
Wondrous item, rare

While wearing these lenses made from carefully-preserved sahuagin eyes, you have darkvision out to a range of 60 feet, and you can magically command any shark within 60 feet of you, using a limited telepathy. If you already have darkvision, wearing the spectacles increases its range by 60 feet.

UNYIELDING MAST

Wondrous item, legendary

This unassuming, wooden mast has a mithral core and is infused with magic. While the mast is affixed to a ship big enough for a crew of at least 10, the ship gains the following benefits:

The ship's damage threshold increases by 5.

The ship is immune to fire damage.

The ship magically repairs 5 hit points of damage each day it hasn't taken damage.

WETSKIN OF THE KUAH-LIJ

Wondrous item, uncommon

If you breathe only water or have the Limited Amphibiousness trait, you can breathe normally out of the water while wearing this wetskin.

In addition, while wearing this wetskin, you can use an action to cast the *thunderwave* spell with it, except the spell deals cold damage instead of thunder damage, and it doesn't create an audible boom. The spell save DC for this spell is 15. The wetskin can't be used this way again until the next dawn or until the wetskin spends 8 hours submerged in water.

WHEEL OF CHAOS

Wondrous item, rare

This ornately-decorated ship's wheel is inlaid with symbols of chaos and destruction. While the wheel is affixed to a ship big enough for a crew of at least 10, the ship's speed is increased by 25%. In addition, you can use an action to cast the *control weather* spell with it. The spell lasts 8 hours, and you don't need to maintain concentration on it. The wheel can't be used this way again until 5 days have passed.

Curse. This wheel is cursed and affixing it to a ship extends the curse to the ship. Once affixed to a ship, the wheel can't be removed unless the ship is targeted by the *remove curse* spell or similar magic. While the wheel is affixed to a ship, denizens of the sea are attracted to the ship. A creature with the Amphibious or Water Breathing trait has advantage on Wisdom (Perception) checks to detect the ship, on Strength (Athletics) and Dexterity (Acrobatics) checks to climb or move on the ship, and on its first attack roll each round while on the ship.

CHAPTER 6: NEW MONSTERS

New and original creatures are presented here to enrich any campaign based on the sea. A random encounter table can be found for these monsters and more in the Appendix.

BLUE-FINNED VANT

These fish are about four feet long, with a broad, thick-ribbed fins across their backs. They are glittery blue in color, with a white underbelly.

Pressure-Based Fish. Blue-finned vants are tropical fish that can control the water pressure around them. They dwell in or near deep coral reefs, particularly near the edges of undersea trenches. They usually go their way alone or in small schools, nibbling on coral encrustations with their bony, beak-like mouths, but can sometimes be found hunting in deeper waters. Blue-finned vants rely upon their ability to control the water pressure around them to drive off or harm potential predators, or to allow them to flee to depths that would crush most other creatures.

BLUE-FINNED VANT
Small beast, unaligned

Armor Class 13
Hit Points 22 (5d6 + 5)
Speed 0 ft., swim 40 ft.

STR	DEX	CON	INT	WIS	CHA
8 (−1)	17 (+3)	13 (+1)	1 (−5)	12 (+1)	2 (−4)

Skills Perception +3
Damage Resistances cold
Senses darkvision 60 ft., passive Perception 13
Languages —
Challenge 1 (200 XP)

Water Breathing. The blue-finned vant can breathe only underwater

Actions

Bite. *Melee Weapon Attack:* +5 to hit, reach 5 ft., one target. *Hit:* 6 (1d6 + 3) piercing damage.

Pressure Shift **(recharge 6).** While underwater, the blue-finned vant suddenly discharges water around it. Each creature within 10 feet of it must make a DC 13 Strength saving throw. On a failure, a creature takes 10 (3d6) bludgeoning damage and is pushed up to 10 feet away from the vant. On a success, a creature takes half the damage but isn't pushed.

BONJO TOMBO

Bonjo Tombo is a gorilla-like creature of truly monstrous proportions. It is a hulking brute nearly 50 feet tall at the shoulder with two pairs of yellowish eyes on either side of its horrific face, one atop the other. The beast has a wide simian mouth exposing a pair of huge curving tusks that protrude from its powerful lower jaw. Nearly hairless, its massive frame ripples with muscle beneath its filthy grayish skin. It has long arms that end in huge clawed hands and short powerful legs that end in apish feet.

Demonic Origins. Bonjo Tombo, the huge Demon Ape, is dumb, fierce, and thoroughly evil. Spawn of a two-headed demon prince and a fiendish dire ape, Bonjo Tombo rules his jungle island through malice, fear, and primeval cruelty. Although enormous, Bonjo Tombo is adept at hiding in the thick jungle vegetation of his island, his shaggy gray fur blending into the surrounding terrain.

Afraid of Water. Bonjo Tombo dislikes running water and refuses to cross it. This may be counted as a blessing by many, as it has kept him upon his island and away from the more civilized locales of the world.

At the onset of any fight, Bonjo Tombo attempts to shatter the will of his foes with an ear-splitting roar.

Bonjo Tombo prefers to attack first with his trample, before grappling opponents with his great reach. He devours many of his opponents whole or hurls them great distances, breaking their bones and softening them up for his feast. If threatened with death, Bonjo Tombo flees.

BONJO TOMBO
Gargantuan fiend, chaotic evil

Armor Class 18 (natural armor)
Hit Points 217 (14d20 + 70)
Speed 40 ft., climb 40 ft.

STR	DEX	CON	INT	WIS	CHA
24 (+7)	14 (+2)	21 (+5)	8 (−1)	15 (+2)	7 (−2)

Saving Throws Dex +7, Con +10
Skills Athletics +12, Perception +7, Stealth +7
Damage Vulnerabilities cold
Damage Resistances fire, lightning; bludgeoning, piercing, and slashing from nonmagical attacks
Damage Immunities poison
Condition Immunities poisoned
Senses darkvision 120 ft., passive Perception 17
Languages Abyssal, Common, telepathy 120 ft.
Challenge 16 (15,000 XP)

Keen Smell. Bonjo Tombo has advantage on Wisdom (Perception) checks that rely on smell.

Legendary Resistance **(3/day).** If Bonjo Tombo fails a saving throw, he can choose to succeed instead.

Standing Leap. Bonjo Tombo's long jump is up to 30 feet and his high jump is up to 15 feet, with or without a running start.

Water Diminution. Each round Bonjo Tombo is immersed in running water or in saltwater, his size is reduced. This trait works like the *enlarge/reduce* spell, except it doesn't reduce Bonjo Tombo below Tiny and it lasts until Bonjo Tombo spends 1 month outside of running water or saltwater.

Actions

Multiattack. Bonjo Tombo makes one Bite attack and two Fist attacks. If Bonjo Tombo hits a Large or smaller creature with both Fist attacks, the target is grappled (escape DC 20).

Bite. *Melee Weapon Attack:* +12 to hit, reach 10 ft., one target. *Hit:* 26 (3d12 + 7) piercing damage.

Fist. *Melee Weapon Attack:* +12 to hit, reach 15 ft., one target. *Hit:* 23 (3d10 + 7) bludgeoning damage.

Deafening Roar **(recharge 6).** Bonjo Tombo releases a deafening roar. Each creature within 30 feet of Bonjo

Tombo that can hear him must make a DC 18 Constitution saving throw. On a failure, a creature takes 44 (8d10) thunder damage and is deafened for 1 minute. On a success, a creature takes half the damage and isn't deafened. A deafened creature can repeat the saving throw at the end of each of its turns, ending the effect on itself on a success.

Legendary Actions

Bonjo Tombo can take 3 legendary actions, choosing from the options below. Only one legendary action can be used at a time and only at the end of another creature's turn. Bonjo Tombo regains spent legendary actions at the start of his turn.

Move. Bonjo Tombo moves up to his speed without provoking opportunity attacks.

Bite (costs 2 actions). Bonjo Tombo makes one bite attack.

Fling (costs 3 actions). Bonjo Tombo throws a creature he is grappling up to 30 feet in a random direction. The grappled creature must make a DC 18 Strength saving throw. On a failure, the creature is thrown 30 feet, takes 21 (6d6) bludgeoning damage, and falls prone. On a success, the creature is thrown 15 feet, takes half the bludgeoning damage, and falls prone. If a creature succeeds by 5 or more, it is thrown only 10 feet, takes half the bludgeoning damage, and doesn't fall prone.

BREATH TAKER

A breath taker is a partially skeletal creature clad in the soggy trappings of a pirate. At first glance, a breath taker might be mistaken for a brine zombie or lacedon. Breath takers are more powerful than those lesser undead, however, and such a mistake in identification can lead to a cruel death.

Underwater Thieves. In life, breath takers were evil thieves who drowned at sea or pirates who took valuable goods from others that plied the waves. Now, in unlife, they seek out and steal that which was first taken from them — the ability to breathe.

Bolstered by Breath. Breath takers attack their victims with long, seaweed-encrusted fingernails before finishing off the creature with their dreaded ability to steal the very breath from a creature's lungs. The breath taker's rotted chest visibly expands as it draws this fresh air into itself.

Undead Nature. The breath taker doesn't require air, food, drink, or sleep.

BREATH TAKER
Medium undead, chaotic evil

Armor Class 14
Hit Points 78 (12d8 + 24)
Speed 20 ft., swim 30 ft.

STR	DEX	CON	INT	WIS	CHA
12 (+1)	18 (+4)	15 (+2)	11 (+0)	8 (−1)	5 (−3)

Saving Throws Wis +1
Skills Perception +1, Stealth +6
Damage Resistances necrotic
Damage Immunities poison
Condition Immunities poisoned
Senses darkvision 60 ft., passive Perception 11
Languages Common
Challenge 4 (1,100 XP)

Breath Eater. If a suffocating creature is within 30 feet of the breath taker, the breath taker's Armor Class increases by 1, and its weapon attacks deals an extra 1d6 necrotic damage.

Actions

Multiattack. The breath taker makes two Claws attacks.

Claws. Melee Weapon Attack: +6 to hit, reach 5 ft., one target. *Hit:* 9 (2d4 + 4) slashing damage plus 3 (1d6) necrotic damage.

Steal Breath. Melee Weapon Attack: +6 to hit, reach 5 ft., one target. *Hit:* 7 (1d6 + 4) necrotic damage, and the target must make a DC 14 Constitution saving throw or begin suffocating. The target continues to suffocate while within 30 feet of the breath taker. If the saving throw fails by 5 or more, the target also gains 1 level of exhaustion. If a humanoid dies from suffocation or exhaustion while within 30 feet of the breath taker, it rises 24 hours later as a breath taker.

CORALITE

Coralites are humanoids who stand four to five feet tall and have a bulky build. Their skin is a deep, rich brown, and their hair is long, dark, and streaked with red or blonde. Both men and women wear garments of diaphanous silk in bright, vibrant colors, to reflect a living coral reef.

Pacifists. Coralite culture and society are founded on one overriding principle: peace. They strongly oppose combat and violence of all types and attempt to live in peaceful relations with all of their neighbors. Overcoming their abhorrence of violence is a significant challenge to their effectiveness at combat.

Artists. From birth, Coralite children are taught history, religion, spellcraft, and the arts: music, poetry, painting, sculpting, and literature. The Coralites are universally skilled at some artistic endeavor, and they follow it their whole life. They are also quite skilled at performing, and even those who don't study music can recite poetry.

Songchangers. The songchangers are the offspring of the Coralites' marriage of magic and music. Songchanger wizards have learned to manipulate the very elemental matter of creation through song and music. They weave powerful magic into their musical compositions and are revered even above the priests in Coralite society.

CORALITE
Medium humanoid (coralite), neutral good

Armor Class 12 (studded leather)
Hit Points 13 (3d8)
Speed 30 ft., swim 30 ft.

STR	DEX	CON	INT	WIS	CHA
14 (+2)	10 (+0)	11 (+0)	14 (+2)	8 (−1)	16 (+3)

Skills Performance +5, Persuasion +5
Senses passive Perception 9
Languages Aquan, Common, Coralite, Elvish
Challenge 1/4 (50 XP)

Hold Breath. The coralite can hold its breath for 15 minutes.

Pacifism. The coralite has disadvantage on an attack roll if the target hasn't harmed the coralite within the last 24 hours.

Sudden Inspiration (recharge 6). As a bonus action, the coralite rolls a d4. The coralite can add the result to one attack roll, ability check, or saving throw it makes before the start of its next turn.

Actions

Spear. *Melee or Ranged Weapon Attack:* +4 to hit, reach 5 ft. or range 20/60 ft., one target. *Hit:* 5 (1d6 + 2) piercing damage, or 6 (1d8 + 2) piercing damage if used with two hands to make a melee attack.

CORALITE SONGCHANGER

Medium humanoid (coralite), neutral good

Armor Class 11 (14 with *mage armor*)
Hit Points 49 (11d8)
Speed 30 ft., swim 30 ft.

STR	DEX	CON	INT	WIS	CHA
8 (–1)	12 (+1)	11 (+0)	18 (+4)	8 (–1)	16 (+3)

Saving Throws Cha +5
Skills Performance +5, Persuasion +5
Senses passive Perception 9
Languages Aquan, Common, Coralite, Elvish
Challenge 3 (700 XP)

Hold Breath. The coralite can hold its breath for 15 minutes.
Inspiring Presence. The songchanger and its allies within 10 feet have advantage on saving throws against being charmed or frightened. Once a creature has succeeded on such a saving throw while within 10 feet of the songchanger, it can't benefit from the songchanger's Inspiring Presence for the next 24 hours.
Pacifism. The coralite has disadvantage on an attack roll if the target hasn't harmed the coralite within the last 24 hours.
Spellcasting. The coralite songchanger is a 5th-level spellcaster. Its spellcasting ability is Intelligence (spell save DC #, +# to hit with spell attacks). The songchanger has the following wizard spells prepared:
Cantrips (at will): *dancing lights, minor illusion, prestidigitation, ray of frost*
1st level (4 slots): *charm person, color spray, fog cloud, mage armor*
2nd level (3 slots): *misty step, shatter, suggestion*
3rd level (2 slots): *hypnotic pattern, water breathing*
Sudden Inspiration (recharge 6). As a bonus action, the coralite rolls a d4. The coralite can add the result to one attack roll, ability check, or saving throw it makes before the start of its next turn.

Actions

Dagger. *Melee or Ranged Weapon Attack:* +3 to hit, reach 5 ft. Or range 20/60 ft., one target. *Hit:* 3 (1d4 + 1) piercing damage.

DECK DEVIL

Deck devils are large porpoise-like creatures with greatly elongated flippers and razor-sharp teeth.

Innocent Appearance. These voracious sea creatures resemble porpoises at first glance, but they are quite unlike their docile cousins. Deck devils have a reputation as being bloodthirsty maneaters. They are carnivorous and use their innocent appearance to move in close to oncoming ships, at which point they attack any sailors they see. These aquatic creatures travel in small schools and are quite territorial. Battles between rival pods stir up the ocean to a froth of sea foam and spilled blood.

Beached Terrors. Like normal whales, deck devils sometimes beach themselves, but this in no way decreases their ferocity. Even a beached and dying deck devil attacks anything that comes near. Though deck devils are vicious combatants underwater, they have become infamous across the Moonsilver Sea for their ability to attack sailors on the decks of passing ships.

DECK DEVIL

Medium monstrosity, unaligned

Armor Class 12
Hit Points 55 (10d8 + 10)
Speed 5 ft., swim 60 ft.

STR	DEX	CON	INT	WIS	CHA
17 (+3)	14 (+2)	12 (+1)	4 (–3)	13 (+1)	7 (–2)

Skills Perception +3
Senses darkvision 120 ft., passive Perception 13
Languages understands Aquan but can't speak
Challenge 2 (450 XP)

Hold Breath. The deck devil can hold its breath for 30 minutes.
Trampling Glide. If the deck devil is flying and moves at least 20 feet straight toward a creature then hits it with a tail attack on the same turn, that target must succeed on a DC 13 Strength saving throw or be knocked prone. If the target is prone, the deck devil can make one bite attack against it as a bonus action.
Water Leap. The deck devil can fly up to 30 feet each round, but it must start its movement in water. If it is flying at the end of its turn, it falls and takes falling damage.

Actions

Bite. *Melee Weapon Attack:* +5 to hit, reach 5 ft., one target. *Hit:* 13 (3d6 + 3) piercing damage, and the target is grappled (escape DC 13). Until this grapple ends, the target is restrained, and the deck devil can't bite another target.
Tail. *Melee Weapon Attack:* +5 to hit, reach 5 ft., one target. *Hit:* 10 (2d6 + 3) bludgeoning damage.

EEL, FIRE

This large eel has a broad, triangular head and a pair of jet-black eyes. Its scales are dark gray on top, lightening to white underneath.

Fire eels are a beautiful but dangerous species of fish that can ignite an oily residue on its skin to drive away predators and attract a mate.

Fiery Courtship. Fire eels can be particularly dangerous to seagoing vessels during their mating season. During this season, they come to the surface en masse to perform fiery courtship rituals, and they are highly aggressive. When they come into contact with air, their bodies burst into flames that can be green, blue, red, violet, or patterns of these colors, depending on the individual eel.

Docile Unless Provoked. Fire eels are normally inoffensive and avoid combat if they can. However, if they are attacked or if it is their mating season, they become more aggressive and use their fire to ward off attacks while they bite until their opponents are driven away.

Fire Eel

Large monstrosity, unaligned

Armor Class 13
Hit Points 75 (10d10 + 20)
Speed 0 ft., swim 60 ft.

STR	DEX	CON	INT	WIS	CHA
12 (+1)	17 (+3)	15 (+2)	2 (–4)	14 (+2)	10 (+0)

Skills Perception +4
Damage Immunities fire
Senses darkvision 60 ft., passive Perception 14
Languages —
Challenge 3 (700 XP)

Fire Shroud. A creature that touches the fire eel or hits it with a melee attack while within 5 feet of it takes 3 (1d6) fire damage. While the fire eel is exposed to air, this shroud appears as bright green, blue, red, or violet flames wreathing it. While the fire eel is immersed in water, this shroud appears as bubbly, superheated water around it.

Water Breathing. The fire eel can breathe only underwater.

Actions

Bite. *Melee Weapon Attack:* +5 to hit, reach 5 ft., one target. *Hit:* 12 (2d8 + 3) piercing damage plus 7 (2d6) fire damage.

Elf, Sea

The creature before you looks like a standard elf, but appears even thinner. Her long green hair reminds you of seaweed.

Aquatic Elves. Similar to their land-bound cousins, sea elves are slender and long-lived. Their skin varies in shades of blue and purple, and their hair often resembles seaweed.

Peaceful Scholars. Sea elves fight to defend themselves and their homes but are, on the whole, a peaceful race. Should the need to fight arise, a sea elf uses whatever means is at its disposal. They spend their years separate from the surface races, studying the many ancient ruins and shipwrecks that dot their realm.

Sea Elf City Defender

Medium humanoid (elf), neutral good

Armor Class 13
Hit Points 26 (4d8 + 8)
Speed 30 ft., swim 30 ft.

STR	DEX	CON	INT	WIS	CHA
10 (+0)	16 (+3)	14 (+2)	10 (+0)	12 (+1)	11 (+0)

Skills Insight +3, Perception +3
Senses darkvision 60 ft., passive Perception 13
Languages Common, Elvish
Challenge 1/2 (100 XP)

Brave. The sea elf has advantage on saving throws against being frightened.

Fey Ancestry. The sea elf has advantage on saving throws against being charmed, and magic can't put the sea elf to sleep.

Actions

Trident. *Melee or Ranged Weapon Attack:* +5 to hit, reach 5 ft. or range 20/60 ft., one target. *Hit:* 6 (1d6 + 3) piercing damage, or 7 (1d8 + 3) piercing damage if used with two hands to make a melee attack.

Net. *Ranged Weapon Attack:* +5 to hit, range 5/15 ft., one Large or smaller creature. *Hit:* The target is restrained. A creature can use its action to make a DC 10 Strength check to free itself or another creature in a net, ending the effect on a success. Dealing 5 slashing damage to the net (AC 10) frees the target without harming it and destroys the net.

Reactions

Parry. The sea elf adds 2 to its AC against one melee attack that would hit it. To do so, the sea elf must see the attacker and be wielding a melee weapon.

Glass Whale

A whale-shaped construct composed entirely of thick, clear glass travels the depths of the ocean, housing researchers. The body is fashioned with a dorsal hump, medium-sized flippers, and a powerful fluke that's as sharp and deadly as broken glass. Its huge, bulky head takes up nearly a third of its total body length. A single, angled blowhole is located on the far left top of its forehead, and the slim and narrow lower jaw of the glass whale is lined with peg-like teeth that fit into grooves along its robust upper jaw.

Research Vessel. The glass whale is painstakingly modeled after the sperm whale, as its massive size and deep-diving ability is ideal for sea exploration. The glass whale is created as a vessel for researchers intending to discover more about the far reaches of the ocean. It takes simple orders from its creator, usually navigational commands. If its creator is slain, the glass whale endlessly drifts the ocean without purpose. A creature inside a glass whale whose creator has been slain can operate the glass whale with a successful DC 20 Intelligence (Arcana) check.

Specimen Collection. The glass whale is not primarily designed for combat. Though imparted with modest offensive ability to protect itself and its passengers, the primary function of its powerful jaw is to collect deep ocean specimens. It grabs and swallows creatures into a throat compartment where it can add or expel water. If there is no water in the throat compartment, the door between the throat compartment and the interior chamber can be opened, allowing a swallowed creature access to the interior chamber.

Passenger Compartment. Used as an ocean exploration vessel for a small team of researchers, the glass whale is capable of holding up to four Large or smaller creatures in its interior compartment. A creature can reach this compartment by accessing a door in the throat compartment when the throat isn't filled with water, or it can enter the interior compartment through a hatch near the glass whale's blowhole.

Constructed Nature. The glass whale doesn't require air, food, drink, or sleep.

Glass Whale

Gargantuan construct, unaligned

Armor Class 16 (natural armor)
Hit Points 188 (13d20 + 52)
Speed 0 ft., swim 60 ft.

STR	DEX	CON	INT	WIS	CHA
21 (+5)	10 (+0)	18 (+4)	3 (–4)	12 (+1)	1 (–5)

Skills Perception +5

Damage Resistances bludgeoning, piercing, and slashing from nonmagical attacks

Damage Immunities poison

Condition Immunities charmed, exhaustion, frightened, paralyzed, petrified, poisoned

Senses darkvision 120 ft., passive Perception 15

Languages understands Common and Aquan but can't speak

Challenge 12 (8,400 XP)

Deep Diver. The glass whale ignores the drawbacks caused by a deep, underwater environment.

Explosive Demise. When the glass whale dies, it shatters in a burst of water and glass shards. Each creature within 10 feet of it must make a DC 17 Dexterity saving throw, taking 33 (6d10) piercing damage on a failed save, or half as much damage on a successful one. Creatures inside either of the glass whale's compartments have disadvantage on this saving throw.

Illumination. As a bonus action, the glass whale can illuminate panels along the underside of its body. While illuminated, the glass whale sheds bright light in a 20-foot radius and dim light for an additional 20 feet.

Passenger Compartment. The glass whale's body is hollow and can hold up to four Large or smaller creatures. This interior compartment holds enough air for 24 hours of breathing, divided by the number of breathing creatures inside. To replenish the air supply, the glass whale must breach the water's surface and collect air through its blowhole for 5 minutes. A creature in the glass whale's interior compartment can see through the whale's glass body, but it has disadvantage on Wisdom (Perception) checks to hear sounds outside the glass whale. A creature in the interior compartment can't be targeted by attacks, abilities, or spells from outside the glass whale. A creature inside the glass whale ignores drawbacks caused by a deep, underwater environment.

Throat Compartment. The glass whale has a throat compartment between its mouth and interior compartment. As a bonus action, the glass whale can fill this compartment with water or expel water from the compartment. A creature inside the throat compartment when it is full of water must hold its breath or suffocate as normal for being underwater. A creature inside the throat compartment when it is empty of water can find a hidden hatch into the interior compartment with a successful DC 20 Wisdom (Perception) check. A creature inside the throat compartment can force the glass whale to fill the throat compartment with water or expel water from it with a successful DC 17 Strength (Athletics) or Intelligence (Arcana) check.

Actions

Multiattack. The glass whale makes one Bite attack and two Tail attacks. It can't make a Bite attack and a Tail attack against the same target.

Bite. *Melee Weapon Attack:* +9 to hit, reach 5 ft., one target. *Hit:* 27 (4d10 + 5) piercing damage, and the target is grappled (escape DC 17). Until this grapple ends, the target is restrained, and the glass whale can't bite another target.

Swallow. The glass whale makes one bite attack against a Large or smaller creature it is grappling. If the attack hits, that creature takes the bite's damage and is swallowed into the whale's throat compartment, and the grapple ends. While in the whale's throat compartment, the creature is blinded and restrained, it has total cover against attacks and other

effects outside the glass whale, and, if the throat compartment is filled with water, it takes 21 (6d6) bludgeoning damage at the start of each of the glass whale's turns.

If the glass whale takes 30 damage or more on a single turn from a creature in its throat compartment, the glass whale must succeed on a DC 15 Constitution saving throw at the end of that turn or regurgitate all creatures in its throat compartment, which fall prone in a space within 10 feet of the glass whale. If the glass whale dies, a creature in the throat compartment is no longer restrained by it and can escape from the glass whale's shattered remains using 5 feet of movement.

The glass whale can't swallow a creature if the hatch between the throat compartment and the interior compartment is open.

Tail. *Melee Weapon Attack:* +9 to hit, reach 10 ft., one target. *Hit:* 23 (4d8 + 5) slashing damage.

GLOWFLUME SWARM

This swarm of plants floats on the surface of the water, glowing various vibrant colors.

The glowflume is a kind of tiny, carnivorous plant that gathers in swarms on the sea's surface and produces a brilliant display of colors to attract prey.

Dangerous Glow. The glowflume's hypnotic glow draws in fish and sea travelers alike. Creatures drawn by the glow swim into the swarm of glowflume only to discover too late the danger they face as the tiny, flesh-eating plants devour the captivated creature.

Scavenger Beacon. Glowflume most commonly grows near reefs and other shallow seas where it can easily draw in land-bound creatures. The glowflume primarily consumes flesh, often leaving organs and bones in its wake. Many reef and coastal scavengers follow a swarm of glowflume on the hunt but are careful not to get too close lest they end up the main course themselves.

GLOWFLUME SWARM
Large swarm of Tiny plants, unaligned

Armor Class 13
Hit Points 82 (11d10 + 22)
Speed 0 ft., swim 30 ft.

STR	DEX	CON	INT	WIS	CHA
3(−4)	17 (+3)	14 (+2)	1 (−5)	8 (−1)	1 (−5)

Damage Resistances bludgeoning, piercing, slashing

Condition Immunities blinded, charmed, deafened, frightened, grappled, paralyzed, petrified, prone, restrained, stunned

Senses blindsight 60 ft., passive Perception 9

Languages —

Challenge 4 (1,100 XP)

Hypnotic Illumination. When a creature that can see the glowflume's glow starts its turn within 30 feet of the glowflume, the glowflume can force it to make a DC 13 Wisdom saving throw if the glowflume isn't incapacitated.

On a failed saving throw, a creature is incapacitated and charmed by the glowflume as long as it can still see the glowflume. If the charmed creature is more than 5 feet away from the glowflume, the creature must move on its turn toward the glowflume by the most direct route, trying to get within 5 feet. It doesn't avoid opportunity attacks, but before moving into damaging terrain, such as lava or a pit, and whenever it takes damage from a source other than the glowflume, the target can repeat the saving throw. A charmed target can also repeat the saving throw at the end of each of its turns, ending the effect on itself on a success.

Unless surprised, a creature can avert its eyes to avoid the saving throw at the start of its turn. If the creature does so, it can't see the glowflume until the start of its next turn, when it can avert its eyes again. If the creature looks at the glowflume in the meantime, it must immediately make the save.

Swarm. The glowflume swarm can occupy another creature's space and vice versa, and the swarm can move through any opening large enough for a Tiny plant. The swarm can't regain hit points or gain temporary hit points.

Water Breathing. The glowflume swarm can breathe only underwater.

Actions

Multiattack. The glowflume swarm makes two Consume Flesh attacks.

Consume Flesh. Melee Weapon Attack: +5 to hit, reach 0 ft., one creature in the swarm's space. *Hit:* 10 (4d4) acid damage, or 5 (2d4) acid damage if the swarm has half of its hit points or fewer. The target must succeed on a DC 13 Constitution saving throw or take 5 (2d4) acid damage at the start of its next turn as the glowflume's acid momentarily lingers, dissolving more of the target's flesh.

HYDROPHANT

The hydrophant appears as a hulking, legless humanoid composed entirely of thousands of moist, diaphanous bubbles. The lower torso develops into a large fluke, similar to a whale's. Two oval-shaped, dark blue water cavities serve as its eyes, while a dense cluster of gray-colored bubbles line the recess that marks its mouth.

The hydrophant is a cantankerous elemental culmination of air and water, renowned for its cruel and territorial nature.

Territorial. Hydrophants are native to the Elemental Plane of Water. However, many find homes in the seas of the Material Plane, where they construct monuments of bubbles, seaweed, and coral. The hydrophant obsessively seeks to increase the size of its territory, resulting in nearby sea life becoming stagnant.

Cruel Trophy Keepers. Sinister ornaments of carcasses and other remains of defeated foes easily distinguish a hydrophant's domain. Hydrophants often carry the remains of recently defeated opponents within their torsos as trophies. Hydrophants have little patience for tactics. Any creature infringing upon a hydrophant's territory is subject to immediate attack. When facing easy opposition, a hydrophant is likely to toy with its foes.

Elemental Nature. The hydrophant doesn't require air, food, drink, or sleep.

HYDROPHANT
Huge elemental, neutral evil

Armor Class 16 (natural armor)
Hit Points 153 (18d12 + 36)
Speed 10 ft., swim 60 ft.

STR	DEX	CON	INT	WIS	CHA
18 (+4)	16 (+3)	15 (+2)	6 (−2)	10 (+0)	8 (−1)

Skills Intimidate +3, Stealth +7

Damage Resistances bludgeoning, piercing, and slashing from nonmagical attacks
Damage Immunities lightning, poison, thunder
Condition Immunities exhaustion, grappled, paralyzed, petrified, poisoned, prone, restrained, unconscious
Senses darkvision 60 ft., passive Perception 10
Languages Aquan, Auran
Challenge 10 (5,900 XP)

False Appearance. While the hydrophant is motionless and isn't carrying a creature inside it, it is indistinguishable from a normal collection of sea foam or bubbles.

Actions

Multiattack. The hydrophant makes one Tail Slap attack and two Slam attacks. If both Slam attacks hit a Medium or smaller target, the target is grappled (escape DC 16), and the hydrophant can use its Engulf on the target.

Tail Slap. Melee Weapon Attack: +8 to hit, reach 5 ft., one target. *Hit:* 20 (3d10 + 4) bludgeoning damage.

Slam. Melee Weapon Attack: +8 to hit, reach 5 ft., one target. *Hit:* 17 (3d8 + 4) bludgeoning damage.

Engulf. The hydrophant engulfs a Medium or smaller creature grappled by it. The engulfed target is blinded, restrained, and unable to breathe, and it must succeed on a DC 16 Constitution saving throw at the start of each of its turns or take 17 (3d8 + 4) bludgeoning damage. If the hydrophant moves, the engulfed target moves with it. The hydrophant can have only one creature engulfed at a time.

Stunning Slam (recharge 6). While underwater, the hydrophant brings its fists and tail together, rupturing some of its bubbles in a small burst. Each creature within 15 feet of the hydrophant must make a DC 16 Dexterity saving throw. On a failure, a creature takes 35 (10d6) bludgeoning damage and is stunned for 1 minute. On a success, a creature takes half the damage and isn't stunned. A stunned creature can repeat the saving throw at the end of each of its turns, ending the effect on itself on a success.

KEEL KELP

A mass of kelp floats near the surface of the water. As a ship approaches, the kelp suddenly comes to life, tangling around the hull of the vessel.

Keel kelp is semi-sentient plant that lives within 2 to 4 miles of certain tropical islands. From the bow of a ship, keel kelp appears to be nothing more than a large floating mass of tangled seaweed and kelp. If found near coral or rocky areas, it is likely to be interwoven with kelp of the standard variety.

Ship Hunter. Keel kelp hardens and sticks to ships that pass over it, entangling and slowing the ship. The keel kelp is equally happy slowly digesting the wood of the ship or the creatures inside. Against particularly sturdy ships, the keel kelp lashes out at the creatures on board, seeking easier prey.

Deadly Delicacy. Keel kelp is considered a delicacy among the nobility, and fresh keel kelp sells for large sums of gold at any large port town. Many sailors have lost their lives chasing the "green gold."

KEEL KELP
Gargantuan plant, unaligned

Armor Class 13 (natural armor)
Hit Points 100 (8d20 + 16)
Speed 5 ft., swim 60 ft.

STR	DEX	CON	INT	WIS	CHA
18 (+4)	12 (+1)	14 (+2)	2 (−4)	10 (+0)	7 (−2)

Damage Resistances fire
Damage Immunities cold
Condition Immunities blinded, deafened, frightened
Senses blindsight 60 ft., passive Perception 10
Languages —
Challenge 5 (1,800 XP)

Amphibious. The keel kelp can breathe air and water.
False Appearance. While the keel kelp remains motionless, it is indistinguishable from normal kelp.
Ship Hunter. When a ship moves within 10 feet of keel kelp, the ship's pilot must succeed on a DC 15 Intelligence or Wisdom check using navigator's tools or the keel kelp sticks to the ship, halving its speed until the kelp is removed. While stuck to a ship, the keel kelp can grapple only two creatures at a time.
Siege Monster. The keel kelp deals double damage to objects and structures.

Actions

Multiattack. The keel kelp makes four Kelp Strand attacks.
Kelp Strand. *Melee Weapon Attack:* +7 to hit, reach 15 ft., one target. *Hit:* 7 (1d6 + 4) bludgeoning damage, and the target is grappled (escape DC 15). Until this grapple ends, the target is restrained.
Squeeze. Each creature grappled by the keel kelp must make a DC 15 Strength saving throw, taking 14 (4d6) bludgeoning damage on a failed save, or half as much damage on a successful one.

KUAH-LIJ

A kuah-lij resembles a gnome that has been stretched vertically to a height of a human. Its features are knobby and elongated. Its hair is light and downy, more akin to a soft fur than anything else, and its skin is white with pale blue undertones.

The kuah-lij are a race of humanoids that inhabit a distant world orbiting a great red sun. They are a lawful and organized but dying people, due to a series of disasters on their home world, and they now search for aid.

Cataclysmic Upheaval. For several millennia, the kuah-lij and their servant race, the weedge, lived in relative peace on an old world in an advanced civilization, though much of the technology was magic-based. This changed with a series of plagues that devastated the population, followed by a gradual, inexplicable advancement of the size of their oceans. Huge floods resulted. These cataclysms were followed by the invasion of a ferocious aquatic race resembling the aboleths. The aboleth-like creatures lurked in the deepest ocean trenches of the kuah-lij planet and attacked by coming up from the depths.

Talented Crafters and Explorers. The kuah-lij, accomplished artisans, retaliated against their deep ocean foes by building a series of magically-enhanced sea craft to travel the deeps and attack these

beings. Thus far, they have arrived at a stalemate, and the kuah-lij now seek aid from other worlds and planes in their battle against their deepwater adversaries.

KUAH-LIJ EXPLORER
Medium humanoid (kuah-lij), lawful neutral

Armor Class 14 (studded leather)
Hit Points 13 (3d8)
Speed 30 ft.

STR	DEX	CON	INT	WIS	CHA
10 (+0)	15 (+2)	11 (+0)	14 (+2)	13 (+1)	11 (+0)

Skills Nature +4, Perception +3, Stealth +4, Survival +3
Senses passive Perception 13
Languages Common, Kuah-Lij
Challenge 1/2 (100 XP)

Cunning Action. On each of its turns, the explorer can use a bonus action to take the Dash, Disengage, or Hide action.
Keen Hearing and Sight. The explorer has advantage on Wisdom (Perception) checks that rely on hearing or sight.
Innate Spellcasting. The explorer's innate spellcasting ability is Intelligence. It can innately cast *mending* at will, requiring no material components.

Actions

Multiattack. The kuah-lij explorer makes two melee attacks or two ranged attacks.
Shortsword. *Melee Weapon Attack:* +4 to hit, reach 5 ft., one target. *Hit:* 5 (1d6 + 2) piercing damage.
Longbow. *Ranged Weapon Attack:* +4 to hit, range 150/600 ft., one target. *Hit:* 6 (1d8 + 2) piercing damage.

KULGREER

This macabre creature possesses no evident features common to other living creatures such as a cranium, appendages, or eyes. It has a long, conical body and a horrific, gaping maw.

Living Whirlpool. The kulgreer is a massive, abominable being of the deep sea that creates powerful whirlpools inside its funnel-like body. It has a 30-foot-long conical body resembling a funnel, beginning in a wide mouth 30 feet in diameter and tapering into a five-foot-diameter outlet of dim, white light.

Slumbering Terror. The kulgreer navigates the depths in a non-cognizant state, pointed-end first; its conical body gradually rotates and propels itself forward subconsciously, amassing various creatures into its frame as it passes through. If awakened from this state, the kulgreer is generally violent. It is popular belief that creatures sucked into the kulgreer's funnel-like body are teleported to another plane of existence. Though not consciously aggressive, the circumstances presented through a kulgreer's presence inevitably lead to conflict. If provoked, the kulgreer typically tramples its opponent in a fit of sudden sentience and conclude in the use of its supernatural ability.

Kulgreer

Gargantuan aberration, unaligned

Armor Class 16 (natural armor)
Hit Points 217 (14d20 + 70)
Speed 0 ft., swim 60 ft.

STR	DEX	CON	INT	WIS	CHA
23 (+6)	10 (+0)	21 (+5)	5 (–3)	14 (+2)	7 (–2)

Saving Throws Dex +5
Skills Perception +7
Damage Immunities cold; bludgeoning, piercing, and slashing from nonmagical attacks
Senses blindsight 60 ft., passive Perception 17
Languages understands Aquan but can't speak
Challenge 16 (15,000 XP)

Echolocation. The kulgreer can't use its blindsight while deafened.
Water Breathing. The kulgreer can breathe only underwater.

Actions

Multiattack. The kulgreer makes two Slam attacks and one Bite attack.

Slam. *Melee Weapon Attack:* +11 to hit, reach 5 ft., one target. *Hit:* 19 (3d8 + 6) bludgeoning damage.

Bite. *Melee Weapon Attack:* +11 to hit, reach 10 ft., one target. *Hit:* 22 (3d10 + 6) piercing damage, and the target is grappled (escape DC 19). Until this grapple ends, the target is restrained and the kulgreer can't bite another target.

Swallow. The kulgreer makes one bite attack against a Large or smaller target it is grappling. If the attack hits, the target is also swallowed, and the grapple ends. While swallowed, the target is blinded and restrained, it has total cover against attacks and other effects outside the kulgreer, and it takes 28 (8d6) bludgeoning damage at the start of each of the kulgreer's turns.

If the kulgreer takes 40 damage or more on a single turn from a swallowed creature, the kulgreer must succeed on a DC 20 Constitution saving throw at the end of that turn or regurgitate all swallowed creatures, which fall prone in a space within 10 feet of the kulgreer. If the kulgreer dies, a swallowed creature is no longer restrained by it and can escape from the corpse by using 15 feet of movement, exiting prone.

If a creature is reduced to 0 hit points while swallowed, it must succeed on a DC 18 Constitution saving throw or be reduced to a pile of goo. The creature can be restored to life only by means of a *true resurrection* or *wish* spell.

Whirlpool (recharge 6). The kulgreer swirls its body and creatures a whirlpool around its mouth. Each creature within 20 feet of the kulgreer must make a DC 18 Strength saving throw. On a failure, a creature takes 42 (12d6) bludgeoning damage and is swallowed by the kulgreer. On a success, a creature takes half the damage and is pulled up to 15 feet closer to the kulgreer, stopping within 5 feet of it.

Lamprey, Burrowing

Long and snakelike, the burrowing lamprey has scaleless skin the texture of supple leather.

The burrowing lamprey is an eel-like fish that attaches to its prey, then burrows into its body, feasting on blood and the rich vital organs.

Adaptable and Indiscriminate Predator. They are a danger to fish and aquatic mammals and can be as deadly as a school of piranha when encountered in large numbers. Burrowing lampreys resemble three- to four-foot-long eels with sphincter-like mouths positioned within hardened cartilaginous beaks. Although they are usually marine creatures, burrowing lampreys breed in coastal freshwater swamps and rivers, and thus can be found in fresh and saltwater environments.

Ambush Hunter. They prefer to either ambush prey by hiding along the silty ocean floor or in rocky crevices, or swarm around a target if traveling in numbers. However, it is possible that they can be encountered inside a dead creature's remains, feeding on its vital organs.

Burrowing Lamprey

Small beast, unaligned

Armor Class 13
Hit Points 10 (3d6)
Speed 15 ft., swim 30 ft.

STR	DEX	CON	INT	WIS	CHA
8 (–1)	16 (+3)	11 (+0)	2 (–4)	12 (+1)	4 (–3)

Skills Perception +3
Senses passive Perception 13
Languages —
Challenge 1 (200 XP)

Keen Smell. The burrowing lamprey has advantage on Wisdom (Perception) checks that rely on smell.

Actions

Bite. *Melee Weapon Attack:* +4 to hit, reach 5 ft., one creature. *Hit:* 6 (1d6 + 3) piercing damage, and the lamprey attaches to the target. While attached, the lamprey doesn't attack. Instead, at the start of each of the lamprey's turns, the target loses 6 (1d6 + 3) hit points due to blood loss.

The lamprey can detach itself by spending 5 feet of its movement. A creature, including the target, can use its action to detach the lamprey by succeeding on a DC 13 Strength check.

Burrow (recharge 6). The lamprey makes a bite attack against a target to which it is attached. If the attack hits, the lamprey burrows inside the creature and can't be removed with a Strength check. While burrowed inside of a creature, the lamprey is blinded and restrained, it has total cover against attacks and other effects outside the host, and the host takes 5 (2d4) poison damage at the start of each of the lamprey's turns.

The lamprey can be removed with a successful DC 13 Wisdom (Medicine) check, causing 3 (1d6) slashing damage to the host. If the lamprey is cut out without the check, the host must succeed on a DC 13 Constitution saving throw or take 7 (2d6) slashing damage.

Once it has killed the host, the lamprey stays within the host's body for up to 48 hours, feeding on the creature's remains.

Lamprey, Dire

This creature resembles an eel 13 feet long and three to four feet in diameter, with a toothy sphincter-like mouth. Its skin has no scales and has the texture of thick, rough leather.

Dire lampreys are large, sphincter-mouthed fish that live in deep waters and prey on large sea-dwelling creatures, attaching themselves and draining their blood from them with their sucking mouths. They are sometimes found attached to whales, the largest sharks, or even sea serpents. Some undersea races such as sahuagin have been known to domesticate them and use them as guard beasts.

Picky Eaters. Dire lampreys normally ignore creatures smaller than themselves as being too small a source of nourishment, though they defend themselves aggressively if provoked. However, if domesticated and trained, they can ignore this instinct and attack any creature they have been trained to.

Dire Lamprey

Large beast, unaligned

Armor Class 11
Hit Points 90 (12d10 + 24)
Speed 15 ft., swim 60 ft.

STR	DEX	CON	INT	WIS	CHA
18 (+4)	13 (+1)	14 (+2)	2 (–4)	12 (+1)	4 (–3)

Skills Perception +3, Stealth +3
Senses passive Perception 13
Languages —
Challenge 4 (1,100 XP)

Keen Smell. The burrowing lamprey has advantage on Wisdom (Perception) checks that rely on smell.

Actions

Multiattack. The dire lamprey makes one Bite attack and one Tail Slap attack.

Bite. *Melee Weapon Attack:* +6 to hit, reach 5 ft., one creature. *Hit:* 11 (2d6 + 4) piercing damage, and the lamprey attaches to the target. While attached, the lamprey doesn't attack. Instead, at the start of each of the lamprey's turns, the target loses 11 (2d6 + 4) hit points due to blood loss.
The lamprey can detach itself by spending 5 feet of its movement. A creature, including the target, can use its action to detach the lamprey by succeeding on a DC 14 Strength check.

Tail Slap. *Melee Weapon Attack:* +6 to hit, reach 10 ft., one creature. *Hit:* 9 (2d4 + 4) bludgeoning damage

Subdue Prey (recharge 4–6). A creature to which the lamprey is attached must make a DC 14 Constitution saving throw, taking 21 (6d6) poison damage on a failed save, or half as much damage on a successful one. If the saving throw fails by 5 or more, the target falls unconscious. A target made unconscious by Subdue Prey doesn't awaken from loss of hit points due to blood loss.

Nisp

These creatures resemble hairless humanoids with smooth, slick skin; their hands and feet are webbed and end in claws, and their faces have large, dark pupil-less eyes. They have no noses or ears, and their small fishlike mouths are filled with tiny, sharp teeth.

Nisps are a race of water-based fey creatures that dwell in swamps, rivers, lakes, and seas. They range from the weak and cowardly spangled nisp to the large, deadly gray nisp found in deep water.

Semi-Sentient and Coastal. Though technically sentient, nisps do not reason the way most creatures do. They have no concept of love, duty, or hatred, though they do seem capable of nearly insatiable curiosity and malice. The weaker nisps dwell in families located beneath the surface, and often scavenge near land-based communities, while the stronger nisps dwell away from communities and are both solitary and territorial.

Burgundy Ambushers. Some nisps have dark, burgundy skin with bellies that lighten to a pale vermilion. They often lurk near the surface, especially under boats or piers, and launch themselves from the water to attack their prey. They live in underwater caves and hollows, often in families and small clans. They may pick up and move to another area frequently or stay in a place for years. They avoid other underwater races and almost certainly avoid living near a community of such beings.

Crested Animal Friends. Some nisps have sleek, colored hides with a finned crest running along their heads and down their spine. These crested nisps are solitary, territorial creatures that prefer to dwell in coral reefs or rocky shoals, often in coastal waters. Because of their affinity with creatures of the sea, they often have predatory marine life positioned strategically about their lairs and are often accompanied by sharks, large eels, or other defenders. They maintain one area for their entire lives, never seeking to leave it, and they become riled when their territory is invaded. When a crested nisp is seriously injured, it retreats to its lair, trusting carefully-placed sea creatures and hazards to weaken or drive off pursuers while it regains its strength.

Gray Terrors. The gray nisp is a fearsome, gray-skinned nisp with a white underbelly. It has large, wicked talons and an unusually large mouth filled with dagger-like teeth. Gray nisps dwell in deeper water, in caves on the ocean floor, or hollows at the bottom of sizeable lakes. They are isolative and territorial like their crested cousins but have more of the curiosity of the lesser nisps. They are just as likely to attempt to communicate with intruders in their territory as they are to eat such intruders.

Spangled Cowards. The weakest of the species, the spangled nisp is named for its pallid skin speckled with moles of various colors. They are the most cowardly and inoffensive of the species, fleeing whenever confronted. However, they do feel the curiosity innate in their species and often come to shore in the dark to rummage through the refuse of land-dweller settlements. Some primitive cultures allow spangled nisps to co-exist, often feeding the nisps in exchange for warnings when outsiders approach. The nisps can understand a few basic words of nearby communities' languages, but they don't speak. Because of their innate cowardice, the spangled nisp flees from any confrontation with a creature its size or larger and may even back down from smaller creatures if the creatures put on a bold enough display. If cornered, spangled nisps defend themselves and seek to escape as soon as possible.

Burgundy Nisp

Medium fey, chaotic neutral

Armor Class 12
Hit Points 18 (4d8)
Speed 20 ft., swim 40 ft.

STR	DEX	CON	INT	WIS	CHA
10 (+0)	14 (+2)	11 (+0)	2 (–4)	12 (+1)	6 (–2)

Skills Stealth +4
Senses darkvision 60 ft., passive Perception 11
Languages —
Challenge 1/2 (100 XP)

Ambusher. In the first round of combat, the nisp has advantage on attack rolls against any creature it has surprised.

Limited Amphibiousness. The nisp can breathe air and water, but it needs to be submerged at least once every 4 hours to avoid suffocating.

Surprise Attack. If the nisp surprises and creature and hits it with an attack during the first round of combat, the target takes an extra 3 (1d6) damage from the attack.

Actions

Claws. Melee Weapon Attack: +4 to hit, reach 5 ft., one target. *Hit:* 5 (1d6 + 2) slashing damage.

CRESTED NISP

Medium fey, chaotic neutral

Armor Class 13
Hit Points 27 (6d8)
Speed 20 ft., swim 40 ft.

STR	DEX	CON	INT	WIS	CHA
10 (+0)	16 (+3)	11 (+0)	4 (–3)	14 (+2)	8 (–1)

Skills Perception +4, Stealth +5
Senses darkvision 60 ft., passive Perception 14
Languages —
Challenge 2 (450 XP)

Innate Spellcasting. The nisp's innate spellcasting ability is Wisdom (spell save DC 12). It can innately cast the following spells, requiring no material components.
At will: *animal friendship, speak with animals*
3/day each: *entangle, faerie fire, locate animals or plants*
1/day: *conjure animals*

Limited Amphibiousness. The nisp can breathe air and water, but it needs to be submerged at least once every 4 hours to avoid suffocating.

Sea Friend. Beasts with an Intelligence of 3 or lower that have the Amphibiousness or Water Breathing traits have disadvantage on ability checks and saving throws against being charmed by the nisp.

Actions

Multiattack. The crested nisp makes two attacks with its Claws.

Claws. Melee Weapon Attack: +5 to hit, reach 5 ft., one target. *Hit:* 5 (1d6 + 2) slashing damage.

GRAY NISP

Large fey, chaotic neutral

Armor Class 15 (natural armor)
Hit Points 136 (16d10 + 48)
Speed 15 ft., swim 80 ft.

STR	DEX	CON	INT	WIS	CHA
18 (+4)	14 (+2)	16 (+3)	3 (–4)	10 (+0)	6 (–2)

Saving Throws Con +6
Skills Perception +3, Stealth +5
Condition Immunities frightened

Senses darkvision 60 ft., passive Perception 13
Languages —
Challenge 8 (3,900 XP)

Keen Smell. The nisp has advantage on Wisdom (Perception) checks that rely on smell.

Limited Amphibiousness. The nisp can breathe air and water, but it needs to be submerged at least once every 4 hours to avoid suffocating.

Actions

Multiattack. The gray nisp makes one Bite attack and two Claw attacks. If both Claw attacks hit a Medium or smaller creature, the target is grappled (escape DC 15).

Bite. Melee Weapon Attack: +7 to hit, reach 5 ft., one target. *Hit:* 13 (2d8 + 4) piercing damage.

Claws. Melee Weapon Attack: +7 to hit, reach 5 ft., one target. *Hit:* 11 (2d6 + 4) slashing damage.

Frightening Roar (**recharge 5–6**)**.** The nisp emits a deep roar. Each creature within 20 feet of the nisp that can hear the nisp must make a DC 15 Wisdom saving throw, taking 35 (10d6) thunder damage on a failed save, or half as much damage on a successful one. If the saving throw fails by 5 or more, the creature is frightened for 1 minute. A frightened creature can repeat the saving throw at the end of each of its turns, ending the effect on itself on a success.

SPANGLED NISP

Medium fey, chaotic neutral

Armor Class 12
Hit Points 13 (3d8)
Speed 20 ft., swim 40 ft.

STR	DEX	CON	INT	WIS	CHA
8 (–1)	14 (+2)	10 (+0)	5 (–3)	11 (+0)	8 (–1)

Skills Perception +2
Senses darkvision 60 ft., passive Perception 12
Languages —
Challenge 1/4 (50 XP)

Limited Amphibiousness. The nisp can breathe air and water, but it needs to be submerged at least once every 4 hours to avoid suffocating.

Actions

Claws. Melee Weapon Attack: +4 to hit, reach 5 ft., one target. *Hit:* 4 (1d4 + 2) slashing damage.

SAIL MOTH SWARM

These gray-white flying swarms appear in clouds, descending upon ships on the open sea.

Sail moths are much like standard moths, save they are somewhat more aggressive and sustain themselves on salt.

Salt Eaters. Sail moths seek out salt deposits. Unable to feast on salt directly from the water, they look for more available salt deposits, namely the fabric found aboard ships that travel the salty oceans. Few sights are more feared by veteran mariners than a gray cloud of sail moths moving toward the ship's vulnerable sails, for in a matter of minutes, the moths can reduce a sail to tatters.

SAIL MOTH SWARM

Medium swarm of Tiny beasts, unaligned

Armor Class 13
Hit Points 60 (11d8 + 11)
Speed 5 ft., fly 30 ft.

STR	DEX	CON	INT	WIS	CHA
10 (+0)	17 (+3)	12 (+1)	1 (−5)	8 (−1)	1 (−5)

Skills Stealth +5
Damage Resistances bludgeoning, piercing, slashing
Condition Immunities charmed, frightened, grappled, paralyzed, petrified, prone, restrained, stunned
Senses darkvision 60 ft., passive Perception 9
Languages —
Challenge 3 (700 XP)

Salt Sense. The sail moth swarm can pinpoint, by scent, the location of large concentrations of dry salt, such as salt-cured meat or a salt-soaked sail, within 120 feet of it.

Siege Monster. The sail moth swarm deals double damage to objects and structures.

Swarm. The swarm can occupy another creature's space and vice versa, and the swarm can move through any opening large enough for a Tiny insect. The swarm can't regain hit points or gain temporary hit points.

Actions

Bites. Melee Weapon Attack: +5 to hit, reach 0 ft., one target in the swarm's space. *Hit:* 21 (6d6) piercing damage, or 10 (3d6) piercing damage if the swarm has half of its hit points or fewer.

SEA ANEMONE, GREAT

This flowerlike creature has a dark green and gray trunk with a brightly-colored interior. It has a smooth top bordered by dozens of fleshy tendrils, and a rougher outer trunk. At the center of the creature's top is a circular opening that leads into its interior.

These gigantic but primitive lifeforms feed on sea life swept near them and may pose a threat to any creature unlucky enough to move within range of its tendrils.

Patient Lurkers. These horrors lurk in areas near the surface of the water, where tidal currents sweep water laden with fish across their surfaces. Great sea anemones in the open are easily spotted and avoided, but they sometimes lurk at the end of rocky channels or around bends, whereupon they pose a hazard to unwary undersea travelers.

Harvested Defenders. In addition to being found in reefs and shoals, many undersea races harvest these creatures when young and plant them in or near their lairs to serve as sentinels against unwanted intrusion. Care must be taken in this process, for the anemone is very difficult to train, and may well snack on the very creatures who cultivated it.

Opportunistic Feeders. Great sea anemones snag anything large enough that comes within their reach with their tendrils. Once their intended victim stops struggling, it is drawn into the anemone's interior, where it is digested. If injured, the anemone withdraws its body into its rubbery trunk; if badly injured, it expels the contents of its stomach in a cloud of acid.

GREAT SEA ANEMONE

Huge beast, unaligned

Armor Class 14 (natural armor)
Hit Points 149 (13d12 + 65)
Speed 0 ft.

STR	DEX	CON	INT	WIS	CHA
18(+4)	11 (+0)	20 (+5)	2 (−4)	12 (+1)	4 (−3)

Skills Perception +4
Damage Resistances acid
Condition Immunities alphabetical lowercase
Senses blindsight 60 ft. (blind beyond this radius), passive Perception 14
Languages —
Challenge 8 (3,900 XP)

False Appearance. While the great sea anemone remains motionless in a coral reef, it is indistinguishable from an ordinary coral plant.

Water Breathing. The great sea anemone can breathe only underwater.

Actions

Multiattack. The great sea anemone makes four tendrils attacks. If two tendrils hit a Large or smaller creature, the target is grappled (escape DC 15), and the great sea anemone can use its Swallow on the target. The great sea anemone can grapple only two targets at a time.

Tendril. Melee Weapon Attack: +7 to hit, reach 10 ft., one target. *Hit:* 7 (1d6 + 4) bludgeoning damage and the target must make a DC 15 Constitution saving throw, taking 7 (2d6) poison damage on a failed save, or half as much damage on a successful one.

Swallow. The great sea anemone swallows a Large or smaller creature grappled by it. The swallowed target is blinded and restrained, it has total cover against attacks and other effects outside the anemone, and it takes 14 (4d6) acid damage at the start of each of the anemone's turns. The anemone can have only one creature swallowed at a time.

If the great sea anemone takes 20 damage or more on a single turn from the swallowed creature, the anemone must succeed on a DC 13 Constitution saving throw at the end of that turn or regurgitate the creature, which falls prone in a space within 10 feet of the anemone. If the anemone dies, a swallowed creature is no longer restrained by it and can escape from the corpse by using 15 feet of movement, exiting prone.

Acid Cloud **(recharge 5–6).** The great sea anemone expels a cloud of acid. Each creature within 20 feet of it must make a DC 15 Dexterity saving throw, taking 21 (6d6) acid damage on a failed save, or half as much damage on a successful one. If the great sea anemone has a creature swallowed when it uses this action, roll a die. On an even number, the swallowed creature is regurgitated with the acid cloud, and the swallowed creature has disadvantage on its saving throw against the acid cloud.

Reactions

Defensive Curl. The great sea anemone adds 3 to its AC against one melee attack that would hit it as it withdraws

Great Hunter Anemone

Legends speak of a species of great sea anemone, called a "great hunter anemone," that is adapted to prey on humanoids by releasing a pheromone into the water that attracts such creatures. The great hunter anemone gains the following additional trait:

Pheromone Lure. A humanoid creature that starts its turn within 100 feet of the great hunter anemone must succeed on a DC 15 Wisdom saving throw or be charmed by the great hunter for 1 minute. While charmed, the target is incapacitated and ignores the pheromones of other great hunter anemone. If the charmed target is more than 10 feet away from the great hunter anemone, the target must move on its turn toward the anemone, by the most direct route, trying to get within 10 feet. It doesn't avoid opportunity attacks, but before moving into damaging terrain, such as a superheated underwater vent or a razor-sharp coral, and whenever it takes damage from a source other than the great hunter anemone, the target can repeat the saving throw. A charmed target can also repeat the saving throw at the end of each of its turns, ending the effect on itself on a success. If a creature's saving throw is successful or the effect ends for it, the creature is immune to the great hunter's Pheromone Lure for the next 24 hours.

into its trunk. Until it emerges, it increases its AC by 3 and can't use its tendrils or swallow action. It can emerge from its trunk as a bonus action.

Sea Serpents

Nearly as old as the dragons that roam the sky are the sea serpents, great snakelike creatures that have roamed the oceans for ages. Unlike the classical dragon, these great, scaly, serpentine beasts are generally agreed to be a product of evolution, though many suspect magical influence, either deliberate or natural, somewhere in their evolution.

Whatever their origins, sea serpents are a highly varied species, with a great variation in size, coloration, intellect, and temperament. However, all sea serpents bear certain similarities. They are long, serpentine, warm-blooded creatures that closely resemble snakes in appearance, though they all have two sets of flippers, which may be large or so small and atrophied as to be nearly unnoticeable. Sea serpents are aquatic creatures, though some can make their way about on land. All sea serpents can breathe both water and air with equal efficiency, and they all possess some level of sentience. Sea serpent bites are venomous, and their sinuous bodies are built for constricting and crushing prey. The largest sea serpents often wrap themselves around sea-going vessels, devouring the sailors on board. Like their draconic cousins, sea serpents have a sense of innate superiority, feeling they are masters of the sea. They aren't beyond reason and can often be bribed or intimidated into leaving a vessel and its occupants alone.

Arctic. This sea serpent is milky white in color, with pale blue undertones that allow it to blend in with icy environments. Its mouth is narrow, filled with a double row of razor-sharp teeth. Living in the coldest part of the ocean are the most intelligent of the sea serpent species, the arctic serpent, which commands great knowledge and magical power. Though they dwell in frigid climes, arctic sea serpents sometimes go far afield in search of knowledge, and they can be spotted even in tropical waters, concealing their appearance with magic to escape notice. Arctic sea serpents delight in learning esoteric knowledge, particularly rare or unusual spells, and may go thousands of miles in pursuit of new knowledge. Because of this proclivity, arctic sea serpents often know spells and lore that have been long lost to most civilizations and are a good place to seek such wisdom.

Fluting. This serpent's body scales are smooth and deep green in color with a blue-gray undertone. It has wide flippers that enable it to move about slowly on land. It speaks with a musical voice reminiscent of the sound of a flute. The fluting sea serpent is an intelligent serpent known for its masterful singing. Though highly individualistic, they may sometimes be hired by civilized beings to serve as court bards, particularly for undersea races. Fluting sea serpents usually live in sea caves along ocean shores, and they love performing and learning. Creatures often seek them out for information on a particular esoteric subject or to listen to a particular performance. Battle is a last resort for the fluting sea serpent, which prefers negotiation. However, fluting sea serpents can be unpredictable, particularly when their performances are faulted, which may cause them to fly into a sulky rage.

Undead. By some quirk of their biology, sea serpents slain by magic have a high chance of becoming one of the restless dead. This quirk leads many scholars to theorize the original sea serpents were not naturally-occurring creatures and were instead magical creations made by some great sea-faring arcanist millennia ago. Undead sea serpents share several traits in common, no matter the type of sea serpents they were in life.

Arctic Sea Serpent

Large dragon, lawful neutral

Armor Class 16 (natural armor)
Hit Points 127 (17d10 + 34)
Speed 10 ft., swim 60 ft.

STR	DEX	CON	INT	WIS	CHA
16 (+3)	17 (+3)	15 (+2)	20 (+5)	12 (+1)	13 (+1)

Saving Throws Cha +4
Skills Arcana +8, History +8, Perception +4
Damage Vulnerabilities fire
Damage Immunities cold, poison
Condition Immunities poisoned
Senses darkvision 60 ft., passive Perception 14
Languages Aquan, Common, Draconic
Challenge 8 (3,900 XP)

Amphibious. The sea serpent can breathe air and water.
Keen Smell. The sea serpent has advantage on Wisdom (Perception) checks that rely on smell.
Innate Spellcasting. The arctic sea serpent's innate spellcasting ability is Intelligence (spell save DC 16, +8 to hit with spell attacks). It can innately cast the following spells, requiring no material components.
At will: *chill touch, detect magic, minor illusion, ray of frost* (2d8)
3/day each: *blur, color spray, invisibility, silent image*
1/day each: *fly, haste, major image*

Actions

Multiattack. The arctic sea serpent makes two Bite attacks and one Constrict attack.
Bite. *Melee Weapon Attack:* +6 to hit, reach 5 ft., one target. *Hit:* 12 (2d8 + 3) piercing damage plus 7 (2d6) poison damage.
Constrict. *Melee Weapon Attack:* +6 to hit, reach 5 ft., one target. *Hit:* 14 (2d10 + 3) bludgeoning damage, and the target is grappled (escape DC 14) if the sea serpent isn't

already constricting a creature. Until this grapple ends, the target is restrained.

FLUTING SEA SERPENT

Large dragon, chaotic neutral

Armor Class 15 (natural armor)
Hit Points 143 (22d10 + 22)
Speed 10 ft., swim 60 ft.

STR	DEX	CON	INT	WIS	CHA
18 (+4)	14 (+2)	13 (+1)	13 (+1)	12 (+1)	19 (+4)

Saving Throws Int +5
Skills History +5, Perception +5, Performance +8, Persuasion +8
Damage Resistances thunder
Damage Immunities poison
Condition Immunities poisoned
Senses darkvision 60 ft., passive Perception 15
Languages Aquan, Common, Draconic
Challenge 9 (5,000 XP)

Amphibious. The sea serpent can breathe air and water.
Keen Smell. The sea serpent has advantage on Wisdom (Perception) checks that rely on smell.
Innate Spellcasting. The fluting sea serpent's innate spellcasting ability is Charisma (spell save DC 16, +8 to hit with spell attacks). It can innately cast the following spells, requiring no material components.
At will: *detect magic, minor illusion, mage hand, prestidigitation, vicious mockery* (2d4)
3/day each: *charm person, hideous laughter, unseen servant*
1/day each: *calm emotions, enthrall, hold person*

Actions

Multiattack. The fluting sea serpent makes two Bite attacks and one Constrict attack.
Bite. *Melee Weapon Attack:* +8 to hit, reach 5 ft., one target. *Hit:* 13 (2d8 + 4) piercing damage plus 7 (2d6) poison damage.
Constrict. *Melee Weapon Attack:* +8 to hit, reach 5 ft., one target. *Hit:* 15 (2d10 + 4) bludgeoning damage, and the target is grappled (escape DC 16) if the sea serpent isn't already constricting a creature. Until this grapple ends, the target is restrained.
Fluting Song (recharge 6). The fluting sea serpent sings a melody that soothes allies and frightens enemies. Each nonhostile creature of the sea serpent's choice, including itself, that is within 30 feet of the sea serpent and can hear the sea serpent has advantage on its next attack roll against a hostile creature within 30 feet of the sea serpent. Each hostile creature of the sea serpent's choice that is within 30 feet of the sea serpent and can hear the sea serpent must succeed on a DC 16 Wisdom saving throw or become frightened for 1 minute. A frightened creature can repeat the saving throw at the end of each of its turns, ending the effect on itself on a success.

UNDEAD FANGED SEA SERPENT

Large undead, neutral

Armor Class 15 (natural armor)
Hit Points 112 (15d10 + 30)
Speed 10 ft., swim 60 ft.

STR	DEX	CON	INT	WIS	CHA
17 (+3)	14 (+2)	15 (+2)	7 (−2)	13 (+1)	5 (−3)

Saving Throws Dex +5
Skills Perception +4, Stealth +5
Damage Immunities poison
Condition Immunities charmed, exhaustion, frightened, paralyzed, poisoned
Senses darkvision 60 ft., passive Perception 14
Languages Draconic
Challenge 6 (2,300 XP)

Keen Smell. The undead fanged sea serpent has advantage on Wisdom (Perception) checks that rely on smell.
Magic Resistance. The undead fanged sea serpent has advantage on saving throws against spells and other magical effects.
Pack Tactics. The undead fanged sea serpent has advantage on attack rolls against a creature if at least one of the sea serpent's allies is within 5 feet of the creature and the ally isn't incapacitated.
Paralytic Poison. When a creature takes poison damage from the undead fanged sea serpent's bite attack, the creature must succeed on a DC 13 Constitution saving throw or be paralyzed for 1 minute. The creature can repeat the saving throw at the end of each of its turns, ending the effect on itself on a success.

UNDEAD SEA SERPENT TEMPLATE

Only sea serpents slain by magic can become undead sea serpents. The residual arcane energies from the killing blow imbue the sea serpent's flesh, turning it into an undead creature. When a sea serpent becomes an undead sea serpent, it retains all its statistics except as noted below.

Type. The sea serpent's type changes from dragon to undead, and it no longer requires air, food, drink, or sleep.

Condition Immunities. The undead sea serpent is immune to the charmed, exhaustion, frightened, and paralyzed conditions.

Magic Resistance. The undead sea serpent has advantage on saving throws against spells and other magical effects.

Paralytic Poison. When a creature takes poison damage from the undead sea serpent's bite attack, the creature must succeed on a Constitution saving throw or be paralyzed for 1 minute. The creature can repeat the saving throw at the end of each of its turns, ending the effect on itself on a success. The save DC is equal to 8 + the sea serpent's proficiency bonus + the sea serpent's Constitution modifier.

Actions

Multiattack. The fanged sea serpent makes one Bite attack and one Constrict attack.

Bite. *Melee Weapon Attack:* +6 to hit, reach 5 ft., one target. *Hit:* 12 (2d8 + 3) piercing damage plus 7 (2d6) poison damage.

Constrict. *Melee Weapon Attack:* +6 to hit, reach 5 ft., one target. *Hit:* 14 (2d10 + 3) bludgeoning damage, and the target is grappled (escape DC 14) if the sea serpent isn't already constricting a creature. Until this grapple ends, the target is restrained.

Sea Sphere (Blubble)

The sea sphere is an odd, spheroid creature composed of a thick membrane. The center of the creature is an air-filled chamber.

The sea sphere (known to sailors as the "blubble") lives in a symbiotic state with other beings. The sphere's home is the ocean and it is always found near vast quantities of water.

The sea sphere is the color of the water where it is found, and it is luminescent in moonlight. Sea spheres see through some innate ability or undetectable magic. They communicate telepathically, and they seek out air-breathers who desire to travel underwater.

Picky Breathers. Blubbles require carbon dioxide to breathe. They can store enough of this gas inside of themselves to last for up to 72 hours. During this time, their respiratory processes use up the carbon dioxide and produce waste oxygen, which is expelled inside their inner bubbles. After 72 hours they run out of breathable gas and die within 1d4 hours. Blubbles stay alive by welcoming oxygen-breathing creatures inside their hollow core. These creatures — usually humanoids — breathe the blubble's oxygen and naturally exhale the carbon dioxide the host blubble requires.

Willing Hosts. Sea spheres can open an aperture in their shells, permitting Medium or smaller creatures to enter their core. The blubble provides travel for these beings, able to swim to great depths where the air-breathers usually couldn't venture. Adventurers often seek out sea spheres and form a symbiotic pact with them: in exchange for travel to the deep places in the ocean, the adventurers simply ride in the blubble's core and breathe, providing their host with the gas it requires to stay alive. The blubble is not violent; however, a suffocating blubble to deep to breech the water's surface is not above forcing air-breathing creatures inside it.

Ooze Nature. The sea sphere doesn't require sleep.

Sea Sphere (Blubble)

Huge ooze, neutral

Armor Class 10
Hit Points 133 (14d12 + 42)
Speed 0 ft., fly 20 ft., swim 60 ft.

STR	DEX	CON	INT	WIS	CHA
18 (+4)	10 (+0)	17 (+3)	10 (+0)	14 (+2)	13 (+1)

Skills Insight +5, Persuasion +4
Damage Vulnerabilities piercing
Damage Resistances bludgeoning and slashing from nonmagical attacks
Damage Immunities acid
Condition Immunities blinded, charmed, deafened, exhaustion, frightened, prone
Senses blindsight 60 ft. (blind beyond this radius), passive Perception 12
Languages Aquan, Common, telepathy 120 ft.
Challenge 5 (1,800 XP)

Air Pocket. The sea sphere must breathe air to survive, and it carries air for up to 72 hours of breathing inside of itself, allowing it to swim beneath the surface of the water for extended periods of time without drowning. If at least one Medium or smaller air-breathing creature is inside of it, the sea sphere can stay submerged indefinitely, the two creatures symbiotically providing air for each other.

Hollow Body. The sea sphere's body is hollow, and it can hold up to six Large or smaller creatures inside it. If four or fewer Large or smaller creatures are inside the sea sphere, the creatures and the sea sphere can breathe indefinitely. If more than four Large or smaller creatures are inside the sea sphere, the compartment holds enough air for 24 hours of breathing, divided by the number of breathing creatures inside. To replenish the air supply, the sea sphere can eject creatures until the creatures inside it are reduced to four or fewer, or the sea sphere can breech the water's surface and collect air through its membranous body for 5 minutes.

A creature inside the sea sphere can see through the sphere's transparent body, but it has disadvantage on Wisdom (Perception) checks to hear sounds outside the sea sphere. A creature inside the sea sphere can't be targeted by attacks, abilities, or spells from outside the sea sphere.

Pressurized But Squishy. A creature inside the sea sphere ignores drawbacks caused by a deep, underwater environment. Due to its soft, spherical body, a creature inside the sea sphere has disadvantage on Dexterity checks and saving throws against being knocked prone. Creatures inside the sea sphere take half of any piercing damage the sea sphere takes, divided among the creatures inside it.

Sea Sphere. The sea sphere takes up its entire space. Other creatures can enter the space, but a creature that does so is subjected to the sea sphere's Engulf attack and has disadvantage on the saving throw. A creature within 5 feet of the sea sphere can take an action to pull a creature or object out of the sea sphere. Doing so requires a DC 15 Strength check, and the creature takes 14 (4d6) acid damage if the sea sphere didn't want to release the target creature or object.

Transparent. Even when the sea sphere is in plain sight, it takes a successful DC 15 Wisdom (Perception) check to spot a sea sphere that has neither moved nor attacked. If the sea sphere has creatures inside it, a creature has advantage on its Wisdom (Perception) check to spot the sea sphere. A creature that tries to enter the sea sphere's space while unaware of the sea sphere is surprised by the sea sphere.

Actions

Multiattack. The sea sphere makes three Slam attacks.

Slam. *Melee Weapon Attack:* +7 to hit, reach 5 ft., one target. *Hit:* 11 (2d6 + 4) bludgeoning damage.

Engulf. The sea sphere moves up to its speed. While doing so, it can enter Large or smaller creatures' spaces. Whenever the sphere enters a creature's space, the creature must make a DC 15 Dexterity saving throw.

On a successful save, the creature can choose to be pushed 5 feet back or to the side of the sphere. A creature that chooses not to be pushed suffers the consequences of a failed saving throw. On a failed save, the sphere enters the creature's space, and the creature takes 14 (4d6) acid damage and is engulfed. When the sphere moves, the engulfed creature moves with it.

If a creature voluntarily allows the sphere to engulf it, the creature automatically fails the saving throw, but it doesn't take acid damage from being engulfed.

An engulfed creature can try to escape by taking an action to make a DC 15 Strength check. On a success, the creature escapes and enters a space of its choice within 5 feet of the sphere. If the sea sphere agrees to allow the creature to exit its body, the creature instead can escape the sea sphere by using 15 feet of movement, entering a space of its choice within 5 feet of the sphere.

Devour Riders. The sea sphere wraps around the creatures inside it, attempting to devour them. Each creature inside the sea sphere must make a DC 15 Strength saving throw. On a failure, a creature takes 21 (6d6) acid damage and is restrained for 1 minute. On a success, a creature takes half the damage and isn't restrained. A restrained creature can repeat the saving throw at the end of each of its turns, ending the effect on itself on a success.

SEA SPIDER

This creature resembles similar arachnids found on land, except in size and habitat. Its color ranges through various shades of blue and green with distinct black markings. It's covered with thousands of fine, sticky hairs.

Sea-Dwelling Arachnids. The hairs on a sea spider's legs trap air bubbles, which aid in floatation and mobility. With its long, strong legs, a sea strider can propel itself underwater as easily as it can glide upon the surface. Sea spiders make their lairs in shallow underwater caverns in secluded lagoons of uninhabited islands. They rarely leave the sea as they cannot long stand the stillness of dry land.

Ship Climbers. Sea spiders usually attach themselves to the ship with the sticky hairs of their hind legs. This brings their mouth to the level of the deck where they can gobble up the tasty morsels on board. If no one is in range, the sea spider relocates to another area of the ship and attacks again.

SEA SPIDER

Huge beast, unaligned

Armor Class 15 (natural armor)
Hit Points 189 (18d12 + 72)
Speed 10 ft., climb 20 ft., swim 60 ft.

STR	DEX	CON	INT	WIS	CHA
21 (+5)	13 (+1)	18 (+4)	3 (−4)	12 (+1)	2 (−4)

Saving Throws Dex +5
Skills Perception +5, Stealth +5
Damage Immunities poison
Condition Immunities poisoned
Senses blindsight 10 ft., darkvision 60 ft., passive Perception 15
Languages —
Challenge 11 (7,200 XP)

Amphibious. The sea spider can breathe air and water.
Sticky Hairs. A creature that touches the sea spider or hits it with a melee weapon while within 5 feet of it takes 9 (2d8) piercing damage and adheres to the sea spider. A Large or smaller creature adhered to the sea spider is also grappled by it (escape DC 17).
Water Sense. While walking on water, the sea spider knows the exact location of any other creature in contact with the surface of the same water within 120 feet of it.
Water Walker. The sea spider can move across the surface of water as if it were harmless solid ground, using its swimming speed instead of its walking speed. It can't use this trait if the water is disturbed by a strong or stronger wind.

Actions

Multiattack. The sea spider makes one Bite attack and four Slam attacks.
Bite. *Melee Weapon Attack:* +9 to hit, reach 5 ft., one creature. *Hit:* 14 (2d8 + 5) piercing damage plus 10 (3d6) poison damage, and the target must succeed on a DC 17 Constitution saving throw or its speed is halved until the end of its next turn. The sea spider has advantage on bite attack rolls against a creature adhered to it.
Slam. *Melee Weapon Attack:* +9 to hit, reach 10 ft., one creature. *Hit:* 8 (1d6 + 5) bludgeoning damage.

STORM RIDER

This fish is barely two feet long, with a body wider than it is high; combined with its broad fins, this gives it an aerodynamic quality, allowing it to leap into the air and glide on winds for an extended distance. The mouth of the fish is filled with many sharp triangular teeth like the blade of a saw.

Gliding Fish. Storm riders are a species of deep-sea fish that are relatively harmless individually, but they become dangerous in great numbers. They are most often encountered gliding in large schools in the violent winds of a storm front, where they can descend upon a ship and ravage its riggings and crew. Ironically, storm riders are quite tasty when cooked, and they are considered a delicacy in many sea ports.

Storm Hunters. When high winds blow upon the surface of the ocean, they leap into the air currents and become aggressive swarm, hunting any living creatures they can see. After they are sated, the swam separates and returns to the sea.

STORM RIDER

Tiny beast, unaligned

Armor Class 12
Hit Points 10 (4d4)
Speed 0 ft., swim 60 ft.

STR	DEX	CON	INT	WIS	CHA
3 (−4)	15 (+2)	10 (+0)	1 (−5)	8 (−1)	3 (−4)

Damage Immunities lightning
Senses darkvision 60 ft., passive Perception 9
Languages —
Challenge 1/4 (50 XP)

Hold Breath. While out of water, the storm rider can hold its breath for 5 minutes.
Water Breathing. The storm rider can breathe only underwater.
Watery Glide. The storm rider can leap out of the water and fly up to 60 feet each round, but it must start and end its movement in the water. If it is flying at the end of its turn, it falls, taking falling damage. If the storm rider uses this trait in a strong or stronger wind, it can instead fly for up to 1 minute before it must return to the water.

Actions

Bite. *Melee Weapon Attack:* +4 to hit, reach 5 ft., one creature. *Hit:* 4 (1d4 + 2) piercing damage.

Storm Rider Swarm

Medium swarm of Tiny beasts, unaligned

Armor Class 13
Hit Points 40 (9d8)
Speed 0 ft., swim 60 ft.

STR	DEX	CON	INT	WIS	CHA
14 (+2)	16 (+3)	10 (+0)	1 (–5)	8 (–1)	3 (–4)

Damage Resistances bludgeoning, piercing, slashing
Damage Immunities lightning
Condition Immunities charmed, frightened, grappled, paralyzed, petrified, prone, restrained, stunned
Senses darkvision 60 ft., passive Perception 9
Languages —
Challenge 2 (450 XP)

Hold Breath. While out of water, the storm rider swarm can hold its breath for 5 minutes.

Swarm. The swarm can occupy another creature's space and vice versa, and the swarm can move through any opening large enough for a Tiny storm rider. The swarm can't regain hit points or gain temporary hit points.

Water Breathing. The storm rider swarm can breathe only underwater.

Watery Glide. The storm rider swarm can leap out of the water and fly up to 60 feet each round, but it must start and end its movement in the water. If it is flying at the end of its turn, it falls, taking falling damage. If the storm rider swarm uses this trait in a strong or stronger wind, it can instead fly for up to 5 minutes before it must return to the water.

Actions

Bites. *Melee Weapon Attack:* +5 to hit, reach 0 ft., one creature in the swarm's space. *Hit:* 18 (4d8) piercing damage, or 9 (2d8) piercing damage if the swarm has half of its hit points or fewer.

Thume

This creature resembles a large jellyfish with dozens of strands dangling from the fringe of its body. The interior of its body is largely hollow, interlaced with razor-thin lines of phosphorescent energy, and many translucent organs cluster around the top and sides of its form.

Intelligent Jellyfish. The thume are an ancient race of deep-sea dwellers that evolved — or were uplifted — from large jellyfish. They bear a close resemblance to their primitive cousins but are much larger, with an obviously complex interior structure composed partly of a pastel lattice of energy.

Grown Cities. The thume live in communities on the ocean floor, usually in well-tended sea gardens, with sculpted stone married harmoniously with carefully-placed sea flora. Thume do not sleep and have no need of houses or other conventional structures. Their "cities" are often no more complex than a large, cultivated area with hundreds of their kind dancing above it, alone or in congregations. Thume do build a few structures, however, to aid in one of their favorite pursuits — the study and use of magic. They sometimes set up forges and research facilities near thermal vents. They often recruit other undersea races, whether as hirelings or through magical compulsion, to aid in the physical process of manufacture.

Peaceful Arcanists. Thume avoid direct combat when they can, relying on summoned or charmed minions and their own arcane powers to protect them. As masters of the art of breeding, thume communities often incorporate dangerous sea life into their defenses, including giant sea anemones. This is sometimes supplemented with charmed monsters and magical traps or with their own formidable talents in the arcane arts.

Grown Magic Items. The thume grow polypites, which are small, roughly walnut-sized lumps of coral. Deep within the core of the polypite is a small fleshy ball — the polyp itself. Two different types of polypites exist: power and spell storing. A power polypite functions as a *pearl of power* and a spell-storing polypite functions as a *ring of spell storing*. A polypite floats harmlessly within its attuned thume's poisonous tendrils, providing its benefits without being worn or carried. These magic items function only while underwater and only for thumes. If a polypite is out of water for 24 hours, the polyp within dies and the magic of the item fades.

Thume

Large aberration, neutral

Armor Class 12
Hit Points 52 (8d10 + 8)
Speed 0 ft., swim 60 ft.

STR	DEX	CON	INT	WIS	CHA
8 (–1)	14 (+2)	12 (+1)	16 (+3)	11 (+0)	10 (+0)

Skills Animal Handling +4, Insight +2
Damage Vulnerabilities piercing
Damage Immunities poison
Condition Immunities poisoned, prone
Senses blindsight 60 ft. (blind beyond this radius), passive Perception 10
Languages Common, Deep Speech
Challenge 2 (450 XP)

Magical Deflection. The thume can't be affected or detected by spells of 1st level or lower unless it wishes to be. It has advantage on saving throws against all other spells and magical effects.

Magical Manipulation. The thume can hold and manipulate objects within 30 feet of it with a spectral, floating octopus-like tentacle. This trait otherwise works like the *mage hand* spell.

Sense Magic. The thume senses magic within 120 feet of it at will. This trait otherwise works like the *detect magic* spell but isn't itself magical.

Water Breathing. The thume can breathe only underwater.

Actions

Stinging Tendrils. *Melee Weapon Attack:* +4 to hit, reach 10 ft., one target. *Hit:* 5 (1d6 + 2) piercing damage and the target must make a DC 12 Constitution saving throw, taking 10 (3d6) poison damage on a failed save or half as much damage on a successful one.

THUME ARCANIST

Large aberration, neutral

Armor Class 12 (15 with *mage armor*)
Hit Points 97 (15d10 + 15)
Speed 0 ft., swim 60 ft.

STR	DEX	CON	INT	WIS	CHA
8 (−1)	14 (+2)	12 (+1)	19 (+4)	14 (+2)	10 (+0)

Skills Animal Handling +8, Arcana +7, History +7, Insight +5
Damage Vulnerabilities piercing
Damage Immunities poison
Condition Immunities poisoned, prone
Senses blindsight 60 ft. (blind beyond this radius), passive Perception 12
Languages Common, Deep Speech
Challenge 6 (2,300 XP)

Magical Deflection. The thume can't be affected or detected by spells of 1st level or lower unless it wishes to be. It has advantage on saving throws against all other spells and magical effects.

Magical Manipulation. The thume can hold and manipulate objects within 30 feet of it with a spectral, floating octopus-like tentacle. This trait otherwise works like the *mage hand* spell.

Sense Magic. The thume senses magic within 120 feet of it at will. This trait otherwise works like the *detect magic* spell but isn't itself magical.

Spellcasting. The thume is an 8th-level spellcaster. Its spellcasting ability is Intelligence (spell save DC 15, +7 to hit with spell attacks). The thume has the following wizard spells prepared:

Cantrips (at will): *mending, prestidigitation, ray of frost, shocking grasp*
1st level (4 slots): *detect magic, expeditious retreat, floating disk, mage armor*
2nd level (3 slots): *hold person, ray of enfeeblement, scorching ray*
3rd level (3 slots): *counterspell, lightning bolt, slow*
4th level (2 slots): *polymorph, stone shape*

Water Breathing. The thume can breathe only underwater.

Actions

Multiattack. The thume arcanist makes two Stinging Tendrils attacks.

Stinging Tendrils. *Melee Weapon Attack:* +5 to hit, reach 10 ft., one target. *Hit:* 5 (1d6 + 2) piercing damage and the target must make a DC 13 Constitution saving throw, taking 10 (3d6) poison damage on a failed save or half as much damage on a successful one.

***Stinging Whirl* (recharge 5–6).** The thume spins with its stinging tendrils extended. Each creature within 15 feet of the thume must make a DC 15 Dexterity saving throw, taking 21 (6d6) poison damage on a failed save, or half as much damage on a successful one.

TIRMANHA SWARM

A tirmanha fish individually reaches 10 to 12 inches in adulthood. Its plump, jagged-edged body is a shimmering white color with deep black features on its belly and fins. The tirmanha's steep forehead, blunted face, and dominant lower jaw complement its menacing demeanor. Its mouth holds columns of razor-sharp, spoon-shaped teeth that are intended to devour wooden objects and materials but are just as hazardous to fleshy subjects.

Wood Piranhas. Tirmanha fish are an abnormal species of piranha that have a boundless appetite for wood and hunt in swarms. Tirmanha fishes' prime source of food is wood, leading them to wreak destruction upon waterbound trees, docks, and ships. Starving tirmanha swarms hunt other creatures if no wooden food source is available, though the swarm must consume twice as much flesh to get the same nourishment it would from a piece of wood.

TIRMANHA SWARM

Medium swarm of Tiny beasts, unaligned

Armor Class 14
Hit Points 82 (15d8 + 15)
Speed 0 ft., swim 60 ft.

STR	DEX	CON	INT	WIS	CHA
10 (+0)	18 (+4)	13 (+1)	1 (−5)	8 (−1)	1 (−5)

Damage Resistances bludgeoning, piercing, slashing
Condition Immunities charmed, frightened, grappled, paralyzed, petrified, prone, restrained, stunned
Senses darkvision 60 ft., passive Perception 9
Languages —
Challenge 4 (1,100 XP)

Water Breathing. The tirmanha swarm can breathe only underwater.

Wood Consumer. The tirmanha swarm deals double damage to objects and structures made of wood, and it ignores the damage threshold of objects and structures made of wood.

Wood Sense. The sail moth swarm can pinpoint, by scent, the location of large concentrations of wood, such as a dock or a ship, within 120 feet of it.

Actions

Bites. *Melee Weapon Attack:* +6 to hit, reach 0 ft., one target in the swarm's space. *Hit:* 28 (8d6) piercing damage, or 14 (4d6) piercing damage if the swarm has half of its hit points or fewer.

TOMBOTU

This creature vaguely resembles a gorilla. It is gray in color and much more powerfully-muscled than any natural ape. Two vicious upward-thrusting tusks sprout from its lower jaw.

Tombotu are the foul offspring of Bonjo Tombo. These gray, apelike humanoids are bred from human or ape mothers, although the resulting spoor often kills the mother.

Leaders of Apes. Tombotu breed true and often build small, tree-dwelling communities, which include dire apes and other apelike creatures. More intelligent than most apes, they communicate with their "lesser" cousins through grunts and body language.

Hunters of Humans. Humans often hunt tombotu to sell them as slaves for southern gladiatorial pits. Because of this regular interaction, the tombotu have developed a taste for human flesh. They hide in the jungle's tall trees and snatch humans that pass below, pulling their unsuspecting prey into the trees where it can't withstand the tombotu's superior strength. If threatened with death or capture, tombotu flee rather than allow themselves to be destroyed or taken as slaves.

Tombotu

Large monstrosity, neutral

Armor Class 12 (natural armor)
Hit Points 45 (6d10 + 12)
Speed 30 ft., climb 30 ft.

STR	DEX	CON	INT	WIS	CHA
18 (+4)	11 (+0)	15 (+2)	10 (+0)	12 (+1)	7 (–2)

Skills Athletics +6, Stealth +4
Senses darkvision 60 ft., passive Perception 11
Languages Abyssal, Common
Challenge 2 (450 XP)

Ambusher. The tombotu has advantage on attack rolls against any creature it has surprised.
Keen Smell. The tombotu has advantage on Wisdom (Perception) checks that rely on smell.
Standing Leap. The tombotu's long jump is up to 20 feet and its high jump is up to 10 feet, with or without a running start.

Actions

Multiattack. The tombotu makes one Bite attack and one Fist attack.
Bite. *Melee Weapon Attack:* +6 to hit, reach 5 ft., one target. *Hit:* 10 (1d12 + 4) piercing damage.
Fist. *Melee Weapon Attack:* +6 to hit, reach 5 ft., one target. *Hit:* 9 (1d10 + 4) bludgeoning damage.

Unrelenting Sojourner of the Sea

This metallic construct appears as a crudely rendered statue of a human, with fully-articulated joints. Though its facial features are nothing more than vague shapes with little definition, its torso is carved with an intricate pattern of runes. Along the area of its left thigh is a long, silvery abrasion, evidence of some ancient battle.

This terrible metal construct, known as the unrelenting sojourner of the sea, is one of a kind, and for that the civilized world is thankful.

Nameless Machine. The sojourner was given its name by a maritime explorer who encountered it, fought it, and retreated with his life to tell the tale. No one knows its true name or even if it has one. It is a human-shaped machine that constantly walks the ocean floor on an unknown quest, destroying anything that attempts to sway it from its inexorable path. The sojourner is fashioned from a special, highly resilient metal of unknown origin, its power source hidden somewhere deep inside its nearly impregnable frame. It continuously and unstoppably walks the lightless ocean floor, having traversed thousands of miles since it was first spotted by adventurers years ago. So far it has proven indestructible. Its purpose remains a mystery. The symbols on its torso are as inscrutable as the sojourner itself.

Staunch Wanderer. During its endless trek along the sea bed, if the sojourner encounters an obstacle it cannot pass through or climb over, it walks around the obstacle's perimeter, regardless of the distance required. It descends into the deepest ocean trenches and slowly advances up the far side. If a living being attempts to impede its progress, the sojourner attacks without hesitation, though it never initiates combat until it is touched or attacked. In combat the sojourner is mindless, fearless, and unremitting.

Constructed Nature. The unrelenting sojourner of the sea doesn't require air, food, drink, or sleep.

Unrelenting Sojourner of the Sea

Medium construct, neutral

Armor Class 19 (natural armor)
Hit Points 171 (18d8 + 90)
Speed 30 ft., burrow 15 ft., climb 15 ft.

STR	DEX	CON	INT	WIS	CHA
25 (+7)	14 (+2)	21 (+5)	8 (–1)	15 (+2)	6 (–2)

Skills Athletics +13, Perception +8
Damage Vulnerabilities force
Damage Immunities poison, psychic; bludgeoning, piercing, and slashing from nonmagical attacks that aren't adamantine
Condition Immunities charmed, exhaustion, frightened, paralyzed, petrified, poisoned
Senses truesight 120 ft., passive Perception 18
Languages understands all but can't speak
Challenge 19 (22,000 XP)

Deep Sea Denizen. The sojourner ignores the drawbacks caused by a deep, underwater environment, and it ignores the penalties for making melee attacks underwater without a swimming speed. Though made of metal, the sojourner is immune to rust and corrosion caused by prolonged exposure to an underwater environment.
Elemental Absorption. Whenever the sojourner is subjected to acid, cold, fire, or lightning damage, it takes no damage and instead regains a number of hit points equal to the acid, cold, fire, or lightning damage dealt.
Freedom of Movement. The sojourner ignores difficult terrain, and magical effects can't reduce its speed or cause it to be restrained. It can spend 5 feet of movement to escape from nonmagical restraints or being grappled.
Immutable Form. The sojourner is immune to any spell or effect that would alter its form.
Magic Resistance. The sojourner has advantage on saving throws against spells and other magical effects.
Magic Weapons. The sojourner's weapon attacks are magical.

Actions

Multiattack. The unrelenting sojourner of the sea makes three Slam attacks.
Slam. *Melee Weapon Attack:* +13 to hit, reach 5 ft., one target. *Hit:* 20 (3d8 + 7) bludgeoning damage.

Legendary Actions

The unrelenting sojourner of the sea can take 3 legendary actions, choosing from the options below. Only one legendary action can be used at a time and only at the end of another creature's turn. The sojourner regains spent legendary actions at the start of its turn.
Detect. The sojourner makes a Wisdom (Perception) check.
Slam. The sojourner makes a Slam attack.
Aquatic Entangle (costs 3 actions). Spiked, grasping sea plants erupt in a 20-foot radius centered on a point on the sea floor the sojourner can see within 120 feet of it. Each creature in the area must make a DC 19 Dexterity saving throw. On a failure, a creature takes 28 (8d6) piercing damage and is restrained for 1 minute. On a success, a creature takes half the damage and isn't restrained. A restrained creature can repeat the saving throw at the end of each of its turns, ending the effect on itself on a success.

WATER PACER

The thin, pockmarked exoskeleton of this creature is a glistening blue. Its body consists of two narrow segments with four pairs of willowy legs. The front pair of legs features a series of serrated hooks that are used to snag underwater prey. A small, circular mouth sits along the underside of its primary body segment, and eight eyes decorate its frontmost body segment.

The water pacer is a mischievous spider-like beast that glides effortlessly along the water's surface. Water pacers dwell in moist dens near coastal areas and swamps but spend most their time upon the open sea.

Peaceful Predators. Though their appearance is rather intimidating, hundreds of years of co-existence with native islanders has mostly removed the water pacer's aggressive behavior toward humanoids. The water pacer generally feeds on small fish and insects near the water, dipping its claws in the water and manipulating food into its mouth.

Water Gliders. Water pacers effortlessly glide along the surface of the water. Their back three pairs of legs have a waxy, water-repelling quality that supports their full weight atop the water's surface. They propel forward with the rowing motion of their middle two pairs of legs, creating mere dimples in the water. Their back legs brace and steer the body in the desired direction.

Docile Mounts. Despite their monstrous appearance, water pacers provide faithful service as mounts to coastal, sea-fairing people. Islanders wishing to travel relatively short distances across water have long developed specialized techniques to train these creatures. Islanders sell trained water pacer mounts for twice the cost of a warhorse.

WATER PACER

Medium beast, unaligned

Armor Class 11
Hit Points 33 (6d8 + 6)
Speed 40 ft., swim 10 ft.

STR	DEX	CON	INT	WIS	CHA
17 (+3)	13 (+1)	12 (+1)	2 (–4)	13 (+1)	7 (–2)

Skills Perception +3, Stealth +3
Senses darkvision 60 ft., passive Perception 13
Languages —
Challenge 1 (200 XP)

Amphibious. The water pacer can breathe air and water.
Beast of Burden. The water pacer is considered to be a Large animal for the purpose of determining its carrying capacity and its ability to carry a rider into battle.
Water Walker. The water pacer can move across the surface of water as if it were harmless solid ground. It can't use this trait if the water is disturbed by a strong or stronger wind or if it is carrying more than 250 pounds.

Actions

Bite. Melee Weapon Attack: +5 to hit, reach 5 ft., one target. *Hit:* 6 (1d6 + 3) piercing damage plus 5 (2d4) poison damage.
Hook. Melee Weapon Attack: +5 to hit, reach 5 ft., one target. *Hit:* 10 (2d6 + 3) slashing damage, and the target is grappled (escape DC 13). The water pacer has two hooks, each of which can grapple only one target.

WEEDGE

This creature is a froglike humanoid, quite wide in the chest but with spindly arms and legs. It is human-sized and is wearing a thick eel skin belt to hold a variety of tools that it can wield in its webbed hands.

On the faraway planet of Lacosta, two races vied for control of the scant resources available. Once the kuah-lij mastered the seas with their machines and magic, the weedge were forced to fall in line. Certainly, the amphibious weedge still have havens, small enclaves that are unimportant to the kuah-lij and their ambitions. **Wise Servants.** The weedge are a storied race, ranging the seas and the coastal lands alike, building cities underwater and advancing a culture of diligent and loyal people. Their wisdom and experience are unequaled on their planet but their younger rivals proved stronger and more aggressive. The kuah-lij have forced the weedge into a servile role, employing them as soldiers in the front line to repel the invaders of their mutual home. The weedge have longed served as workers in kuah-lij factories and as craftsmen and farmers in their villages. They also make up a large part of the army set to defend the kuah-lij. Their sacrifices as the front line against the invasion of their world has made the weedge a wise people accustomed to the rigors of a centuries-long war.

Artisans and Fighters. Before becoming servants of the kuah-lij, the weedge were artisans, scholars, and architects. After they lost to the kuah-lij, the devoted weedge refused to mourn the loss of their people's dominance and turned their passions toward bettering themselves and their equipment. They begin training at an early age, and, after reaching a certain level of expertise in a particular skill or weapon, they go into careers as servants and soldiers for the kuah-lij. Though trained in various weapons, they prefer the shortspear for its versatility underwater. The weedge serve in companies of five and fight well in concert with their teams. A group of weedge fighters that has been together for years is a formidable opponent.

WEEDGE

Medium humanoid (weedge), neutral good

Armor Class 11
Hit Points 18 (4d8)
Speed 30 ft., swim 30 ft.

STR	DEX	CON	INT	WIS	CHA
15 (+2)	13 (+1)	11 (+0)	8 (–1)	14 (+2)	8 (–1)

Skills Insight +4, Perception +4
Senses darkvision 60 ft., passive Perception 14
Languages Weedge
Challenge 1/2 (100 XP)

Amphibious. The weedge can breathe air and water.
Pack Tactics. The weedge has advantage on an attack roll against a creature if at least one of the weedge's allies is within 5 feet of the creature and the ally isn't incapacitated.
Standing Leap. The weedge's long jump is up to 20 feet and its high jump is up to 10 feet, with or without a running start.

Actions

Spear. Melee or Ranged Weapon Attack: +4 to hit, reach 5 ft. or range 20/60 ft., one target. *Hit:* 5 (1d6 + 2) piercing damage, or 6 (1d8 + 2) piercing damage if used with two hands to make a melee attack.

Weedge Captain

Medium humanoid (weedge), neutral good

Armor Class 14 (chain shirt)
Hit Points 55 (10d8 + 10)
Speed 30 ft., swim 30 ft.

STR	DEX	CON	INT	WIS	CHA
17 (+3)	13 (+1)	13 (+1)	10 (+0)	14 (+2)	10 (+0)

Skills Insight +4, Perception +4, Persuasion +2
Senses darkvision 60 ft., passive Perception 14
Languages Common, Kuah-Lij, Weedge
Challenge 3 (700 XP)

Amphibious. The weedge can breathe air and water.
Pack Tactics. The weedge has advantage on an attack roll against a creature if at least one of the weedge's allies is within 5 feet of the creature and the ally isn't incapacitated.
Standing Leap. The weedge's long jump is up to 20 feet and its high jump is up to 10 feet, with or without a running start.

Actions

Multiattack. The weedge captain makes three Spear attacks.
Spear. *Melee or Ranged Weapon Attack:* +5 to hit, reach 5 ft. or range 20/60 ft., one target. *Hit:* 6 (1d6 + 3) piercing damage, or 7 (1d8 + 3) piercing damage if used with two hands to make a melee attack.
Attack as One (recharge 6). The weedge captain makes one melee attack against a creature within 5 feet of it. If the attack hits, each weedge ally within 10 feet of the captain can move up to 10 feet toward the target creature and make one melee attack against it as a reaction.

Whale, Deep Singer

This creature looks much like a sperm whale, though it is slightly larger and has midnight blue skin.

Only in the deepest oceans can one find the deep singers, a race of intelligent whales that sing with an entrancing harmony and that are said to be the repositories of all the sea's wisdom.

Air-Breathing Singers. A deep singer can travel to any depth in the ocean without harm, but it breathes air, nonetheless. It is occasionally seen by sailors as it breaches the surface to replenish its air supply. Its haunting songs can be heard echoing among the waves, rising from the deeps. Its songs are of such melancholy beauty that even the most hardened sailors find tears in their eyes.

Celestial Origins. Deep singer whales are often accompanied by a retinue of dolphins and intelligent, sea-dwelling humanoids such as merfolk, who come to learn from the whales' song and bring the whale information from the world beyond. Some believe that deep singer whales are the first stage in the evolution of the celestial whales that swim in the oceans of the Outer Planes. Others believe they are avatars of those beings, come to the world to increase their knowledge and experience before returning.

Deep Singer Whale

Gargantuan celestial, neutral good

Armor Class 19 (natural armor)
Hit Points 248 (16d20 + 80)
Speed 0 ft., swim 90 ft.

STR	DEX	CON	INT	WIS	CHA
27 (+8)	14 (+2)	21 (+5)	16 (+3)	23 (+6)	19 (+4)

Saving Throws Con +11, Wis +12, Cha +10
Skills History +9, Insight +12, Performance +10, Persuasion +10
Damage Immunities poison, radiant; bludgeoning, piercing, and slashing from nonmagical attacks
Condition Immunities charmed, frightened, paralyzed, poisoned
Senses truesight 120 ft., passive Perception 16
Languages all, telepathy 120 ft.
Challenge 19 (22,000 XP)

Deep Diver. The deep singer whale ignores the drawbacks caused by a deep, underwater environment.
Hold Breath. The deep singer whale can hold its breath for 1 hour.
Innate Spellcasting. The deep singer whale's innate spellcasting ability is Wisdom (spell save DC 20, +12 to hit with spell attacks). It can innately cast the following spells, requiring only verbal components:
At will: *mage hand, message, minor illusion, prestidigitation, ray of frost* (4d8)
3/day each: *major image, shatter, silence, sleep* (11d8)
1/day each: *arcane eye, legend lore, scrying*
Legendary Resistance (3/day). If the deep singer whale fails a saving throw, it can choose to succeed instead
Magic Weapons. The deep singer whale's weapon attacks are magical.

Actions

Multiattack. The deep singer whale uses its Entrancing Song. It then makes one Bite attack and two Tail Slap attacks.
Bite. *Melee Weapon Attack:* +14 to hit, reach 5 ft., one target. *Hit:* 21 (2d12 + 8) piercing damage.
Tail Slap. *Melee Weapon Attack:* +14 to hit, reach 10 ft., one target. *Hit:* 19 (2d10 + 8) bludgeoning damage.
Entrancing Song. The deep singer whale sings an entrancing song. Each creature of the whale's choice that is within 120 feet of the whale and that can hear it must succeed on a DC 19 Wisdom saving throw or be charmed for 1 minute. While charmed, a creature is incapacitated, enthralled by the song. A creature can repeat the saving throw at the end of each of its turns, ending the effect on itself on a success. If a creature's saving throw is successful or the effect ends for it, the creature is immune to the whale's Entrancing Song for the next 24 hours.

Legendary Actions

The deep singer whale can take 3 legendary actions, choosing from the options below. Only one legendary action can be used at a time and only at the end of another creature's turn. The deep singer whale regains spent legendary actions at the start of its turn.
At Will Spell. The deep singer whale casts one of its at will spells.
Bite. The deep singer whale makes one bite attack.
Move. The deep singer whale swims up to half its swimming speed without provoking opportunity attacks.

CHAPTER 7: CHARACTER RACE OPTIONS

CORALITE

Back in the Age of Kings, before men had come to terms with the monthly moon vanishings and the accompanying assault from below, civilization was unable to cope with the horrors that unfolded on Moonless Night. Soon that civilization began to collapse. People were terrified. They revolted, they fled, or they died. The Yalts suffered as much or more than anyone, trying to hold the fabric of society together and protect the people who endured their beneficent rule. They failed. The land was overrun, the populace decimated. The Yalts gathered what was left of their people, built tall ships, and sailed into the dawn, intent on rebuilding their peaceful society in some idyllic setting.

When they reached the broad expanse of coral reef, they halted, broke apart their ships, and used the lumber to build shelters. A thousand years later, Hawkmoon has been established and gone through several evolutions, as has the new Yaltic city. They called their city Coralis and themselves Coralites. While Hawkmoon was settled by pirates, killers, and thieves, Coralis became a haven of peace and knowledge. Coralis became a city of legend, encountered rarely by wayward travelers and built up in mortal minds as the earthly abode of the gods.

PACIFISTS

Coralite culture and society are founded on one overriding principle: peace. When first they began this quest, they hoped to escape the turmoil of their kingdom and start a way of life based on establishing equilibrium among each other and with the world around them. They would devote their lives to learning, loving and living fully, enjoying the fatness of life. They disdain violence, greed and wealth, keeping only what possessions they need and sharing them throughout the community. They have no need of weapons or money. They number no thieves in their ranks.

The Coralites strongly oppose combat and violence of all types and attempt to live in peaceful relations with all of their neighbors. Their wizards and priests learn and know offensive spells, but seldom have cause to use them. There are a few fighters among their number because they view martial training as an art form. They are fundamentally skilled but lack experience. Overcoming their abhorrence of violence is a significant challenge to their effectiveness at combat.

COMMUNITY-ORIENTED ARTISTS

The Coralite society is intentionally simple. They bond together in family units — what they call "tribes" — and several tribes choose to inhabit the same common area. They call these groups "communities." Each community houses together, primarily in large towers constructed of various materials and held together by magic. However, some communities prefer to live in primitive huts on the various islands along the reef. Everyone is responsible for the needs of the community and, as an extension, the nearby communities as well. Out of each member's particular skills arise what is required to supply each individual need in the community.

The Coralites are slow to reproduce and most couples have but one child in their lifetimes. This has kept the total population rather small, perhaps a few thousand. From birth, Coralite children are taught history, religion, spellcraft, and the arts: music, poetry, painting, sculpting, and literature. The Coralites are universally skilled at some artistic endeavor, and they follow it their whole life. They are also quite skilled at performing, and even those who don't study music can recite poetry. Learning is a key part of their lives, and they spend many hours each day studying the multitude of books they brought on their journey or have written since. Ancient history, magic, and religion are their favorite subjects. The Coralites have an affinity for creation rather through art or craft, which has led to their crowning achievement of marrying magic to music.

SONGCHANGERS AND THE PRIESTHOOD

The songchangers are the offspring of the Coralites' marriage of magic and music. Songchanger wizards have learned to manipulate the very elemental matter of creation through song and music. Through their skill, they produce everything from mundane kitchen utensils to the very towers that make up the city of Coralis. They weave powerful magic into their musical compositions and are revered even above the priests in Coralite society.

The Coralites are pious and devoted to their religious pursuits, though in proportion to their other interests. They have perhaps the definitive collection of material on Majium, god of magic and mercy. Their priests spend hours in prayer and devotion and lead daily sessions of worship and teaching for any who wish to participate, which defines most of the inhabitants at least once in a month's span.

CORALITE NAMES

Coralites pull their names from history or from the ocean. Communities that prize a particular type of fish, for example, might name the first born in a generation after that fish and the other children of that generation after fish with similar traits. Similarly, a great scholar or entertainer of a community may see their name gifted, with variations, to generations of Coralites after the person has passed. A Coralite's surname often reflects the primary function of their home community, or the surname reflects the individual's unique skill. Communities and an individual's talents are irrespective of

---

NEW DEITY: MAJIUM

God of Mercy and Magic
Domains: Good, Healing, Knowledge, Magic
Typical Worshippers: Wizards, sorcerers, healers, the charitable, and those who put mercy before justice, and magic before life.
Favored Weapon: Dagger, quarterstaff

Unlike deities of other pantheons, the divine beings worshipped in the Domain of Hawkmoon defy description and subscribe to no single alignment. They have no set forms and no gender. For the purpose of bringing their inscrutable natures closer to human understanding, worshippers have given them names and anthropomorphic characteristics, and attempted at least to surmise their realms of control and the areas they influence. All gods have been assigned a primary dichotomy, and several lesser fields of influence. Because of this complexity, beings of various alignments and vocations might pray to the same deity.

The followers of Majium, among whom the Coralites have perhaps the most knowledge, characterize him as a wise old man with a kind smile and a gentle touch. Majium is basically good, but those who revere his more magical aspect usually care nothing for moral and ethical considerations. They are wholly devoted to the pursuit of arcane knowledge and its acquisition at any cost.

Spellcasters often incorporate prayers to Majium into their verbal spell components. Alchemists tend to devote a small corner of their labs as shrines to him. Healers universally consider him the father of their arts. His beneficence knows no bounds, or so say the tomes that chronicle his encounters with humanity.

their gender, and, as such, Coralites don't distinguish gender in their naming conventions.

Coralite Names: Bluefin, Fungia, Goby, Labroidei, Lamprey, Rayfin, Scyphozoa, Snapper, Trevally, Tuna, Veratra, Wrasse

Coralite Surnames: Boatwright, Coralsmith, Dyer, Fisher, Reedweaver, Songchaser

CORALITE TRAITS

Your coralite character has the following racial traits.

Ability Score Increase. Your Dexterity score increases by 2, and your Charisma score increases by 1.

Age. Coralites reach adulthood around the age of 20 and can live up to two centuries.

Alignment. Most Coralites are neutral good. As a people they are peaceful and good-hearted, seeking to aid and enlighten those around them.

Size. Coralites tend to stand just under 5 feet tall with a bulky build and average about 150 pounds. Your size is Medium.

Speed. Your base walking speed is 30 feet, and you have a swimming speed of 30 feet.

Artistic Upbringing. You are proficient in your choice of two of the following skills: Arcana, Medicine, Performance, and Persuasion.

Hold Breath. You can hold your breath for up to 15 minutes at a time.

Pacifist. You have disadvantage on an attack roll against a target if the target hasn't harmed you within the last 24 hours. You have advantage on saving throws against being charmed or frightened by creatures you haven't harmed in the last 24 hours.

Sudden Inspiration. A child of artists, you sometimes find yourself struck with sudden inspiration. You can use a bonus action to roll a d4 and add the result to one attack roll, ability check, or saving throw you make before the start of your next turn. Once you use this trait, you can't do so again until you finish a short or long rest.

Languages. You can speak, read, and write Common and Aquan.

ELF, SEA

Similar to their land-bound cousins, sea elves are slender and long-lived. Their skin varies in shades of blue and purple, and their hair often resembles seaweed. They typically stand around five feet tall and weigh about 100 pounds.

PEACEFUL SCHOLARS

Sea elves fight to defend themselves and their homes but are, on the whole, a peaceful race. Should the need to fight arise, a sea elf uses whatever means is at its disposal. They spend their years separate from the surface races, studying the many ancient ruins and shipwrecks that dot their realm.

SEA ELF TRAITS

As a sea elf, you have an appreciation for the sea and for the ancient history of the world. Even the boundless sea can't hide all history, and you believe the past should be embraced as it is the best teacher. You have the traits of an elf in addition to the following sea elf traits.

Ability Score Increase. Your Wisdom score increases by 1.

Aquatic Weapon Training. You have proficiency with the net and trident.

Water Dweller. You have a swimming speed of 30 feet, and you can breathe air and water.

Extra Language. You can speak, read, and write one of the following extra languages: Deep Speech, Primordial, or Sahuagin.

KUAH-LIJ

The kuah-lij were at once a peaceful race of explorers, living in an organized society on a distant planet orbiting a great, red sun. Though the course of their lives was regimented, their culture allowed them scope for individuality, and, in fact, encouraged it. This, and the natural propensity of the kuah-lij for order, resulted in a society that had remained fresh and vigorous for over 10,000 years.

The kuah-lij had civilized their planet millennia ago and had settlements across its lands and beneath its seas. Many areas they deliberately kept undeveloped, and they took great pleasure in long sea voyages and extended exploration of back country. The weedge, a race they consider mentally and culturally inferior, have over the years taken on the role of servants to the kuah-lij, if not slaves. See the "weedge" entry in **Chapter 6** for more information.

Their innate tendency to organized society also helped them immeasurably with mass production and technology, in particular a merging of science and magic. Though it never reached the pinnacles seen in other exotic cross-planar cultures, it was highly polished, with many of their technological marvels being as much works of art as useful items.

COMMUNAL CITIZENS

Kuah-lij young are placed into a public crèche within days of birth, to be raised by child-care specialists. As they grow and are educated, their affinities and talents are assessed, and at age 15 they are assigned a vocation based on their talents and an avocation based on their preferences. They then study more intensely in these two areas, until they reach maturity at age 25. Kuah-lij youths have the option of changing vocation or avocation if they insist upon it, though this almost never occurs.

Upon reaching maturity, they fully enter society, where they spend 10 months of the year working at their vocation 10 hours per day, and the final two months on sabbatical, traveling, exploring, or doing whatever else strikes them as interesting. Their culture is based on a complex system of credit, with currency reserved only for dealing with non-kuah-lij. Medicine, vacation time, and other services are all socialized, but, due to their innately organized, cooperative mindset, there is remarkably little corruption within their culture.

CATACLYSM SURVIVORS

Their idyllic existence came to an end over 300 years ago, when a strange darkness crept into the deepest places of their oceans. Kuah-lij explorers that investigated did not return or came back reporting nothing amiss — but with a strange gleam in their eyes. They merged back into the kuah-lij culture and immediately set about sabotaging it, destroying it from within.

Despite their placid lives, the kuah-lij had many thousands of years of history to draw upon and took this in stride. Yet even as they isolated the tainted members of their society and set about investigating the cause of this in detail, the invaders of the deeps struck, poisoning food supplies and attacking kuah-lij undersea cities, often overwhelming them without warning or survivors.

As the years passed, the kuah-lij culture became more militant, fighting a war against a race they had almost no information about. The battle has entered a kind of stalemate: the kuah-lij have many sea-based vessels and devices to use against their foes, but the enemies of the deep, which resemble aboleths, are surmised to have secret aid from an extraplanar source and almost limitless numbers.

The kuah-lij have turned some of their efforts to exploring distant worlds, in this plane and beyond, for answers to the origins of their attackers and how to defeat the creatures. This is their single, overriding concern.

KUAH-LIJ NAMES

Kuah-lij young are given short, quick names by their caretakers to facilitate easy discipline and training. When a kuah-lij youth reaches age 15, it is given a name based on its vocation. These youth names are often used as surnames to the child name or hyphened with the child name to distinguish individuals. When a kuah-lij reaches adulthood at age 25, it chooses a name for itself, replacing its child and youth names. The kuah-lij tend to prefer vowel-heavy names, but their adult names can come from anywhere, including other cultures they have observed. Though most kuah-lij leave their child and youth names behind when they reach adulthood, some keep the names as private names between loved ones or as reminders of their past.

Child Names: Bir, Erk, Kip, Lin, Tess, Vil, Wend, Zep

Youth Names: Builder, Cook, Dancer, Fisher, Hunter, Swordsmith, Tanner, Weaver

Adult Names: Asosi, Bazoij, Foroco, Jugil, Inooqi, Miwib, Tyjeku, Yekuki

Kuah-Lij Traits

Your kuah-lij character has the following racial traits.

Ability Score Increase. Your Intelligence score increases by 2, and your Dexterity score increases by 1.

Age. Kuah-lij reach adulthood around age 25 and can live to be just over 200 years old.

Size. Kuah-lij tend to stand just over 6 feet tall and have slender builds. Your size is Medium.

Speed. Your base walking speed is 30 feet.

Natural Crafter. You know the *mending* cantrip and can cast it without requiring material components. Intelligence is your spellcasting ability for it.

Skilled Artisan. When you use downtime to craft an item, you can craft an item with a total market value not exceeding 7 gp instead of the standard 5 gp. If something you want to craft has a market value greater than 7 gp, you make progress every day in 7-gp increments until you reach the market value of the item. You must still expend raw materials worth half the total market value to craft the item, as normal.

Kuah-Lij Training. You are proficient with two artisan's tools of your choice.

Languages. You can speak, read, and write Common and Kuah-Lij.